MYTH STALKER: WENDIGO NIGHTS

SHANNON LAWRENCE

WARRIOR MUSE PRESS

ISBN
979-8-9898381-0-3

*To my husband: the best spouse, father of our children, and cover designer a girl could ask for. You are the one thing in this life I can depend on.
I can't wait to discover new places with you.
Thank you for everything.
You're my forever.*

1

EXPLOSIVE BEGINNINGS

Selina Moonstone ducked as a small tree, roots dangling, swung at her head. She threw herself into a somersault, deftly coming to her feet and breaking into a run toward the giant red rock formation before her. The thundering footsteps and rancid stench told her the creature wasn't far behind. If she could lead it to the cave about five-hundred feet around the sandstone abutment, she'd have a chance.

A burst of air hit her backside, as if something had just missed her. She leapt sideways, bounding off the rock wall and twisting in mid-air. Her feet hit the packed dirt with a *whump*, and she risked a glance at the creature behind her. The inky blackness of the night hid his full color, but he was tall, over seven feet, and covered in hair. His eyes caught the light of the moon and glinted yellow. One of his massive hands swung toward her, barely missing as she turned, darting sideways into a copse of pinyon pines. Though their low branches snagged at her clothing and hair, she hoped they would be far more daunting for the pursuing behemoth. Their piney scent surrounded her as she fought through the needles.

Behind her, the creature let out a great growl that sounded like a bear, only deeper and more drawn out. A quick glance back showed her the rough branches pulling at his hair as he batted frantically at them, trying to force his way through. Selina ducked low and squat-walked her way through the remainder of the trees, quick flicks of pain telling her she wasn't escaping the sharp needles entirely. She broke through the last of them and grabbed the flashlight from its casing at her left hip, flashing the light three times in quick succession in the direction of the next rock face, the top of which towered above her like a city building. Three flashes were returned telling her everything was in place.

"Come on, Gog, darlin'." She blew a puff of air up at the dark hair laying across her face. "I've got things I'd rather be doing."

Huffs and growls sounded behind her. She was happy to hear them getting closer. An entire pinyon pine flew out of the cluster of trees, landing close beside Selina. Bits of dirt and bark struck her, stinging along her right arm and cheek. She brushed the fragments from her face and backed away, ready to sprint as soon as he broke out.

Instead, silence greeted her, everything completely still.

She stopped, using her enhanced vision and hearing to try to detect what was going on. Small sounds reached her ears, none of them coming from the creature. She could smell him again, that rank odor that spoke of unwashed fur and a carnivore's spoils.

A sharp intake of air indicated he was moving again. Just as he burst from the trees, she fell onto her back, lifting her legs to meet the creature's advance. Her feet met his midriff, and she used his own momentum to send him over her where he landed in a heap. He got up right away, as did she, and they faced each other.

He was on the wrong side of where she needed him to be.

In this position, she could see the intelligence in Gog's eyes. He studied her, just as she studied him. His arms fell to his sides, and he tilted his head to the side, gaze boring into her. She spoke to him in a gentle, quiet voice. "You know you shouldn't be out here. There's no place for you. You'll be shot or captured, and I don't want that." She tilted her head to match his. "I don't suppose you understand any of that, do you?"

He continued to look back at her, and for a moment she entertained the thought that maybe he really could understand what she'd said. Then he straightened, fuzzy brow furrowing, eyes narrowing, and lunged.

Selina jumped to her right and darted around Gog. She figured he'd follow her, and she was now back in position to get him where she needed him.

Up ahead, a figure rose from behind some brush, his curly hair a blond halo around his head against the backlighting of the moon. He held something in his hands. It was too dark to make anything else out, and she didn't have time to try, but he was in position. An extra wave of confidence swept over her. Straightening her shoulders, she diverted to the left of him, hoping Gog would continue to pursue her instead of becoming interested in the man in the scrub.

Gog's footsteps gained, which reassured her that he still followed. She looked around to gain a better sense of her location. Surely, she must be nearing her destination.

Finally, a sheer rock face loomed before her. Gateway Rock, she'd know it anywhere. Its presence helped her pick up speed and she put more distance between herself and Gog. She picked out the cave entrance she was looking for and ducked inside as a boulder smashed against the rock wall over her head. Shards of rock peppered her back, slicing exposed flesh with sharp slashes of pain. She winced, but continued on.

Behind her, Gog struggled to get inside. His head, torso, and one arm jutted through the hole. He scraped at the ground with his giant hand, trying to pull himself across the strewn shards and gravel-crusted surface. Despite a small entrance, the inside of the cave was plenty big enough for him to stand up once he got through. She had only seconds before he would join her inside, trapping her.

Selina unbuttoned a pocket on her thigh and pulled out a signal flare. She snapped off the lid and struck the end of the flare against it. Hot red sparks shot out of it, sending a phosphorescent glare throughout the cavern.

Gog broke free, pulling himself inside and standing cautiously to his full height. She threw the flare behind him, ducking behind a rock to the side of the slanted passageway. He flinched and looked back, belting out a terrified roar. He ran toward the tunnel, which carried him straight past Selina's hiding place.

She leapt from behind the rock, jumped over the flare, and escaped through the entrance of the cave. Before she could get her flashlight out to signal, a small explosion occurred behind her. Sandstone rubble fell, blocking the entryway to the cave, and she slid to a stop, placing her hands on her knees and gasping for air. Her lungs burned.

The crunch of gravel alerted her to someone walking toward her. She straightened and looked toward the sound. The owner of the curly hair approached her along the path. He handed her the remote apparatus he'd used to set off the explosives, which she stuffed in the now empty thigh pocket.

"Thanks, Brent."

"Did it work? You think he's okay?" Brent's eyes traveled from the cave to Selina like he was reluctant to look away from where the beast had disappeared.

"He should have been far enough in that it didn't hurt him; he might have a headache and crappy hearing for a bit. I think it was the only thing we could do. Besides, you're the one who checked the cave out and told me the tunnel will bring him further into the mountains. He'll be happier there. Safer."

"I guess."

"I'm fine." She smiled. "Thanks for asking."

"Sorry. I'm glad you're okay. I'm worried about Gog, is all." He looked back at the rubble blocking the entrance, a wistful look on his face. "I wish I could have met him."

"He wasn't much for conversation. You know he'll be safer in the mountains than in the middle of suburbia. He's survived this long in that network of caves and tunnels. He'll be fine." Selina approached the cavern entrance. She checked the stability of the rocks, looking for any holes that might be exploited. It seemed to have done the job. The entrance appeared to be well blocked. She only hoped there had been no major rock slides or damage inside, but the charge had been relatively small and set near enough the entrance to minimize damage elsewhere.

"I got some good footage of you and Gog," Brent said. "Want to see it?"

"Let's head back to my place. You can help me patch up while we watch."

His eyes widened in concern, and he looked her over, grasping her arm to examine it. "You badly hurt anywhere?"

"No, just a few cuts, I think. Still, a lot of it's on my back, some I can't reach."

Brent rushed to get his stuff from the brush in which he'd concealed it. Selina went to help, but the aches were setting in now, and she slowed her movements. As she approached, he hopped out of the brush, carrying a large rucksack and a small video camera.

She paused to wait for him, and they headed out via a sidewalk that wound through the sandstone rock formations. It was hard to make out the reds and grays of these towering rocks, but Selina knew them well. This was where she came to relax. Nothing grounded her quite like being surrounded by rock formations that rivaled the skyscrapers downtown. Even in the dark they were an awe-inspiring sight, yet peaceful.

Her Jeep sat in the large visitor parking lot. Luckily, Garden of the Gods was closed at night, though that didn't stop people from coming in sometimes. This also meant the police occasionally rode through to check for drunk teenagers and people with spray paint, which had made this mission slightly more treacherous. No one had interrupted them, and she was relieved to see the Jeep remained unmolested.

The desert air had cooled, and with her no longer running around, the chill bit into her skin. The moment she started the Jeep, she hit the switch to her butt warmers and set the heat blasting. It was cold at first, but Jeep heaters were fast and hot. She let the warmth soak into her skin before putting it into gear. Her various cuts prickled with the constrained movements inside the vehicle.

As they drove away, Selina studied the Kissing Camels rock

formation. She'd always thought it looked more like a camel and a squirrel. Now that she'd had the opportunity to meet the Garden of the Gods monster—really just a regular old Sasquatch—that had been terrorizing nearby neighborhoods, the park took on a whole new mysticism that hadn't been there before.

She'd loved it here since she was a kid. When she hadn't been on a mission with her father, she'd spent quite a bit of time hiking the paths and climbing these rock structures, yet the only animals she'd discovered previously had been deer, squirrels, rabbits, bighorn sheep, and birds. Even the odd rattlesnake, fox, coyote, mountain lion, or bear.

This park had been sacred to the Ute. Though her people, the Cherokee, had never been here, the quiet power of the place pulsed through her, recharging her energy stores.

What else did the red and gray rocks of Garden of the Gods hide?

2

IN STITCHES

After a stop for nachos at a twenty-four-hour roadside stand, Selina and Brent arrived at her three-bedroom Victorian right outside downtown Colorado Springs. It was big for a woman alone, but she hadn't been able to resist the gorgeous originality of the house, or the giant elms and maples that lined the street. Every home in this area was different from the others, setting the neighborhood apart from the boxy cookie-cutter houses that made up the surrounding suburban areas. Plus, she was walking distance from restaurants and her bank, with only a short drive to outdoor recreation.

Selina took a quick shower, reveling in the heat of the water as it pelted her body. It stung when it touched the multitude of tiny cuts, but she sucked it up and soaped everything down to be sure there'd be no infection. The water pooling around her feet ran red from the sandstone grime covering every inch of her. Pine needles and leaves swirled down the drain. She didn't get out until the water ran clear and clean.

She dried off then wrapped herself in a thick towel, cinching it over her breasts. Glancing at the hair dryer, she dismissed it, not wanting to make Brent wait any longer. Instead, she wrapped her dark, unruly hair up into a sloppy bun on top of her head then dabbed at the moisture that speckled her shoulders. A quick glance in the mirror revealed small nicks on the unblemished skin of her face, especially over her forehead and right cheek. She leaned in and used a finger to rub dirt out of the corners of her eyes. Clean as she was going to get, she went into the living room.

Brent sat on the sofa waiting for her. They settled in to watch the video, Selina perched on the sofa in front of Brent as he used tweezers to pick out bits of wood and rock from her injuries. She'd received a few good lashings as she went through the trees, and virtually her entire body was covered in scratches and gashes. She used a second pair of tweezers to go over her legs and arms. It was tedious, but important. Who knew what a creature as old as Gog might be carrying around in his fur, and what she may have come into contact with. With her rapid healing abilities, she wanted to be sure nothing remained inside once the cuts sealed.

The video wasn't the best quality, but she could make herself out, pale against the night. Oddly, Gog looked larger to her on the video than he had in person. It was strange to see herself running in front of the massive creature. She couldn't make out his color on the video, but she'd pulled thick, brown hairs off her clothing.

"There goes the tree he threw at you!" Brent whooped. "For a second I thought it was going to take you out. Good thing you're so fast."

"I felt that puppy go right over me."

She watched in fascination, right up to the moment the cave blew. As comical as Gog's struggle to get into the cave had been from her side, it was twice as funny watching it from the outside. They both burst out laughing as the poor monster's feet scrabbled at the dirt, trying to push his way inside.

Once it finished, Brent started it again. "He's so smart. Watch how he responds to your movements."

"How did you know about the cave?"

"Spaulding's Cavern? It's been around for ages. A trapper found it in 1848. When I was doing research on Bigfoot in that region, I kept coming across information about this cave that had been sealed in 1963 and was thought to have housed a creature. Articles talked about the network of caves and tunnels running beneath the park and Manitou Springs, but they'd never fully explored them. It was only a matter of time before it opened back up, considering it's been discovered after erosion several times since Spaulding claimed it."

"Why'd they keep sealing it up then? Sounds like a fun place to explore."

"The sandstone's too fragile. The park rangers were afraid someone would get injured by falling rock, so they closed it off." Brent paused. A sharp pain followed as he extracted a particularly large piece of something from her right shoulder. "You've got a nasty gash here. Might benefit from a few stitches."

"I don't suppose you'll do the stitches? I really don't feel like going to the doctor, and if it heals like this I'll have yet another scar."

"I don't have anything to stitch you up with."

"I do. If you're willing, I'll go get it." Selina turned to look at Brent, who hadn't replied. He had paled, lips pinched. "You don't want to do it, do you?" She thought for a moment. "Can you hold a mirror while I do it?"

"That I can do." He visibly relaxed and eased back against the sofa.

Selina went to her main floor bathroom to grab her first-aid kit, the one she took along on her bigger myth stalking expeditions. Inside was everything she needed, including curved surgical needles and thread. She settled back in front of Brent and handed him a medium-sized mirror. Pouring a small amount of rubbing alcohol into a shallow dish, she put the thread in it to soak.

Brent cleaned the wound then applied an ice pack to her back while she waited, numbing the area.

Once she'd become numb enough, Selina removed the thread from the alcohol and inserted it through the surgical needle. She then lit a lighter and held the needle in the flame for a few seconds. At her request, Brent applied some antiseptic to her back then held up the mirror until she nodded that she could see it. She craned her head to look over her shoulder and stuck the needle in below the gash.

Brent promptly shut his eyes, still holding the mirror up.

"Wimp." She laughed as she pulled the thread through her flesh. It stung, and the laugh came out as more of a gasp. She gritted her teeth.

The gash wasn't too bad, so it didn't take long to get it stitched. Brent taped a sterile bandage over it, and they returned to picking out slivers and rock chips, the second play of the footage long over.

"You think any of that footage will allow you to publish about this one, Brent?"

"I don't know. I got some clear shots, but I'm not sure how the Cryptid community will feel about what I helped you do."

"What would they have wanted us to do?" she asked. "Leave him out to keep eating people's pets? Eventually, he would have hurt a person, possibly killed them. Or someone would have killed him. This is too populous an area to leave something like Gog free."

"I know that, you know that, but convincing other Cryptos will be harder. They weren't here. They'll probably say we should have left him alone or relocated him."

"Yeah, not sure how we would have accomplished that." Selina threw her hand up in exasperation.

Done removing the bits and pieces buried in her skin, Brent cleaned the other wounds, careful to keep the bandage around her stitches dry.

"Well, just tell them my job is normally to kill these creatures, but you helped me keep him alive."

"We'll see. Either way, I'll be going through the footage to see what I've got. This was an awesome night. Thanks for calling me in to help."

"I missed you. Thought it was about time we got together again."

Selina said this quietly, turning to face Brent. She smiled at him, grateful for his help. It had been a while since they'd worked together. They both traveled heavily for their jobs, rarely together. They'd been friends for over two decades; he was someone she always felt comfortable talking to and being around. She leaned into him to give him a quick hug, but he reached for her, eyes meeting hers as he cupped her chin and pulled her in for a kiss. His lips were soft and warm. He tasted spicy.

She slid a hand up his chest, feeling the firmness of the muscles beneath the soft cotton of his shirt. He smelled like the outdoors, an earthy scent that went right to her middle. Underneath that was a musky, citrusy scent. She'd always loved the way he smelled.

As nice as this would be, and as much as she wanted it, their friendship was more important to her. Her eyes jerked open and she used the hand on his chest to push away from him. She clutched the towel at her chest. "I'm sorry, Brent. I can't do this. We can't do this. I didn't mean to—"

"It's okay. I should have known better."

Selina could see him closing off to her, the light in his eyes dimming. His shoulders hunched forward and he pulled away. She wanted to reach out to him, but feared it could send the wrong signal. Instead, she got up. "I need to get dressed. Will you be here when I'm done, so we can talk?"

He looked away from her, and she tensed, but then he said, "Yes, I'll be here."

With a sigh of relief, she headed into her bedroom to throw on a pair of sweatpants and a t-shirt. Her hair had mostly dried, and she released it from the bun so it wouldn't be a bird's nest when it fully dried. She grabbed a pair of fluffy socks and slid them on, her feet whispering across the floor as she went back into the living room.

Brent still sat on the sofa. He was watching the video for the third time, and he didn't look up when she came in. Selina slid into the overstuffed chair next to his side of the sofa and waited for the video to end.

When he had stopped it and set the remote down on the coffee table, she said, "I'm sorry."

"You don't have to keep apologizing, Selina. I'm the one who should be sorry. It just...it felt right."

She looked down at her sock, picking at a thread hanging off it. "I don't want to lose our friendship over this." She raised her eyes to meet his. "This isn't going to mess things up, is it? It's been so long since we saw each other. I value our friendship."

His solemn face softened, and a small smile touched his lips. "We're okay, Selina. But I think it's time for me to head home for tonight. It's after three, and my ego needs some time." He reached forward and grasped her hand, gave a quick squeeze, then stood and gathered his things.

She watched as he packed away the camera. When he'd finished, she got up and walked him to the door, locking it behind him.

She hoped he hadn't been lying. She wasn't exactly swimming in friends these days.

3

AN OLD FRIEND CALLS

Selina awoke the next morning to a persistent ringing. She rolled over and looked at the bedside clock. 10 A.M. Groaning, she grabbed the phone. "Who is this?"

The person on the other end hesitated a moment then said, "I see I woke your sunny ass up, hey?"

It took Selina a minute to process the rich, warm voice on the other end, but she perked up when she did. "Nathan! How goes it in the other North America?"

"Not good, Selina. I need to ask you a favor." It wasn't like Nathan to skip the friendly preliminaries.

She instantly sobered. "Anything."

"I need you to come up here. We have a Wendigo situation, and you're the only person I trust to deal with it."

"Wendigo?" A knot formed in her stomach. Wendigo was her least favorite type of creature to stalk, but it was also her specialty. Go figure. "Do you know who it is?" She sat up, the blankets pooling around her waist. She kept a small pad and pen in the bedside table drawer, and she pulled them out. Faint light came around the edges of the blinds, lending just enough helpful illumination.

"I do," Nathan said. "I'll explain everything when you get here. Can you do it? I'll pay your normal fee, plus a bonus for the rush."

"Of course. I've just come off a local case, but I can be in Alberta by tomorrow. Is that soon enough?"

"Yes, that'll be fine."

"Okay, Nathan, stay safe. You remember the basic protection?"

"Seeing as how I'm the one who taught you, I do." He chuckled. "I'll see you tomorrow. I've got most of the materials you'll need for the basics, so just bring your personal gear." He paused, the silence buzzing over the phone line. "It's bad, Selina. Get here as fast as you can. There isn't much time."

"I understand. I'll be there. I'm calling the travel agent as soon as we hang up."

"Bye, kiddo."

"Take care."

A click, and the dial tone sounded in her ear. She settled the phone back onto its charger. Nathan, who was typically laid back, had sounded scared. He was never an alarmist, never dramatic. Something bad must be going down, and it would take her a while to get everything packed, the necessary items shipped north to Alberta.

She lay back against her pillow, worry seeping in. There had been Wendigo issues in the Canadian Rockies before, which is how she'd met Nathan. She'd been sixteen, just starting out, "realizing her full potential," as her dad had said before sending her off on her own to "sink or swim." He'd given her basic equipment, made sure she packed her oversized reinforced leather motorcycle pants and jacket to keep her safe from claws and such, and bought her a plane ticket. He hadn't even walked her to the airport gate, not wanting to go through security.

She'd arrived, scared and unsure what to do next. She'd never been to Canada, though her dad said it wasn't any different from the U.S., not really. "You don't even need to know how to speak a different language," he'd told her. "Well, not in the area you're heading, anyway."

While true overall, she'd been heading to a pocket with a high

Cree population, where many spoke Plains Cree. Luckily, the vast majority there spoke English, though some of the older folks didn't. She wasn't sure if they actually couldn't or merely chose not to, but it was all the same to her when trying to ask them about their experiences and to hunt down the creature she'd been sent there to kill. Detective work was always easier if people would actually talk to you, maybe hand out a few clues.

Then Nathan entered the picture, then only thirty-nine to her sixteen years. Though not a father himself, he'd been very comforting, almost paternal. He'd taken her under his wing and been her translator, the lubrication some needed to even be willing to talk to her. Though she was mixed blood, with Cherokee from her mom, it was not enough to make it obvious in her features. She'd gotten the dark hair and a tan complexion, but her eyes were green, not brown, and her face shape was more European than Indigenous. To Caucasians she wasn't white enough; to Natives she wasn't brown enough.

In that first case, the Wendigo had been a mother of three. They'd been poor and desperate, a harsh winter closing in. The mother beseeched a spirit of the forest for a solution, and this curse was the answer. She told the spirit she would do anything for its help. What it wanted turned out to be flesh. Not only had she been unable to save her children this way, but they'd numbered among her victims. Only the youngest, a six-month old baby, survived. Her sister saved her by hiding her in a cabinet, fast asleep, right before their mother killed the rest of the children.

Nathan had been kind, both to Selina and the woman whom they were after. She remembered his quiet strength, his rugged features, and how he'd helped her. An adolescent crush developed then, something her father mocked her for later when he'd figured it out. Twelve years later, she and Nathan were good friends, nothing more. Nathan had never returned her feelings, and the schoolgirl crush faded as they all do.

Nathan had told Selina stories of the past, some from his own history, some from long before him. Everything she knew about hunting Wendigo, he'd taught her in a matter of days. The best way to kill them, what weapons to use, how to be prepared for what could happen. He'd also helped Selina deal with the body after she'd killed the woman. It was an involved process, which took a lot of time and effort. He had held her as she shook and retched, this being the first beast in human form she'd slain.

Then, as always, he had been calm about it all. Not desensitized, no, but he'd come from a culture that accepted Wendigo as a real thing, and he'd been prepared as much as anyone could be. His own grandfather was a Stalker, like Selina, but the genes had not passed to Nathan or his father before him, probably because of the lessening of the problem. Modern day living had brought about many ways of keeping starvation at bay, which decreased instances of people being trapped in their homes without enough food, which thus decreased the need for cannibalism in order to survive. Modern technology had whittled down the number of Wendigo, ensuring fewer people were exposed. Every once in a while, environmental factors stepped in, accidents happened, emergencies occurred. Worse, there were people, usually young, somewhere in their twenties or teens most commonly, who thought it was fun to perform an old ceremony they found, seeing as they didn't believe in Wendigo or sorcery.

Knowing what she knew of Nathan, her alarm grew by the minute. He wanted her there now; he was desperate. Normally, he would be able to take care of the issue on his own. Not this time.

What did that mean?

Selina rolled out of bed, stretched, and headed into the kitchen for breakfast, creating lists in her head of what she'd need to pack. This was more a comfort measure than anything else, as she had checklists for various types of beasts, as well as certain types of prepared packages. In her line of work, it paid to be prepared.

Remembering her promise, Selina placed a call to her travel agent, who vowed to call her back within an hour. With as much travel as she did, it was helpful to have a professional to book Selina's trips for her whenever possible.

In the meantime, she had a quick breakfast of eggs and toast, then set about packing. She split everything between a suitcase and two trunks, one small, one large. She'd have to ship her specialized blades and guns in the larger trunk, but she'd do it under the guise of a weapons shop. She and Nathan knew a legal weapons dealer who helped them by receiving these packages. She'd cultivated a lot of similar relationships in places she frequently traveled, and Alberta was one of those places. Though Nathan had said he had the basics, she felt more comfortable using her own tools, so she did whittle down what she was taking from what she would normally pack, but she still took more than strictly necessary.

Some women over-packed shoes; Selina over-packed weapons.

Into her trunk went her reinforced motorcycle gear, holsters and similar apparatuses. She also put a tube of bone ash, her trusty first aid kit, and various other items that would come in handy, but that weren't weaponry in non-Myth Stalkers' eyes. She scanned her Wendigo checklist, threw in a couple more items, and finished packing her clothes for the trip.

She decided it would be a good time to check her cuts. The ones on her arm were mostly healed, but the others were harder to see. One of the benefits of being a Myth Stalker was the ability to heal more quickly. Pulling her collar down, she turned her back to the mirror in her bathroom and examined the wound with the stitches. From the look of it, the stitches could stay in another day. It looked good, but not fully healed yet, the skin around it pink with new growth.

The phone rang, and she was ready to go for her early morning flight the next day. Nothing was available for today on such short notice. That gave her time to run out and ship her box next day air, so it would be waiting for her when she got there. It sounded like she'd need her weapons right away.

She called Nathan to update him. "Hey, Nathan. I got a flight tomorrow morning. I'm shipping a package to Steve. Can you let her know?"

"No problem. I'll give her a call. She'll be happy to see you. Bryan's been asking after you, too."

"I'm looking forward to seeing everyone. It's been a while."

"That it has." Nathan sounded sad, which didn't help Selina's concern.

She'd purposely backed off Wendigo cases the last two years, and had avoided going to Alberta, even though it had been somewhere she'd gone several times a year previously. There'd been no shortage of work elsewhere, and she'd taken advantage of that.

"See you soon," she said.

"And you."

Selina hung up. Tomorrow she'd find out what was going on. Until then, she'd brush up on her Wendigo lore and see if the papers had any information for her on odd occurrences and disappearances happening in the area. It never hurt to be prepared, and she intended to hit the ground running the moment she got to Alberta.

4

AN UNPLEASANT SURPRISE

Selina walked along the airport hallway, leaving her arrival gate behind. She strained for any sign of Nathan. Hundreds of faces greeted her, all a bit gray, as faces tended to be in drab, airless airports the world around. Everything was stark, only neutral colors decorating every surface, save the food area in the distance, which boasted neon and colorful signs. The strange scent only found in airports drifted around, reminiscent of claustrophobic spaces, new car smell, and flop sweat. She brushed her fingers across her nose, feeling the tickle of a sneeze trying to break through.

None of those surrounding faces belonged to her old friend and mentor. She stopped at the front doors, all glass and metal, wondering if she shouldn't go to the luggage carousel and find him after. Where could he be? He was usually prompt, if not early.

She turned in the direction of the luggage claims area. Fine, she'd grab her stuff and look for him after. Otherwise, she feared she'd have to go hunt everything down when the carousel was needed for a different flight's luggage.

Someone grabbed her sleeve. She jerked it away, turned, and stepped forward into the owner of the hand's space, something no one ever expected. A young man stumbled backward away from her, panic pinching his dark features. Fear shone in his brown eyes, and he held his hands up, palms out, in a defensive position.

"I'm sorry. Don't hurt me! Nathan sent me."

Selina paused, looking at him again. His features did seem to be consistent with the Cree bloodline. Maybe someone from Nathan's community.

"Why didn't he come himself?"

"He's not well, Miss Selina. You are Selina Moonstone, yes?"

"Yeah, that's me, and you should definitely skip the 'Miss' portion of that name."

"Okay." He clamped his mouth shut.

"We need to get my luggage first, but then where do we need to go...what's your name, anyway?"

"I'm Johnathon Child." He held his hand out to Selina, who took it in a firm grip and shook. His grip was weaker than hers, but it firmed as she held his hand. Quick learner, this one.

"Where are we going after this, Johnathon?"

"You can call me Johnny." At her nod, he continued. "We'll be going to Nathan's cabin. You've been there before?"

"Not this one." She pointed behind him with her lips at a rack of trolleys. "Here, grab one of those trolleys for me, would you? I've got a sizable trunk full of books and other heavy items. Cost me a fortune in luggage fees to get the sucker on the plane."

He got a trolley from its place against the wall, rushing after her as she continued walking. One wheel wobbled and squeaked as they walked, and the sound dug into Selina's spine, working its way upward to her shoulders and neck. It managed to stand out against the roar of voices all around her, the sounds of suitcases on plastic wheels, and the slap of feet against the tiles. Six hours' worth of flight and layover time, and she wasn't in the best mood. Her senses were raw, overstimulated, picking up every sound and smell around her.

They passed another free trolley, and she jogged over to snag that one. When it proved quieter than the one Johnny'd chosen, she gestured at the now blank space against the wall. "Go ahead and put that one over there. This one's quieter."

He quickly did as she'd said, catching up to her right away. She noticed him looking sideways at her, obviously curious. She watched him in her peripheral vision for a moment, thinking how young he looked. What was he, twenty? He couldn't be very old, his face still open and naïve, his black hair cut short, though not drastically so. How did he know Nathan? She knew Nathan had no kids, had never married, in fact. So who was this kid?

Conjecture was getting her nowhere. "So how do you know Nathan?"

"I'm apprenticing with him. He put out word that he was looking to train someone a few months back. My parents weren't too excited when I took him up on it. They want me to do something else."

"I'm betting they'd prefer you go into a less dangerous career. And one that pays better."

"That, and they don't really believe in what we do." He stopped and swallowed. "What you guys do."

They arrived at the carousel and she stood back, watching for her luggage. It was mostly empty now, no one else standing around them, and she hoped she wasn't too late, that this was still the luggage from her flight. Right as she started getting nervous, her blue suitcase came around the loop. She stepped forward, set her feet, and grabbed it as it moved in front of her. Johnny pushed the trolley forward, knocking her in the shins in the process, which sent a wave of pain up her legs. She plopped the suitcase onto the trolley's flat, carpeted platform and rubbed one shin with the opposite foot, glaring at the boy.

His lips pulled back in horror at what he'd done, and he opened his mouth, probably to apologize again.

Selina held up a hand to stop him. "No sweat, kid. There's one more piece coming: the trunk."

They waited and waited, but still no trunk. Growing concerned, she followed the path of the carousel, moving around the curve. A man bent over something there, struggling to cover it with a blanket. When he looked up, she saw light brown hair, a firm jawline, and eyes traced by lines made by years of squinting. A trio of frown lines furrowed the skin between his eyebrows, accentuated as he frowned up at her.

At that moment, she recognized her trunk beneath the blanket. She stepped toward him, wondering what the hell was going on. "Hey, what do you think you're doing with my trunk?"

"Oh, is this yours? Sorry about that. Selina." His brow relaxed, and a grin spread across his face, making him look roguish.

How did he know her? Who was this asshole? She'd been accosted by press before. And by individuals who followed the Cryptozoological publications.

"What did you say?"

"Don't you recognize me? I know it's been years, but I'd think you'd find me a bit more memorable. I knew your dad."

She continued looking at him, squinting in thought. At last she got a flash of him in her memory, something deep within her subconscious. Hold on, yes, last time she'd seen him his hair had been darker, his skin paler, and he hadn't had quite so many lines on his face. He'd apparently spent a lot of time in the sun since then.

"Life hasn't treated you well, has it, Charles?" A smirk creased her face.

His grin faded, but he quickly pasted it back on.

"That's not a nice thing to say."

"I wasn't going for nice. Why are you stealing my trunk?"

"I wasn't stealing it, just borrowing it."

"Oh, bullshit, Charles." She snorted. "Why are you here?"

"I've heard there's a good case out here. A vicious predator in the woods. Nice body count; good for the press. Whoever captures this one will be able to capitalize, for sure."

She'd found a few stories about recent deaths by predators. They always thought it was bears or wolves, of course, but actual attacks by those animals were rare. Still, she wouldn't have thought there were enough of those attacks to raise eyebrows unless someone was looking at this area specifically. "That *would* be what you'd be after. I've already been hired. Why don't you take a hike?"

"I plan to, but it will be a real hike in the woods." He looked her up and down. "You can come along if you'd like. I'd prefer you walk in front, though. Better view for me, and less chance of a blade in the back." He chuckled at his own joke.

"Considering our history, I'd say it's me who should fear a good back-stabbing."

He winked at her and pulled the blanket off her trunk. The blanket went over his shoulder, and he hefted the trunk. "Where do you want it? We might as well be civil, don't you think? We'll be seeing plenty of each other for a while."

Selina sighed and turned to go back around the carousel. Johnny still stood there, keeping an eye on her suitcase. His brow furrowed when Charles came up behind Selina carrying the trunk, but he recovered quickly and picked up the suitcase, pushing the trolley toward them.

Selina rubbed her temples, chewing on the inside of her cheek. Great, all she needed was Charles getting in her way. He was a fellow hunter, though not a Myth Stalker like her. He hadn't been born to the work as she had been, was merely human, with no exceptional traits. Sure, she was human, too, or she thought so anyway—it had never been clear to her what a Myth Stalker was, it being a small group made up of typically gung-ho folks that didn't set much store in passing down their histories—but she possessed heightened senses and reflexes, and she healed faster than the average joe.

She had been born to hunt these creatures, to deal with them as was required. What she did know about Myth Stalkers was that they existed to keep a balance. Some creatures were evil and needed to be killed. Others weren't evil, but were misunderstood and could be a danger to those who might run across them. Gog was an example of one of these, a creature who was large, but not typically aggressive, except when provoked, which she'd done masterfully. It was her job to know the difference and to act accordingly.

Charles, on the other hand, was in it for the glory. He'd once been a Cryptozoologist, like Brent, but had grown bored with the work, wanting the excitement and press that came with ridding the world of the monsters others believed were myths. He'd become a gun for hire. After a bad experience involving him, her father, and a herd of Chupacabras when she was a teenager, she'd kept her ear out for news of him. Cryptos talked about him a lot, which made Brent a natural resource. Charles showed up in Crypto and conspiracy periodicals, but he looked different in person than on the page, and it had been a while since he'd been in one of them. Of course, the regular press always heralded him as a hero who had slain a wolf or a bear. But in the circles where these creatures were a known reality, he'd become more infamous than famous, frequently sought out for jobs others were afraid to take.

Before her mind could drift back to their last meeting, Johnny cleared his throat and spoke up. "Are you ready to go, Selina? I've got a truck waiting in short term parking."

"Of course. Let's get out of here." She looked at the obnoxious hunter. "Charles, I trust I'll see you again sometime soon?"

"What, you aren't going to offer me a ride?" Charles stuck out his bottom lip in an exaggerated pout. "That's not very friendly."

Johnny opened his mouth, possibly to offer Charles a ride, but Selina spoke before he could. "That's not a good look for you, Chuck. And you'll do fine on your own. See ya'."

Johnny led the way, pushing the trolley ahead of him in the direction of the parking lot. Selina followed, with Charles right behind her as they cleared the doors. She looked behind her once she'd crossed the road, but he had disappeared, lost somewhere in the crowd. She could try to locate him, but there was absolutely no part of her that had any interest in that, so she followed Johnny to a beat-up truck and helped him load the luggage.

Besides, Charles would turn up soon enough, and probably at an inopportune time. That was his super power, as she recalled. That, and using teen girls as bait. Given, her father had allowed that to happen. She'd always been conflicted as to whose fault it really was that she'd ended up tied up in someone's backyard, being stalked by Chupacabras. Either way, she didn't plan on giving him a chance to put her at risk like that again.

With her things in the truck, she climbed into the worn seat beside Johnny. She took out her phone and sent a series of texts to Brent.

On a case in Alberta for about a week.

Guess who showed up?

Charles Lancaster.

The question that remained was how he'd known she was going to be here.

5

MOUNT UP

Johnny took her to see Steve first. Her weapons shop wasn't far from the airport, and Selina's weapons should have arrived by now. Pulling up out front, Selina took in the familiar wood plank façade. The sign read *Steve's Weapons & Ammo*.

Selina hurried through the glass front door, eyes scanning the dim interior for Steve. She was excited to see her old friend.

A woman with short blond hair stood behind the counter, hunched over some paperwork. She didn't look up at the sound of the door. Instead, she held up a finger as if to signal for a moment. "Go ahead and look around. I'll be with you in a minute."

Selina cleared her throat once, then again, louder this time.

Slowly, the woman put down the pen and looked up, one eyebrow quirked in irritation, but the second she saw Selina, her face lit up, other eyebrow bopping up to join its friend. "Selina, there you are! I got your package and wondered when you'd be showing up." She ran out from behind the counter and picked Selina up in a hug. "I've missed you!"

Selina hugged Steve back fiercely. The shop owner had gotten rounder in the middle, though she was already no beanpole. She'd always been long limbed, her wrists slim, despite the weight she held elsewhere. Her hug felt like a steel girder wrapping around Selina, and she smelled of coconut shampoo.

"I've missed you, too, Steve."

People were frequently taken aback when they discovered this blonde was the owner of *Steve's*. If they didn't leave right away out of some misguided misogyny, they quickly grew to respect her knowledge of weaponry and hunting. She'd been doing this all her life, helping her dad, the original Steve, with the shop. Her name was actually Stevie—not because he'd wanted a son, as folks usually thought, but because he'd been proud to have a daughter who he'd hoped would follow in his footsteps—but once she'd taken over after her dad's health had declined, she'd adopted Steve as her official name.

Steve released her. She nodded at Johnny, then asked of Selina, "What are you here for, woman? I've heard rumblings about disappearances in the mountains. That yours?"

Selina nodded. "I think so. Nathan called me up, but hasn't given me any information other than a Wendigo being around. It sounds serious. I'm betting those disappearances are related."

"Can you stay and chat a while?"

"I can't, but if I have a chance I'll try to drop by to visit before I leave. I'm not sure how long I'll be here, but I'm figuring about a week, maybe two."

"All right, let me run back and get your box." She looked over at Johnny, who had been standing quietly near the door throughout this exchange. "Why don't you come grab it? You're young, and your back's not been destroyed yet."

He followed her meekly into the rear of the shop, leaving Selina to chuckle. No one questioned Steve's demands. Ever. Selina had long wished Steve was her kind of hunter, rather than the regular kind. She'd be a powerhouse in the Myth Stalker world, purely mortal senses notwithstanding.

Johnny came from the back carrying her box. Steve sauntered in behind him, a small package in her hand. She went behind the counter, set the package down, and gestured for Selina to join her, which she did, stepping up to the other side of the glass showcase that also served as the counter. Beneath the glass, on the top shelf, were knives of all sizes and types. Underneath those were swords and larger knives. The guns were in other cases, but Steve was a knife girl at heart, and always kept them close. She believed everyone should have a knife, male or female, starting when they were old enough to be taught to be careful with them. Selina's dad had been the same. Selina felt naked without a knife clipped to her belt, but that would soon be remedied.

"This is for you, too, honey. I'd been intending to mail it to you, but since you're here..." She slid the package over the glass surface with a *shush*.

Selina took it and pulled the top open. It hadn't been taped up yet. Inside, nestled amidst foam packaging material, lay a knife. She recognized the symbol on the leather sheath: a fanged mouth atop a long-clawed paw. It had been her dad's logo, and was hers now. She gasped. "Oh, Steve, you fixed it?"

A huge grin spread across Steve's face. Her teeth were large and white, save one brown one on the side, which had been damaged when she'd helped Selina on a case years ago. It startled Selina to see it still wasn't fixed, but then her friend had never cared much about appearances. She didn't use cosmetics, and she kept her hair close cropped for ease of styling.

"I sure did," Steve said. "Go on, pull it out."

Selina did just that, lifting it from the box and pulling the knife from its sheath. The blade gleamed, silver and ornate. It was engraved with the same logo as that on the sheath, but the blade had five lines running along it, one offset from the other four, which ran parallel. They were meant to represent the scratch marks of an animal with five claws.

"You did a beautiful job, Steve. Thank you."

This had been her dad's knife. He'd broken it during his last stand, before the Wendigo took him over fully. He'd been about to use it on her, but had regained enough of himself to shatter half the blade on the ground and throw it away.

Right before she'd killed him.

Her chest and throat felt as if they were packed full of cotton. Expanding, spiked cotton.

"I mean it. Thank you for doing this." Her voice choked with emotion. She slid the knife back into its sheath and tucked it back safely into the box. "This means a lot to me."

Steve reached over the counter and pulled Selina into an awkward hug. "I was happy to be able to do that for you." Drawing back from her, she asked, "You'll take care of it now, won't you?"

"Definitely." Selina held so much anger for her dad, but it would never quell the love she'd felt for him, nor the guilt she still experienced over the way he'd had to die. It had been three years, the catalyst for her avoiding Alberta. And Wendigo. "Okay, I've got to go, but I'll try to see you before I go."

"All right, honey," Steve said. "Tell Nathan hello for me. He still owes me a drink."

Johnny led the way outside with the bigger box. Selina carried the smaller one clutched to her chest.

Now to get answers from Nathan. She found she was nervous. No amount of rationalizing and guessing explained why he couldn't handle this himself, and why he'd called her to do so.

6

GUT PUNCH

The drive wasn't too long, about ninety minutes, but it felt longer due to Selina's anxiety and her eagerness to see Nathan and talk to him, find out what was going on. How sick was he that he hadn't bothered to come pick her up? She wracked her brain, trying to remember how he'd sounded on the phone. She'd been so happy to hear a familiar voice that she hadn't really paid attention. Had he sounded weak? Ill? Had his nose been stuffed up? Both phone calls had been brief, which was unusual for the two of them, but her sense of urgency and the sound of fear in his voice had drowned out everything else. She couldn't remember for sure, but supposed he might have sounded weak.

Johnny turned out to be a competent driver, calm, with quick reflexes. They drove in silence, windows open to let in the cool autumn air. As they followed the road, the Canadian Rockies looming in the distance, Selina gazed at their peaks, content to know she was near the Rockies, even if these were farther north of those she typically had a view of. It had always made her feel more at home to have them hovering over her, keeping her safe with their granite strength and unimaginable age. The things they'd seen. How many monsters had they witnessed in their time? How many had scaled their heights or swooped above them, catching prey in the air? Certainly more than she'd dealt with.

As she pondered the rugged mountains before her, Johnny entered forested land, where she promptly lost sight of the peaks. He steered around the narrowing curves, eventually getting them to a gravel road that broke off from the paved one. Branches reached toward the truck, scraping along its side as they passed them. She winced, looking over at Johnny to gauge his reaction to the possible damage being done to his truck. He looked straight ahead, relaxed, uncaring.

He must have felt her gaze on him, because he turned to her and smiled. "It sounds bad, but it really doesn't do much damage. Plus, this is a clunker; it's okay if it gets a little scratched up."

Selina nodded. Made sense. Most people in areas like this cared more about how a vehicle ran than what it looked like. If it was dependable, it didn't have to be pretty. Her Jeep took a regular whooping when she needed to go off-road to get to a site for work.

Johnny concentrated on the road, taking them farther into the evergreens. The gravel ended and the road became overgrown, just dirt, with clumps of weeds growing from the furrows. The shocks didn't appreciate it, and they passed their displeasure onto the passengers inside, causing them to bounce around, sometimes landing quite hard.

Selina grabbed the door handle, clenching in an attempt to keep herself from being knocked silly against the doorjamb or even the ceiling. Her fastened seatbelt allowed maybe a bit too much leeway, and the ceiling grew frightfully close at times.

Finally, a nice-sized wood log cabin became visible ahead of them, closely surrounded by pines and brush. This was the first she'd seen this house, his old one having burned down the last time she saw him. Dusk had fallen, and the warm flicker of a fire danced in the glass windowpanes to the right of the front door. She kept expecting Nathan to come to the porch, greet her, but there was no sign of his presence other than the fire.

She climbed out of the truck, massaging her aching tailbone, and took a solid stretch. Vertebrae popped along her spine. She'd been sitting far too long today, between airplanes and cars, and her body wasn't happy with her. There was also a trace of ache from yesterday. Her flesh might heal quickly, but it didn't let her forget her sins.

Johnny got out and opened the hatch, struggling with the trunks. She rounded the vehicle to help him, but he waved her off. "I'll get these. Mr. Thrush, er, Nathan has been looking forward to you getting here since he decided to call you. The door won't be locked."

It never had been.

The slip-up with the name told her he was new to working with Nathan. Still adjusting to not calling him by his formal name. He'd mentioned it had been a few months ago that the call had gone out, but she wasn't sure how long he'd actually been working closely with her mentor. Their ride had been a quiet one. Brent hadn't texted her back yet, but he didn't live by his phone like so many did. Instead, she'd used the time to figure out what she needed to do once she had the rest of the information.

She hurried toward the cabin, taking a beat to inhale the fresh piney scent that surrounded her. A hint of vanilla hovered, telling her there were ponderosa pines mixed in with the rest. She climbed the short steps onto the wooden porch, enjoying the give and creak of the planks beneath her feet, and tapped on the door before pushing it open.

Despite the rustic appearance of the outside, the sight that greeted her was warm and welcoming. She stood in a small foyer, a cushioned bench beside the door for one to remove their shoes. Faint yellow light reached out from a dainty light fixture on the wall. She slid her shoes off without using the bench and stepped into a hallway with a door on either side of it. Following the hallway, she could see the firelight growing ahead, dancing to and fro on the walls, and casting shadows of unidentifiable furniture. The wood smoke provided a comforting smell, and she took a deep breath to enjoy it.

"Nathan?"

"In here."

His voice came from the direction of the fire, and she kept going. When she reached the end of the short hallway, a comfortable looking living room greeted her. Nathan sat on a long leather sofa, his feet resting on an ottoman. He looked thin, haggard, as if he was wasting away. A jolt of dismay shot through her when she glimpsed a sharp collarbone sticking out from his shirt collar.

She ran to meet him, kneeling in front of him. "Nathan, are you all right? You look terrible." No wonder he couldn't fight the Wendigo on his own. He was too weak. It would take about two seconds for it to take him out.

He laughed, reaching a scrawny arm out to pat her shoulder. "Gee, thanks, Selina. That's the very thing a guy wants to hear from a beautiful young woman."

"What's going on? Why didn't you tell me you were sick? I had to hear it from Johnny, and he's good at following directions, because he told me absolutely zip other than that you were sick."

"It's a long story, and one I needed to tell you in person. I want you to get a drink and some dinner before we talk. I'm afraid what I have to tell you is going to come as a shock."

"Are you dying?"

They looked at each other a moment. Selina wasn't willing to let this go, and she could see some sort of internal conflict reflected in Nathan's eyes and the expression on his face.

Finally, he sighed, shoulders slumping. "Yes, but not in the way you probably think. Humor me, would you?"

Selina wanted to resist, wanted to tell him she wouldn't wait, but Nathan Thrush was stubborn. If he didn't want to tell her yet, she'd never get the words out of him. He could be infuriating. He'd sent her into a rage many times in her youth. Rages that had done nothing but amuse him, which made her all the angrier. But when she'd persisted against him, he had closed himself off. She knew if she pushed too hard, insisted, he would clam up. Then she'd have to wait until he came back around.

He leaned forward, using his arms to try and push up. He didn't make much headway. At first, when she attempted to help he waved her off. After two more tries, where he instead fell back onto the sofa, she moved to his side, lifting him and putting his arm over her shoulder. He was so light that it made her sick to her stomach.

Could it be cancer? That was the first thing that came to mind when she saw him in this wasted state. Of course, he'd said it wasn't what she'd think. It could be countless other things, but she couldn't think of anything else. Her mother had wasted away like this when her breast cancer spread. She'd been teeny in the end, a sparrow of a woman.

Memories of her mother sent her panic into high def. "Do we really have to wait, Nathan? I'm not sure I can eat until I know what's going on."

"Believe me, you won't be able to eat afterward. I'm hungry. I'm sure you are, too. I know Johnny will be. Food first."

His shoulder popped as he pulled it from around her. She hovered near, readying her hands when it looked like he might fall. She'd seen many a mother do the same thing when following a toddler, and that thought caused her to pull back and let him walk on his own.

He merely grinned, shook his head, and leaned in to give her a kiss on the cheek. "My little Selina, tell me how things have been. Any new critters for you lately?"

"I did get to hunt down a Sasquatch, or what I believe to be in that family. I named him Gog. Ever heard of a 'Squatch at Garden of the Gods or thereabouts?" She had fond memories of visiting Garden of the Gods with Nathan when he'd come down to visit.

"No, can't say that I have. A Sasquatch, though, eh? I'd say it makes sense, you being in the foothills, but it's such a busy area, what with the tourists and a big city nearby. I've never heard of them in the Rockies. Not confirmed, anyway. I always figured it had to be the altitude. One of the reasons they're sighted in the Cascades so often. Smaller mountains, lower altitude. Of course, altitude doesn't stop the bears, does it?"

"Not this guy either."

"Did you have to kill it?"

"No, just trapped him. He's in a cave system where he lived perfectly well until a tunnel opened. He'll be fine, but so will the pets he won't be stealing from nearby homes anymore."

They'd arrived in the small, but clean kitchen. Nathan opened the fridge, still standing of his own accord, despite looking frail and unsteady. Selina stayed close by, but leaned against a counter so she wouldn't look like she was hovering over him anymore. He patted her on the arm, likely knowing precisely what she was doing. Too bad. He'd have to deal with it. At least she wasn't glued to him, holding him up and waddling along behind him anymore.

He pulled out a platter covered in plastic wrap and handed it to her. "Put this on the table, would you?"

She did so without a word, returning to take a large bowl and then a smaller one. She set these on the table and removed the wrap from each of them, bunching it up into a ball. Next, Nathan opened a breadbox and pulled out a plastic bag with rolls in it. He held them out to her until she took them and set them on the table.

This was a routine he'd long followed, a dance she knew well. "I'll get the butter," she said, voice firm. "You sit down."

He actually listened, settling into a chair with a sigh. His clothes hung off him, looking about four sizes too big. A sick feeling filled Selina's stomach once again as she noticed that his once large, strong hands even looked diminished, skeletal. He had a vague stoop in his back, and his mouth sloped downward, an occasional grimace pulling it taut. He was obviously in pain.

She poured water over ice for the three of them, setting the glasses at three spots on the table already set with old, chipped plates. Even the silverware bore scars. She ran her thumb over a familiar groove cut into the butter knife from when it had gone into the garbage disposal.

Johnny came in with a lot of shuffling, followed by a loud *thunk*. A sigh floated into the room, and he shuffled back out to get the rest of the luggage from the porch.

"Did you warn him how much crap I'd have?" she asked.

"Nah. He's learning the trade. Might as well learn it all as he goes." His laugh was rich and warm, familiar.

Selina felt her chest squeeze as she watched him. He looked like a stranger, but the voice was the same one that had comforted her through the years.

"Stop looking at me that way, young lady. You'll understand soon."

"Tell me, Nathan. I can't do this. Give me a hint, anything. Is it cancer?"

"No, but I figured you might think that. That's not what it is." He sighed and locked his hands together on the table in front of him. He studied them for a second, not saying anything, while Selina waited. Anything from her right now might shut him down.

He drew a deep breath and looked up at her, reaching one hand for hers and taking it firmly in his grip. They were still strong, his hands. The flesh was thin, but his iron strength still came through in the grip. "I wanted you to get sustenance and rest first, but I can see that's not going to happen. You're as stubborn as I am, and it was stupid of me to think you'd wait. Not when it's so obvious something is wrong." He paused and took a breath. "Why'd I call you here?"

"A Wendigo. You said you knew who it was."

"And I do. Better than anyone else, but you're not going to like the answer."

Her mind raced as she tried to think of someone she might know in the area. It obviously wasn't Steve. There was her old brother-in-training, Bryan, who she had hunted many a beast with. She had a hard time imagining him being infected, despite his rashness and need for adventure. Still, it couldn't be anyone else. "Is it Bryan?"

He shook his head.

Who else? She didn't care about anyone else as much as Nathan, and Steve and Bryan were the only close friends she'd made here during her training. Still, Nathan was the one she relied on for true friendship, and to help with everything else.

Then it dawned on her. She shook her head, snatching her hand out of his. Pain cascaded through her chest, made it hard to breathe.

"No!" The blood rushing to her head made her dizzy, on the verge of blacking out.

She saw the truth in his face before he said the words. "I'm afraid so. I'm the problem you've come to take care of. I'm the Wendigo."

7

ORIGIN OF A MONSTER

Selina stumbled over to a chair and slumped into it. She couldn't look at him, couldn't process anything. A roar filled her ears, and it took her a moment to realize he was talking to her. She couldn't hear his words, could barely make out his face through a growing tunnel of black closing in on her vision.

It couldn't be. He couldn't be Wendigo. He was no cannibal, of that she was certain. And he definitely wouldn't have beseeched the forest spirits for help. He knew better. More than just about anyone else. There were other, rarer options, but he didn't meet those definitions either. Surely he hadn't been weak before this had made him ill. He wasn't evil.

She realized she was hyperventilating and put her head between her knees, her hands grasping the hair at her temples, pulling her head downward, refusing to look in his direction so she wouldn't have to see the seriousness in his face. The pity being directed at her, when he was the sick one. No, not sick. Possessed. Either way, he was dying.

It took a few minutes, but she began to calm down, the blackness receding, normal sound filtering through the rush and roar besieging her. As she calmed, thoughts began to circulate in her mind. The most typical way someone became Wendigo was to become a cannibal, to feast on the flesh of another human being. Once this happened, an evil spirit of the woods would enter, pushing out the weakened spirit of the flesh eater, and taking over their body. He wouldn't have done that. She ran through a rapid checklist in her mind of the possible causes, but none of them made sense.

"How did it happen?" she asked. "You're a good man; it shouldn't have been able to overtake you, no matter what you did."

"That's true, but I took it willingly to save someone."

"You what? Why? How many lives have you taken? How was this one different?"

Nathan ducked his head. When he looked up, his eyes sparkled with unshed tears. "You remember how we met?

"Of course."

"You remember the survivor in that case? The baby?"

"Yes."

"It was her that was possessed. She's thirteen now, almost fourteen. She was on the way to turning. I couldn't let it take her, too, not when she'd barely survived once already, so I consulted elders until I discovered a ceremony, one that would allow me to take the spirit into myself and rid her of the pestilence. They weren't sure it would work; no one in recent history had tried it. But it did." A sense of pride trickled through his words.

"This isn't right." Anger overpowered the sadness. "If there's a way to transfer the spirit, there must be a way to banish it entirely. Let me research it, find an answer. You don't have to die, Nathan. Not now."

His face was sad, but calm, as he looked at her. He shook his head and gave her a faint smile, resting his hand over her clasped ones. She freed her own and took his in a tight grip.

He squeezed back. "I've lived a good life. Who wants to get old, anyway?" He winked at her. "All the years I've spent cleaning up these monsters, it was inevitable something would happen. If you think about it, I avoided it for a surprising amount of time."

"You're talking like you're a hundred years old instead of fifty-one. And what does this say about me? How long do I have then?"

He shook his head. "You're different. You're meant to do this. You were blessed with extra physical resources to help you. I've always been a sidekick, a man who grew too big for his britches."

"In what way? You were doing important work, whether you think you were born to do it or not. You've saved countless lives—"

"By taking many lives, Selina. Don't you see? There's not some infinite repository of sin. Eventually, one pays the price. Yes, I've killed people who were turning, but they started out as good people. Desperation or situations outside of their control forced them into this, and I killed them instead of healing them. I am supposed to be a healer."

"But you were saving their souls." Her voice rose. "You know that one's soul is lost once they make the full turn. You were doing them a favor."

"I know this, my dear, but there must be another way. Shouldn't I have tried to find that alternative before it affected me directly?"

"No, there is no other way or we would have heard of it by now. Someone would know it."

"Did you hear what you just said?" Nathan asked. "There is no other way. We can't stop this. You know what you have to do."

"But we hadn't heard you could take the spirit into yourself, either," she countered. "Obviously, we don't know everything."

"Yes, and the same people who taught me how to take in that spirit said there was no way to rid myself of it after. You know our elders pass on the knowledge of the past, our history. They speak the truth of our ancestors."

Selina squeezed his hand once more before releasing it. She paced the room, hands clenched, eyes unseeing as she looked inward for answers. There had to be a way to save him, and she would find it.

She turned back to him, stood over him. "How long do you have?"

"I'm already considerably weakened. I feel my soul losing its grip more and more each day. I would say less than a week."

"Give me three days. Three days to find an alternative."

"I can try."

"Don't try, do. Fight it, Nathan. You have means."

"I've already been employing those same means, but I'll continue. Charms and fetishes can only do so much good, for so long."

"I know. Just do what you have to in order to stay alive and whole."

"I will." He nodded then gestured at the food on the table. "Now will you eat some food?"

Selina paused in her pacing. "I'm really not that hungry."

"Sit down with me, Selina. Eat. Tomorrow is plenty of time for you to start."

"I'm starting tonight, but I'll eat dinner first. Will that make you happy?"

Nathan smiled. "Very. Now please sit down and join me."

Johnny came into the room as Selina settled into the chair across from Nathan. He looked between the two of them, probably trying to gauge if she knew. His gaze settled on Nathan, who nodded and gestured to the seat across from Selina's. Without a word, Johnny sat down, nodding once to Nathan, and doing the same when Selina met his eyes.

She handed plates to both men and started serving food onto her own plate. Fish, potatoes, bread, mixed berries, and veggies. The aromas of seasoned fish, butter, and yeast mixed, making her mouth water. She was actually quite hungry now that she'd decided to eat something. Her stomach growled in agreement, causing both Nathan and Johnny to smile.

"You see?" Nathan asked.

"Yeah, yeah, just eat."

"Tell us about this Gog/Sasquatch creature you dealt with."

Johnny looked up. "Gog?"

Selina told them about her and Brent's adventure in Garden of the Gods, and they spent the next hour chatting, pretending there was nothing wrong. In the back of her mind, she ran through all the things she'd have to do to find a treatment for Nathan. She didn't want to have to kill him, but she would if it would mean saving his soul and keeping him from turning into the rabid beast he feared becoming. Her thoughts strayed to her father, his face overlaying

Nathan's. She pushed his image away, turned her mind to what she needed to do now.

First, she'd go to her room to read up on her notes. She'd learned a lot about Wendigo over the years, and she possessed the notes each Myth Stalker in her lineage had passed on. Her family had been better about it than other Myth Stalker families, though it lacked order. The Monsternomicon, as she liked to refer to it, was chock-full of information. Nathan had also given her his family's meager journals, as she could do more with them than he could. She carried these with her on every unusual or unknown case, as there was no way to memorize everything within the yellowed pages. Given, she'd read it enough times that it should have rung a bell if there was anything in there about the current situation, but perhaps she had just forgotten, or even missed it in those previous perusals.

She'd also need to pay the young woman he'd saved a visit. Find out where she lived, what her name was now. Any clues she could gain as to the one that caused this would help. One never knew what would break a case and produce answers.

There was no chance Selina could get any more information out of the elders than Nathan had. She was sure he would have done plenty of his own research with them, and they weren't likely to talk to Selina without him there to assist. Johnny had already said his family was against him being part of this world, which meant they wouldn't be any help. She'd see if Brent had any information, but this wasn't his expertise. The killers among the Crypto creatures didn't interest him.

Selina laughed at the tale of a particularly confused Wendigo spirit Nathan had dealt with. He threw his head back and laughed in his wonderful loud way. She'd always thought he must be filled with such joy to make that sound. Now she sensed the lie in that. There could be no joy left within him, yet still he laughed like there was.

"So this man is sitting in front of the fire, and the spirit inside him is too stupid to make him move, despite the fact that they hate fire. Well, too stupid and too weak. You see, the man refused to follow the urges that came to him; they were so weak. He hadn't knowingly eaten human flesh, so the spirit had no true hold. It would have had better luck had it entered the woman who cooked up the flesh. It was hers. She was so angry that she cut a piece of her own skin from her stomach, thinking that he would be possessed by Wendigo and she'd get her revenge."

"She didn't think that this was a good way to get eaten once he turned?" Selina choked on a piece of bread as she laughed.

"Oh, she was long gone. She fed him the soup then invited the spirit and left later that night while he slept. Was so kind as to leave him a note letting him know he'd consumed a piece of her, which she said was only fair as he'd consumed her soul in the course of their marriage."

Selina laughed again. "Damn."

Johnny asked, "Did you have to kill him?"

"No. The spirit had nothing to hold onto, and the man's soul was too strong."

Selina sobered. "Your soul is strong."

"It's different, Selina." Nathan's smile dropped from his face.

"Different how?"

"I accepted it. I took it into myself. This spirit had already strengthened by feeding on Nell, the young woman, and I cannot reverse the invitation I issued it. You know the truth in this." When he said this, he looked deep into her eyes, concern reflected in the deep brown of his. He knew what she had contended with when her father suffered the same fate. And by that time she hadn't loved her father nearly as much as she loved Nathan.

"We'll see about that, Nathan. We'll just see."

And she saw in both Nathan's and Johnny's eyes a glimmer of hope, that her conviction was enough to make Nathan think there might be something beyond what he thought he knew. Some truth that might save him yet. Her chest swelled with the reflection of that hope.

Selina would find that truth. She would not fail again to save someone she loved.

8

A LITTLE OVERKILL NEVER HURT
ANYONE

Selina felt the irrepressible urge to be doing something, physically chasing down a solution to Nathan's problem. Her body thrummed with the need to be running, fighting, chasing. She had tried sitting to go through her notes, but she couldn't sit still, couldn't focus. While research was important, it didn't feel like she was actually doing anything useful.

Instead, after getting details from Nathan on how he'd ended up in this situation, she asked to borrow the truck. He said yes as soon as she asked, looking at her knowingly. She could see he'd expected as much, knew her so well. He hesitated when she asked for Nell's information, telling her he'd have an answer for her by the time she was ready to go back out. It was late, and her visit could wait until tomorrow.

She packed up the journals she'd left out in case she reached a point where she could sit down somewhere and peruse them, but right now that didn't feel possible. She also suited up in her protective leathers, arming herself with some bare minimum basics, just in case. A custom made silver-plated long blade slipped into a sheath built into her pants. The handle was small, and the entire thing stretched the length of her femur, allowing her to sit and move comfortably, even with the knife hidden against her leg. A spray container, similar to that of mace, held a chemical with various materials in it, including silver, bone ash, sage, tobacco, and pepper. The intention was for the spray to work on as many beasties, human or otherwise, as possible. She'd invented it based on years of experience.

Studying the knife Steve had fixed for her, she pondered putting it on, as well, but for now she placed it back in its box, safe. Instead, she strapped a wrist sheath onto her left hand, and placed the smaller trigger blade into it. This one was also silver plated, as were the majority of her blades. An ankle sheath went on next, custom-built for a slim, but strong wooden stake. She'd had it made out of bubinga, or African Rosewood, a strong hardwood imported into the United States. When she couldn't get bubinga, her next choice was hickory. Luckily, these stakes could be used repeatedly, as long as she managed to retrieve them.

Thinking this quite enough, and, yes, likely overkill, seeing as how she wasn't even sure what she'd be doing, she pulled her armored leather jacket on, tested the wrist sheath, which sprung out on command, tucked it back in and walked to the living room from Nathan's bedroom. He was sleeping on the sofa these days, so he'd insisted she take his room. He wanted her and Johnny to be able to lock themselves into their respective rooms at night, though she'd pointed out to him that no wooden door and basic lock would keep him out if he did change and try to get into their rooms.

"So you'd rather take no precautions then?" he'd asked.

"I didn't say that; just making a point."

"I want your doors locked at night, a fire burning in the fireplace, and alarms set at the front and back door to keep me from getting out without you knowing. I've also made you each a medicine bag to protect you. I know you can take care of yourself, but Johnny can't yet. Our training isn't complete. Not even close."

"I'll do whatever you ask of me, Nathan. You know that."

He already had the alarms readied, which Johnny had been putting out each night. They were made from a series of cans, bells, and fishing line. She knew that Johnny had a shotgun by his bed, full of silver shot, which had a lead ball at the center, as silver was so soft, but that would, at most, slow the Wendigo down. Silver bothered them, yes, but was not the automatic death sentence that would be best. She made a note to ask if he had a silver stake. If he slowed it (and yes, she was referring to the beast that might come out as "it," because it most certainly would not be Nathan) with the silver shot, he could probably stake it through the heart, which would keep it down long enough to complete the entire process required to ensure a Wendigo did not return for its killer.

In the living room, Nathan sat on the sofa, a blanket tucked around him. He'd lost most of his fat and muscle mass, the first step in becoming Wendigo. She knew he was vomiting, as he'd had to run to the bathroom several times. This was another step, and she was afraid to ask if he was vomiting blood yet. Soon, his raven hair, threaded through with strands of white, would become all white, and he'd begin developing a fine white layer of hair over his entire body, which would thicken and lengthen as he became the beast. His eyes would poke out, becoming yellowed. His teeth and nails would grow longer, thick and sharp. She shuddered as she pictured these changes coming over someone she loved so much. Again.

Nathan looked up and waited for her to settle on the sofa beside him. Johnny, who had been sitting by the fire, got up and left. Going to his room to give them privacy, Selina assumed.

"I will not tell you where Nell is today," he said, without preamble.

"What? I need that information. I need to know who bit her and caused all of this to start. Maybe finding him will provide the answers I need."

"No. It won't." He held up a hand when she made to interrupt him. "I've already killed him. It made no difference."

"You didn't think this was an important detail to tell me right off? You can't hide things from me and expect me to be able to find anything. Not if I'm doubling up on steps you've already taken, treading the same ground."

"I understand that."

"You're not acting like you do." She paused to rein her anger in.

She was not accustomed to speaking to him in a disrespectful manner, and he certainly wasn't used to being spoken to that way. Given, he was blocking her by not giving her more information, and she wondered if he had completely given up, if that touch of hope she'd seen on his face had been false. "Who turned the guy you killed? How did he become Wendigo?"

"He was too far gone to get any answers from him on how it happened. It was Nell's uncle, and I had to kill him in his sister's home."

"Tell me his name so I can track backwards from him and find out what I can."

"It won't do any good."

"How would you know? It can't do any harm, either. Just tell me, Nathan."

Nathan puffed out a breath, hunched deeper into the blanket. To her dismay, he was shivering, no fat on his body to keep him warm. The comforting scent of him had been overtaken by the scent of impending death, vomit, and the stench of freezer burned rot that accompanied the presence of Wendigo. "His name was Curtis Lansing. He lived in town, wasn't a good person. However he ended up being turned, I'm betting he earned it."

"Aright. I'll need his address and where he worked. It would help me to be able to go to Nell's house since that's where he was killed. "

He merely looked back at her.

"Fine. You took all precautions in seeing him destroyed? You weren't too weak immediately after taking the Wendigo on?"

"Yep. The heart is in the churchyard right outside town. I burned the rest of his remains and scattered them to the four winds. He is quite thoroughly gone."

"Okay. I figured, but had to ask."

"I know."

"I know it's too late to visit an elder, but I'd like to know someone around here I might speak to that could have more information. Someone that might know something, even if they don't know they know it."

"I've spoken to anyone I thought could help." He pointed at a piece of paper sitting on the table. "I've made a list of the people I've talked to and any pertinent information I gained from them. This includes the elders I spoke with and an address for Lansing."

She picked it up and zipped it into a jacket pocket, then shrugged. "What if I think of questions you didn't? Given, they likely won't talk to me without you there, anyway. I may have more questions for you. Is there a historical section at the library? Anything that might have old mythology texts?"

"Yes. I've found useful information there in the past. I warn you, I've been there, as well."

"Maybe there's something you missed." She paused. "No offense."

"None taken." He chuckled, a dry and quiet sound. One thin arm snaked out of his blankets, and he patted her on the knee. "If anyone can find these answers, it's you. But I also need you to be prepared for what will likely end up being necessary."

"You know I'm more than capable of that." She looked him in the eye.

"I know."

"I realize I choked with my dad, Nathan. But that was years ago. I was a kid. It won't happen again. You don't have to worry."

"I'm not."

She turned her body to face him better, and leaned forward. "You're really not. Why are you so calm about all this?"

"It is what it is, Selina. I made that choice and came to terms with it before I took this curse. There was no other way for me to act."

"There really was, but we won't get into that discussion."

He shook his head, a small smile tugging at the corners of his downturned mouth. She took in how exhausted he looked, how drained. Lines were appearing around his face, neck, and hands as the substance beneath his flesh melted away. He looked twenty years older than his real age, and that was significant, considering he'd always looked young, aging with a smooth and handsome grace.

"You're so strong, my dear. So determined. But also so stubborn and angry. I keep waiting for you to outgrow that anger, but I suspect it will always be a part of you. Be careful while you're looking into this. Don't force me to take on a second curse."

Selina leaned all the way over and pulled him into a hug, his frail body feeling as if it would break in her arms. There was nothing familiar in this embrace, not the feel, not his scent. The strength she'd relied on since childhood was gone. He wrapped his arms around her in turn, and they sat that way for a moment, Selina looking into the flickering flames and preparing herself for the days ahead.

Finally, she pulled back, kissing him on the cheek before standing up. He pulled his arms back into the blanket. She helped him tuck it back around him, stoked the fire to keep it burning. Johnny had stacked plenty of firewood in here. One whole wall was lined with it. It looked like furniture had been moved out of the way to allow for it, as two chairs were crammed together against the wall behind an end table.

"I'm out of here, Johnny," she called on her way to the front door. She plucked the truck keys off the hook beside the doorway and stepped into the brisk evening air. As she went down the porch steps, a set of headlamps came through the trees. Someone was on their way up the drive.

Jogging back up the porch, she stuck her head in the door. "Johnny, there's someone coming."

The sound of his footfalls preceded him into the hallway. He reached for Nathan's shotgun, which leaned against the wall, but she shook her head. He pulled his hand back and followed her onto the porch. They watched together as the SUV pulled into the drive. A short, bearded man got out, wearing a pair of denim over-alls. He snugged a thick flannel around him, looked up at them, and waved.

Johnny waved back as Selina watched the stranger warily.

In a whispered aside, Johnny said, "It's Herb. He owns several cabins around here, including one next door, through the trees over there." He gestured to their right with his lips. "Just bought that one about six months ago."

"Does he usually stop by at seven in the evening? What the hell does he want?"

"No idea. He stops by to be social occasionally. He's got a couple brothers, one he used to bring with him. Tim, I think. But I haven't seen that guy in a couple months. Never met the other one, but they talked about him sometimes. I gathered he wasn't their favorite person."

The two of them walked out to meet Herb halfway. He held out a hand to Johnny, which Johnny took and shook. Then Herb offered his hand to Selina, giving her a firm handshake. "Hey there, Johnny. Who is this lovely young woman?"

"This is Selina," Johnny answered. "She's visiting from the States."

"Nice to meet you, Selina. I'm Herb."

Selina nodded. "Hi, Herb. Nice to meet you. What brings you here this evening?"

"Ah, I took a new tenant to the rental cabin and thought I'd stop by. He's an interesting fella'. Some kind of hunter, I believe. Lots of gear."

Selina filed this away for later. They'd have to be careful now with someone occupying a nearby cabin. This was a common area for hunters to camp or go on vacation, so it didn't set off any alarm bells, though she'd be paying the new tenant a visit, probably tomorrow, to make sure "gear" was actually the normal hunting apparel and nothing more. She'd also like to see how much they intended to be at the cabin. It felt like one more thing to worry about when she was already overloaded.

"I'm afraid Nathan isn't feeling well," she said. "We just left him asleep in there. Nasty bug, fever and everything. Can I pass him a message to call you, maybe?"

"Nah, that's okay. Just thought I'd come shoot the shit." His eyes widened, and he licked his lips. "Sorry about that, young lady. Shoot the breeze, I meant."

Selina laughed. "No problem. I'll tell him you stopped by."

Another round of handshakes, and Herb climbed back into his car, reversed into a turn, and drove away down the drive. Johnny went back inside, his face creased with worry. He'd let Nathan know what was going on, and she figured they'd take the appropriate precautions. She had things to do, and Nathan was more than capable, even in his weakened state, of dealing with there being a new neighbor.

In the meantime, it was time to stop by Curtis Lansing's house and learn something about the man who started it all.

9

CIRCLE IN BLOOD

Curtis Lansing had lived in a quiet, but fairly ritzy, neighborhood. His house stood on a flat lot behind the rest of the houses, with a long driveway leading up to it. The dark kept her from being able to make out the minor details, but it appeared to be well cared for. The lawn had become overgrown, which probably caused the neighbors some suburban angst, but no one knew he was dead. The amount and quality of landscaping showed he'd taken care of the lawn when he was alive. There was no visible chipping paint on the house itself, and everything was tidy. It struck Selina as being way too large a house for a man living alone.

Then again, she lived in a house too big for her, too, so she couldn't judge.

The surrounding houses were also dark, for the most part, though a smattering had outside lights on that probably stayed that way all night. She drove on, parking the truck in a church parking lot, and went back to the house on foot. The night was cool, but not horribly so, and she enjoyed the walk, despite the leathers making her feel like a roast cooking from the inside out. Sweat ran down her back and between her breasts.

"Blech." She fanned the leather jacket away from her chest. Once she got in the house and had a chance to go through it, she'd probably take her jacket off, at least.

She walked with quiet, purposeful steps, but didn't sneak, as that would grab someone's attention before someone walking along at a normal pace would. She did try to keep in the shadows of the trees, over at the side of the driveway. Night creatures sounded off around her, tiny paws creeping through the brush. Some supernatural beings scared night creatures off, making them go silent. Luckily, they didn't respond to Myth Stalkers that way.

She enjoyed the chirps and squeaks that sounded from the trees and bushes around her, glancing up to take in the moon, which looked like a Cheshire cat grin tonight. The midnight blue of the sky bordered on being black, tiny stars scattered throughout. The air smelled of suburbia, with a touch of oil and gas, fresh cut grass, fabric softener, dog poop from a couple yards, and wood smoke from someone's chimney.

Before going inside, Selina walked around the entirety of the property, scoping out the building to be sure it was empty, but also making sure no one lingered outside. Though Curtis was gone, it paid to be cautious in case anything else lurked in the vicinity. There was no way to know if he'd turned a neighbor before disappearing, or if something had sensed him previously and been drawn to his house. Like often called to like.

The same tidiness reflected in the front yard existed around the perimeter, and it was an easy matter to get around the house in just a few minutes, despite it being pitch black under the trees. She was grateful for her advanced night vision at times like this. That, and her keen hearing. Other than the small wild animals, nothing snuck around that she could hear.

She walked up to the front door and studied the doorknob, which was fairly basic, no gimmicks or electronics involved. She pulled out her lock picks and went to work, inserting the tension wrench and applying torque. Unlike in the movies, it usually took time to get the lock properly jimmied. The darkness would help her out here, her black leathers keeping her out of sight of anyone taking a quick glance in her direction. The brightest thing would be her face and hands. She loosed her hair from its ponytail and shook it around her face to hide as much of it as she could while still being able to see what she was doing.

Next came the pick, which she used to rake across the pins inside the lock, once, twice. A quiet click told her at least one pin had set, so she put the pick back in and started working on the individual pins. It took her several minutes, back aching, ears straining, but then she felt the give that told her she'd finally gotten all the pins set on top of the cylinder. With great relief, she used the tension wrench to spin the cylinder, unlocking the door.

Selina ejected her wrist blade and pushed the door open a tiny bit, seeing if anyone, or anything, would respond. She didn't breathe, didn't move.

Nothing, so far. Nothing growled. There was no sound of a shotgun being pumped. Nobody screamed. These were all good signs.

She nudged the door open a little more. Happily, her eyes were already adjusted to the dark, but it was darker inside. She took a moment to finish adjusting to the deeper darkness of a room that obviously had the curtains pulled. Not that there was a ton of light outside with only a sliver of a moon, either. Stepping inside, she closed the door behind her and locked it to make sure no one could slip inside after her. At the very least, it would take them a few minutes, and she'd hear them well before they came inside.

Her feet sunk into what must have been deep carpeting. She pulled out the penlight she carried in her jacket. Though she could see better in the dark than the average human, things were still clearer with some light. Why squint into the darkness when she could light it up? Its beam illuminated a room that had obviously been decorated by a professional, not a bachelor. The sofas looked like something children would get shrieked at for touching, the tables were all delicate, and the lamps were girly, but attractive. Art on the walls reflected a woman's touch, as well, with landscapes that should have been rugged had it not been for the pastels and gentle lines throughout.

There was, indeed, a deep carpet in a muted gray, almost white. Everything in the room was impeccable in order and cleanliness. It didn't appear that he'd been reported missing, or that anyone had come looking for him.

Double doors opened up to the right, and Selina went to investigate. The room held a large wooden desk, polished to a shine, with a glass-doored bookcase standing behind it, curtained windows on either side. The books in the case were all classics, nicely bound, which probably meant he wasn't a big reader, and that the case existed for show. On the other hand, he might just love the classics.

Grooves in the wood of the desk were the first sign Selina had seen that everything wasn't perfect here. They were deep and thick, and could quite possibly be those of talons, such as a Wendigo might have. Selina had started wondering if he'd been staying elsewhere when he'd turned. He must have a great cleaning lady.

In fact, when she glanced back into the living room, she noticed a dark rectangle on the wall where a painting or large framed photo had likely hung before, as well as a rip in the back of the full-sized sofa. Small things were starting to filter through. Still, considering the usual amount of damage a Wendigo did, it seemed minimal. He had to have gone through the majority of the process elsewhere. Nathan had said he killed him at his sister's house. That must have been where Curtis infected Nell, and where the bulk of the change occurred.

Selina finished a quick walkthrough of the house to be sure she was the only one there. Once positive, she pressed the blade back down into its sheath and shed her coat, laying it across the back of a sofa in the living area. There were other slight hints at damage, but still nothing major. A bag of garbage in the garage confirmed there had been damage cleaned up by the maid—stuffing and fabric from the sofa, a broken wooden frame and glass, a shattered lamp.

They usually made themselves a nest, but she found no sign of one. A note on the bedside table in the master bedroom told her the cleaning lady quit after lack of pay. She couldn't have been his cleaning lady for too long if she hadn't figured out something was wrong and called the police. And considering the amount of damage she had possibly had to clean up, she couldn't be terribly bright, either. Surely, someone with half a brain would have grown concerned if her employer were missing, the house torn up. Even by bachelor standards. There was also the possibility that she simply hadn't liked him enough to care.

Selina headed back into the office to look for a Rolodex, among other things, curious as to whether she'd find Nell's name somewhere in there. It wouldn't matter if Nathan wouldn't give her the address if she found the information on her own, and yes, she'd cross him to save his life. In a heartbeat.

"Where are you, Nell?" She dug through the drawers of the desk, muttering. He didn't seem to have a physical Rolodex or an address book. Maybe he kept it on a smart phone, a laptop, or another form of technology.

As she continued to look through the desk drawers, her foot hit something under the desk. The light of the penlight revealed a power strip. Curious. There was no computer on this desk.

Wait a second. There's no computer on this desk.

The meaning of that hit her. She followed a cord from the power strip to a printer, sitting on a desk against the left-hand wall. Her search revealed a spray can of air used on computers, re-writable CD-ROMs, a USB drive, etc. All evidence that there should be a computer somewhere. She searched the house one more time without finding a computer or laptop. As no keyboard had been left behind, she thought perhaps he had used a laptop. Otherwise, someone had taken all the pieces of the desktop computer, which seemed weird.

It was also possible he'd taken the laptop with him somewhere. She'd only done a cursory examination of the garage earlier, not going through the sporty red car that sat in the space big enough for two vehicles, oil stains in the empty spot telling her he had more than one vehicle. She headed back out there now to look through the car.

"Gotta' love a mid-life crisis car," she said aloud. "How sweet."

The top was down, which made it easy to go through. There were coins inside an old mint tin, a couple CDs, a tube of lip balm, and a tire pressure gauge in the center console. The dashboard held the usual documents—insurance cards, vehicle manual, etc. She popped the trunk to be sure, but found nothing there. The car didn't hold anything important, and it was undamaged. In fact, it was impeccably clean like his house. He may have been a jerk, according to what Nathan had said, but he wasn't a slob.

Back in his office, she found the title to a Forerunner. He'd taken off in the more rugged vehicle before changing. Interesting. Did he know what was happening? Is that why he had left early enough in the transformation for the damage to his home to be so minimal? Perhaps he'd tried to head up into the mountains. Still, he'd gone somewhere, and that vehicle had to be there. She suspected it was at Nell's family's home. Either that, or he'd been dropped off there.

Selina went through the house more thoroughly, looking for anything that might give her hints. Family photos lined the wall near his bedroom. In them were a couple, a teenaged girl, and a young boy. The teenager was First Nations, from her appearance, but the rest of the family were light skinned with blond hair. His sister must have adopted Nell. Odd, as it was typically discouraged for a white family to adopt a First Nations child. It usually took help from inside the tribe to make that happen, as the hope was to keep the child within the tribe so they could stay within their own culture and learn the ways of their people. They were, after all, trying to keep their heritage alive.

The last thing she found that was of interest, though she wasn't sure what it meant yet, was a leather bag with a variety of herbs in it, likely a fetish or charm of some sort. She wasn't sure if it was protective or otherwise. In that bag, she found a business card for one Oliver Benson III. His name had been circled in a brown substance that appeared to be dried blood.

Who was Oliver Benson III? And why was his card in a charm? Selina had a new lead. Was this the man who had infected Curtis? Or someone else entirely? Only way to find out was to do more digging, this time on Oliver Benson III. First, she needed to go to impound and see if a Forerunner had turned up. Her to-do list kept getting longer, yet she wasn't learning anything that would help Nathan.

And time was running out.

10

NICE NIGHT FOR A RUN

Selina arrived at the impound lot to discover it wasn't a twenty-four hour one. She walked around the fencing, looking for cameras and ways in that weren't destructive or unnecessarily dangerous. There were a couple cameras arranged to take in most of the small lot, and a couple guard dogs. The security was surprisingly high for such a small town, and it wasn't worth trying to break in when she could return the next day and not risk prison or a dog mauling. A second trek failed to reveal a Forerunner, and as far as she could tell, the entirety of the lot was visible. Still, she'd check tomorrow.

Seeing as how everything else would be closed, and dropping in for personal visits would be very much unappreciated in the middle of the night, she decided to head back to Nathan's to get some sleep. She climbed back into the truck and took her cell phone out of her pocket. It shuddered, letting her know she had a text or a message.

Sorry to hear about Charles. Dealing with some stuff here, but let me know if you need my help. Brent had finally responded to her texts from earlier.

Okay, thanks, she texted back, surprised he didn't have more to say about Charles, considering they'd butted heads in the past. He was obviously preoccupied. She considered asking him what was going on, but figured he would have told her if he'd wanted to. Instead, she put the phone down and headed home.

The fire burned bright and warm when she arrived back at Nathan's. He was asleep on the couch, his breathing labored. Beads of sweat dotted his forehead, and when she crept closer waves of heat came off his body. His pulse was so fast it visibly pounded in the artery in his throat, throbbing at an astounding and strong rate. Something was definitely happening inside him for him to have gone from freezing cold to putting off massive amounts of feverish heat.

She picked up his glass and refilled it with ice water for him, setting it back on the table with a quiet *tick*.

His eyes popped open, no initial stirring or warning, and she startled, stepping back from him. His eyes glowed red in the warm light of the fire, and he stared directly at her.

Shivers crept up her spin. He didn't speak a word, and after a moment she backed away and went to her room, testing Johnny's door on the way to assure herself he'd followed Nathan's instructions, and making sure the alarms were in place.

Exhaustion hit her like a Mack truck, and she stripped off her leathers, folding them neatly on a chair by the bed. Her weapons went into the chest. She tucked a stake under her pillow, a gun in the drawer next to her bed, and her long blade beside her, under the covers. If his change went more quickly than they were expecting, she wanted to be prepared.

She fell asleep the second her head hit the pillow, something that rarely happened for her. Her dreams were crazy and rolled through her head like a silent film on fast forward, jerky and frantic. She saw her father in the moments before turning, white fur covering his body, eyes glowing red. In her dream, the red cleared and he became himself, pleading for his life, asking her why she was doing this to him. Even in her sleep, her chest clenched and she registered that discomfort, struggling to breathe past the monstrous obstruction in her chest.

Just as she was about to finish him off, he changed to Nathan, as he was now. No fur, no talons or long teeth. Just Nathan, scrawny and broken. Weak. He threw his head back and laughed, the warm tones of his usually infectious laugh becoming a hacking cough, which turned into an evil chuckle. He reached a hand toward her, but as she tried to grab it, talons sprouted from it, longer than blades, and he stabbed her in the abdomen.

"This is for even thinking of killing me," he said in a garbled voice.

"No, I don't want to kill you. I'm trying to find a cure."

"You're not trying hard enough. What is this? Are you sleeping? As I die slowly in another room?"

"There was nothing else I could do. I'll start first thing in the morning. I promise."

He jerked his claws out of her, ripping more on the way out, and she bent over, gripping her abdomen, arms wrapped around herself.

"Please, I love you, why are you doing this to me?"

He laughed again, and then Johnny's sweet, innocent face replaced his. All that youth.

Johnny reached for her, beseeching her, his face full of disappointment in her for not saving him. His face melted, changed shape, went from her dad to Nathan to Johnny, then back through it all again. It was as if they were all there together, all blended into one, a puddle of familiar faces, the mouths open and screaming, full of pain.

It was so loud, resounding in her ears, bouncing off the walls, and she jerked up to a sitting position before realizing that there really was someone screaming. She threw back the covers, grabbed her long blade and the gun, and ran out the door, dressed only in a tank top and her panties.

Johnny's door stood open, and she threw a quick glance in as she raced by, fearful of what she would see. It was empty.

Oh lord, where is he?

The living room was also empty, so she dashed toward the front door, which stood open. Johnny stood on the front porch, shivering in a pair of sweatpants, raking the woods surrounding the cabin with his gaze. He held the shotgun from beside the door.

"Where is he?" she asked.

He shook his head. "I don't know. I heard the alarms, wasn't sleeping well anyway. Then the screams started. He went through the door right as I got mine open. Nowhere to be seen when I got out here." He looked at her, eyes wide in the dark. "How did he move so fast? He can hardly get around inside the house."

She knew exactly why he was suddenly able to move so quickly. "It's common at this point. The spirit is asserting itself. His body is weak, but the spirit doesn't care about the physical discomfort, so it pushes through where he can't. We have to be even more cautious now. These bursts of energy can occur at any time, but only when the spirit wants something."

Selina slipped her feet into her boots, which still rested by the door. "Go get dressed, check your weapons, and lock yourself in your room."

"I'm not leaving him out there. I can help."

"I don't know how bad he might be. He was feverish when I got in. there's never any telling how fast this process will go. Do you want to die?"

"I'd die for him." He set his jaw. "You do what you need, but I won't be locking myself up and leaving you two alone to fight this."

She locked eyes with him, studying his face. He obviously meant it, though she wondered if he'd thought through what would happen if he wasn't lucky enough to be killed. His jaw bulged out at the side from being clenched so hard, and his lips pressed together into a firm line. No point arguing with him; there was no time.

"You got it, kid. My priority is getting him back here and making sure he can't hurt anyone else. You're on your own, got it?"

He nodded and turned, entering the house. She stayed there on the porch for a minute, studying the woods, focusing on her night vision. There was no sound of night creatures now, and that spooked her. Even they could sense that something was wrong with him, and she began to fear that he had less time than they'd thought. Then again, animals were drawn to Wendigo, not put off by the spirit, so it struck her that this was a small positive sign. Had he changed all the way, they wouldn't be scared.

A feral scream sounded from her right, deeper into the forest, in the direction of Herb's cabin. She leapt off the porch, sprinting into the woods, weapons clasped in her hands. She should have asked Johnny to get her stake. It was the only true thing that could put Nathan down, even temporarily, if he had changed.

Branches slapped her in the face, ripped at her bare skin, lashes of sharp pain. She ducked around them the best she could, almost dancing through the woods as she deftly avoided tree trunks and grounded logs. She could smell Nathan, the sick scent he exuded now, and she followed his trail as she ran.

Up ahead came the sound of something making its way through the brush. She slowed, listening. A huff sounded, followed by a pained whimper. Her blood ran cold, hairs standing up along her body, as something screamed, high and in pain. She sped up again, though not quite running. Was it him making the sounds, or did he have someone or something? The person renting the cabin, perhaps. That would be one of her worst fears realized.

She broke through a thick copse of trees and saw a small cabin, no lights on. Something hunched over near the porch. She approached with caution, eyes only leaving the form long enough to check for anyone else, though she couldn't smell any other presences, nor hear them. What she could smell, other than Nathan, was blood, coppery and thick. Behind that was the scent of an animal, but Nathan's smell was so strong that she couldn't read her sense of smell as much as she should have been able to. She didn't know for a fact that this was Nathan—his scent could be coming from anywhere at this point, it was so thick—but whatever it was, it presented the biggest hazard right now.

As she got closer, the form stilled, froze really. The head swiveled in her direction. Eyes glowed red in the moonlight.

She stopped. "Nathan, is that you?"

It whimpered, still not moving. She took a step closer, another. It didn't rise to defend or attack. Didn't move at all.

Selina took a deep breath, another step. Still no movement from it.

Now only a few feet away, she could make out the features. It was Nathan, she could see that now, but he seemed different. She couldn't quite put her finger on it. He picked up something large. A doe. The fur was dark and matted—dry, not wet.

She nodded at Nathan, understanding. Someone had hurt the deer, not him. At her nod, he screamed again, an inhuman sound that sunk to the primal core of her, made her want to run screaming, but she resisted. Her subconscious lashed out, making her bowels turn to liquid.

This was Nathan, but it also wasn't.

"I'm sorry," she said. "Something hurt her?"

It/Nathan nodded, cradled the deer to his body. Nathan was an animal lover, yes, but it was well known among Cryptos that Wendigo had a deep connection with the animals of the forest. It hungered for human flesh only, never animal. That didn't explain how he'd known it was out here. Perhaps he'd felt it.

"We need to go back home, Nathan. Would you like to bury her? We can do that." She spoke in a soft voice, calm. Hopefully it would comfort him, lull him into calming down.

"She's been shot." His voice was garbled, as it had been in her dream, rough, not quite his.

"When?"

"I don't know. I heard her crying."

"Is she dead now, Nathan?" Maybe if she kept calling him by name he'd come all the way back around. Maybe.

"Yes." He whimpered, released a soft sob.

"Let's take care of her then. Let's take her home, okay?"

"This is her home! She should have been safe."

"I know, Nathan. It's not fair. Come on, let's put her to rest."

He rose, still slightly hunched. But he seemed taller, wider maybe. The doe's limp body lay over his arms. "A man killed her. I have his scent now."

Selina's mouth went dry.

Not good.

11

THE SCENT OF DEATH

"Let's bury her, and then we'll talk about what needs to be done. Take care of her first, Nathan, okay?"

He nodded, and they headed back toward home, him in the lead so she could keep an eye on him. She shot a glance at the cabin. No one had stirred, even with all that screaming, and there was no vehicle outside. They'd lucked out this time, but there was no telling how long their luck would hold.

Footsteps sounded in the direction of Nathan's. "That's just Johnny, Nathan."

"I know. I can smell him."

The changes were definitely coming faster.

They continued forward, a sad funeral procession for a murdered doe, and came across Johnny within a couple minutes. He had a flashlight taped to his shotgun, and he aimed it at them as they approached.

"It's okay, Johnny. He's mostly him. That's a dead deer in his arms. We're burying her."

"Ooookay." Johnny frowned, drawing the word out, but he lowered the gun/flashlight combo and waited for them to catch up to him entirely, turning to walk beside Selina.

"Did he...?" Johnny started to ask, voice fading away at the end as he stared at Nathan's form ahead of them.

"No. He found her. Heard her crying. Wendigo doesn't harm animals."

"That's right. I'd forgotten that part of the lore."

"Listen, don't let your guard down. He wants the man who shot her. He's slipping."

Johnny gulped and straightened in her peripheral vision. He understood what that meant, which was good. She wouldn't have to do near as much explaining as she'd thought.

"I can hear you back there, you know." That was a little more Nathan.

Selina allowed herself a hint of a smile. "We know. Maybe hearing it will get you under control, yes?"

"I will not go hunt that man tonight, if that's what you mean. There's still enough human left in this shell that I can fight that urge."

"Sounds good," she replied.

They walked the rest of the way in silence, nothing more to say. Relief filled her. She wasn't going to have to fight to get him inside. There definitely wouldn't be any more sleep for her tonight, because she'd have to make sure he stuck to that. The good thing being that hunters usually didn't stay in any area for long. Whoever had done this was probably back home in their cozy living room, possibly with a different deer carcass in their garage. Hunters were usually more responsible than this, not leaving a wounded animal out there to die slowly.

She sighed. The adrenaline had started to drain away. It left behind a complete lack of energy, and she was starting to feel the various cuts and scrapes on her body.

As they neared their house, a pair of headlights shone through the trees. She looked at Johnny, brows drawn together in a question.

"It's the drive up to the cabin we were just at," he said. "Guess we got lucky tonight."

She nodded, a tiny additional spurt of adrenaline coursing through her. They'd escaped an escalation of events, but this had been close. Now it occurred to her to worry about whether the new tenant had shot the doe. What if he'd been there? Where had he been so late at night?

Checking in on this neighbor moved up her to-do list. Not now, of course. Dawn crept in, a stealthy burglar on pink and gold feet, and appearing on one's property at this time of day when they were likely armed wouldn't be a good idea.

She'd have to stop in when she could, though. No more mistakes like tonight. No more trusting to luck.

THE DOE BURIED, they all went inside, filthy and sore. She saw to it that Nathan bathed first, so she could get him settled while Johnny took his shower. That probably meant there'd be no warm water for her, but she could use a cool shower at this point. Her skin felt shrunken from the dried sweat covering her, and heat suffused her body from the work she'd done digging the hole. Exactly what she wanted to do on a couple pitiful hours of sleep.

While Nathan showered—Johnny standing outside the bathroom door to make sure nothing happened—she set up the trip alarms again, adding extra cans to ensure it would wake them up. Had he not screamed as he'd done, she might not have woken up at all, leaving Johnny to take care of the issue on his own if he hadn't thought to wake her.

Was there enough humanity in there that he wouldn't have chased down the hunter either way? She could no longer answer that definitively. She and Johnny were going to have to take shifts at night from here on out if they wanted to avoid anything horrible happening. It would have killed Nathan to have harmed someone, and she didn't want to let that happen.

Once she'd reset the alarms, she moved to the disarray he'd left behind. His water had been spilled when he'd leapt up from the sofa, or so it appeared. His blanket had been thrown over the back of the sofa, the glass knocked over, and the table sat several feet from its original position. She grabbed a fresh glass of water and set it on the table, then folded the blanket onto the foot of the sofa so he'd be able to pull it over him. She usually wasn't so maternal, but he apparently brought it out in her.

Nathan came out of the bathroom, nice and clean, wearing sweatpants and no shirt. She looked at the torso that had once been muscular and tan, a pleasure to look at. Now, he appeared pale—almost gray—and thin, the muscle mass gone, his skin sagging. However, as she'd noticed in the dark, his shoulders were broader, his back hunched, and he towered above her. He had definitely grown, the mass changing from muscle to height, which seemed like it should be physically impossible. She knew from experience it wasn't.

Selina helped him settle on the sofa. "Tell me what happened tonight." She tried to wrap the blanket around him, but he pushed it off.

"No, thank you. I'm roasting."

He clasped his hands together, leaned forward, forearms balanced on his knees. For a moment, he looked into the fire, which had burned down to embers. She allowed him the time to collect himself while she built the fire back up, throwing in two more logs. The light of the flames licked at his face, accentuating the gauntness there, his cheekbones standing out in stark relief, eye sockets black holes.

Finally, he spoke, his voice sad and quiet. "I woke up to crying. It was loud, close, so I stopped outside your room then Johnny's. It wasn't coming from either room, though I heard you breathing heavily. Nightmares?"

"Yeah." She'd always had an issue with nightmares, which he was aware of.

He unclasped his hands long enough to squeeze her arm, then continued. "I'm sure you're thinking about your dad a lot."

"Not as much as you might think. That was years ago, and I'm worried about you right now. But, yeah, he's been on my mind." She paused. "Steve fixed his blade. It's sitting in my room right now."

Nathan nodded. He knew their relationship hadn't been great, her and her father's, which is probably why she'd latched onto a man twenty-three years her senior as a father figure. He was kind where her father had been strict and indifferent. He worried about her, tried to train her, while her father had thought more along the lines of throwing her to the wolves to see if she would survive, literally at times, and figuring she would learn from her mistakes.

Her father had meant well in his own way, she knew that now, but he also hadn't wanted to be stuck with a child. And when he'd learned that she was one of them, a Myth Stalker, he'd been disappointed more than proud. Sure, there was a part of him that was proud, of that she was certain. Most Myth Stalkers were male. It was just the way it worked out. Having a daughter who happened to be the only known female Myth Stalker currently alive was a boon to his pride. But having to train her meant having to put in effort, to spend time with her, and that had been something he had never been good at. Suddenly, he was saddled with a kid who had to go on his trips with him, an extra body to care for and protect. Before that, she'd been left at home with her mom, her problem, while he disappeared on his adventures, surfing a wave of adrenaline. "Myth Stalkers are solo creature, lone wolves," he'd told her.

Nathan knew her well, but sometimes he still didn't understand how removed she'd become from memories of her father. Until this trip, he hadn't crossed her mind in months, possibly a year.

"I see," Nathan said. "Well, sorry to throw you back into all of it. You were the only person I knew I could trust."

"S'okay. Tell me what happened after you realized it wasn't one of us."

"Right. I went to the front door, heard the crying, knew something was in pain. It filled me. And suddenly I could feel the pain, and I couldn't stop screaming. White hot agony, filling my body, but also an ache behind it all. So tired. I felt all her sensations. She'd been shot earlier, but either wasn't feeling it then or she was too far out of some kind of radar. I just know that I could hear her, out there in the woods, and I could feel her pain. I had to make it end, had to help her.

"When I found her body, so weak from the pain and blood loss, rage filled me, white hot. I held her to me as she died, felt her spirit go. She looked into my eyes like she knew I wouldn't hurt her, like she knew what I was. She recognized Wendigo inside me."

"You said you smelled him? The killer? What...how does that work? What did you smell?"

"Ah, yes, it's hard to explain. At first, all I could smell was her, the scent of blood overwhelming, and yet not entirely unpleasant. I smelled gunpowder. Don't know if that means he'd gotten close to her or that it comes with the bullet. I smelled the metal of the bullet, the scent of burned flesh from where it had seared her. But then I smelled human smells. Grease, probably from whatever he'd eaten, cologne, scented deodorant, unwashed socks."

His nose wrinkled as he continued explaining what he'd smelled, and Selina found her own nose scrunching in response. She had a heightened sense of smell, but his might rival her own. Unless this guy had rubbed on the doe, it seemed far-fetched that his smell could have so encompassed hers. If he'd actually touched her, he would surely have finished her, kept his trophy. Unless she'd broken away after he made contact with her, which was entirely possible. Or perhaps Nathan had smelled the man through the deer's sense memory.

"Are your other senses heightened at all, or only your sense of smell?" she asked.

"Good question. I could see really well. I could see the bark on the trees, even in the pitch dark. I could see the night critters hiding, an owl in a tree, a rodent under the leaves. They were quiet, but they didn't seem scared of me, so much as...reverent? Maybe that's wrong. Maybe they were scared. They were quiet. So were the bugs."

"The doe wasn't scared, so maybe they weren't either. I'd assumed they were quiet because they were afraid of you, but sounds like that isn't so."

"True." He stopped to think again, maybe running through the events that had occurred. He kept running his thumb over the top of his index finger, something he did when he was nervous or thinking.

Faint signs of the real Nathan still in there heartened her, told her he had a better hold than she kept allowing herself to think.

"I suspect I know a little of what you usually feel as a Myth Stalker now. It's amazing." He looked at her, wonder showing on his face, voice low in awe. "My hearing was heightened, too. I heard you coming, knew from the speed that it had to be you. No regular person can run that fast, especially not in the night woods. Johnny was much slower, stumbling, running into things, though I see that you met your share of sharp items."

He reached over, plucked a couple pine needles out of her hair. It had been loose as she'd been running, and she'd probably picked up all manner of interesting things in her long hair.

She studied her arms, which had possibly taken the worst of the lashings. She'd seen them coming, but it was more important to avoid the large items than the small, better to get smacked with a light branch than brained by a thick one. Dried blood covered her arms in slashes, and she knew it would sting when she first stepped into that shower. Speaking of which...

"Does that boy take the longest showers ever, or what?"

12

HIGH TIMES IN A HIGH RISE

The next morning, a clean and somewhat better rested Selina got dressed and hit the impound lot. It smelled of motor oil. There was a woman working the front, red hair feathered around her face. She wore a mechanic's overall with the name Bonnie on the nametag, a pair of cubic zirconia earrings winking from her ears. Her gum chewing resembled a cow chewing cud, and Selina resisted the urge to pinch Bonnie's lips together to still her jaw.

"Can I help you?" Bonnie asked.

"Yes, I'm here for a Forerunner with Alberta license plate BKBM 637." Selina slid a piece of paper across the counter with that information written on it.

Bonnie turned to an ancient computer monitor and tapped the keys. She frowned, tapped some more. Finally, she looked up at Selina. "We don't have anything like that. You sure you came to the right lot?"

"I guess not." Selina reached across the counter and took the piece of paper. "Is there another impound lot I should go to?"

"We're the only one in this town. Do you have the notice? Maybe I could help figure out where it was taken, though I don't know why it would be anywhere else. Were you in the city when it was impounded?"

"I left the letter in my car, but I had just assumed it was here. It wasn't here, but in Cascade. Thank you for your help. Sorry to have wasted your time."

So his vehicle hadn't been impounded. Where was it then? He had to have left it somewhere. Nathan hadn't mentioned anything about a vehicle, so she didn't think he'd done anything with it, and she'd completely forgotten to ask. Not that she'd had the opportunity. Nathan had been passed out cold when she'd left this morning.

One item off her to-do list, she headed to the library for some internet time. Nathan didn't have a computer, let alone internet, and she wondered how he survived. He didn't even have cable! She searched for information on Curtis Lansing. Lansing hadn't been in the news, so all she found were his social media accounts. None of these yielded anything too interesting. His Facebook page was largely unprotected, which allowed her to see photos and status updates. What she saw made her agree with Nathan—this guy had been a jerk. Between tacky, sexist memes, political rants, and asinine jokes, he'd covered pretty much every means of annoying people via social media. There were even gym selfies.

Aside from all this, she found nothing damning, and certainly nothing stating who'd turned him into a monster. The last thing he'd posted was a status saying, "Off to the cabin. Don't miss me too much." No one had responded to it in any way, so she figured no one had missed him. She scanned down the page to see who he might have gone with. There were several likely candidates, and she jotted down their names so she could check them out. Clicking on their names took her to protected accounts, and she couldn't see anything about them.

She plugged their names into a search engine one by one. One was nowhere to be found except for his Facebook account. Another name brought up two local articles about some men killed in an animal attack. Authorities were leaning toward a bear. Lansing's name didn't come up in the article, so maybe he hadn't been with them. Or the families hadn't known he was. Nowhere did it say where the cabin was located. She'd have to find someone who knew. A quick search produced the second man's address, and she jotted it down in case she couldn't find the information elsewhere. It wouldn't do to bring anyone unnecessary in on this, or to harass a recently bereaved family.

Now it was time to search for Benson. Apparently, he was quite the giver, donating funds to various charities, as well as time. He worked in soup kitchens, visited schools, you name it. On the surface, he looked pretty good. His photos showed him as a handsome man with a friendly smile. So how in the hell was he mixed up in all this?

As she clicked through to read one of the many articles about what a phenomenal human being he was, she felt a presence behind her, smelled cologne and sweat.

"What are you looking at there?" asked a deep male voice.

She quickly closed the window and turned to confront Charles. "What are you doing here? I didn't think you could read."

He chuckled and reached forward to pick up a lock of her hair, running it through his fingers. "I can do a lot of things that would surprise you."

"Is bathing one of them?"

"Touché. So, what was it you were looking at? Anything interesting?"

She yanked her hair out of his hand, flipping it over her shoulder.

He smiled and brought his fingers up to his nose, drawing in a long breath before bringing it to rest at his side again.

"That was creepy and stalkerish. Again I ask, what are you doing here, Charles? I thought you had a mission. This is none of your business and, seriously, have you never heard of sexual harassment?"

"Have you found your Wendigo yet?"

"If I haven't made it clear, I won't be speaking with you about this." She gathered her things, stuffing them into her bag.

He nodded, rubbing a hand over his scruffy chin. "Fair enough. That means I don't have to tell you what I know, either. See you soon."

He turned, though not before tossing a smirk her way, and walked to the back of the library, disappearing behind a set of shelves.

She watched for a while, wondering if he really knew something, or if he was merely trying to get her to talk. When he didn't return, she turned the computer back on. Casting glances over her shoulder and tuning into her sense of smell, she quickly cleared the history. Satisfied, she headed out to the truck. She'd have to return later to continue her searches, but she'd gotten enough for now, including confirming the address on Benson's business card.

Once outside, she watched through a window as Charles sauntered over to the computer and turned it on.

"You won't find what you're looking for." Laughing, she climbed into the truck and headed into the city.

BENSON'S OFFICE was downtown amongst several tall buildings. Selina looked up the length of the building, the face sparkling as sun danced off the glass and metal. The windows were lightly tinted, probably a blessing for the employees stuck inside.

She pulled out the card and glanced at it one more time, verifying the address. Yep, right place. It showed Suite 1301. From the looks of it, he was at or near the top.

Grasping the card, she went up the steps and pushed through the glass front door, skipping the rotating door in the center. She always had images of herself getting stuck in one of those things, everyone staring at her like a fish in a bowl. Or perhaps being chopped in half as she tried to step out. Either way, it was easier to use the regular door when that was an option.

The lobby was spacious, a desk sitting off to the side, manned by one perky quasi-adult, her hair perfectly coiffed, teeth glittering all the way across the lobby. She appeared to have more energy in one finger than Selina would have all year, greeting the people sidling up to the counter with enthusiasm and bounce.

It was painfully obvious that she wouldn't be arriving in a beast-infested office up on the thirteenth floor, and she was made very aware of how severely she stood out in this setting with her leathers on. Good thing her weapons were all hidden. Maybe next time she'd do a bit more research before showing up at a location. Nathan was always telling her she should, but she wasn't a planning kinda' girl. It was why she never played chess. She just wanted to plow across the board and take out any piece that got in her way, not sit and strategize how to do it in twenty moves, or whatever the aim was. At the same time, the clock was ticking and she didn't know if she'd be going straight from this office to somewhere far more dangerous. She probably would have worn them either way.

As she approached Miss Perky, it gave her a small thrill of amusement that her gigantic smile faltered at the sight of Selina. Good. Who did she think she was, Julia Roberts?

"Hi, is there some way I can help you?" asked Miss Perky, sounding vaguely as if she were eating her own face as she spoke.

"Yeah, if I'm going to an office upstairs, do I need to sign in, or do I just go on up?"

The girl studied her, taking in her clothes, disdain and a shadow of fear playing across her pretty face. "You can go on up. You want me to call ahead for you? Let them know to expect you?"

She was probably trying to figure out how to warn them, maybe see if she should call security. Selina realized she was being uncharitable, and perhaps slightly paranoid, but this girl brought it out in her. Why, was an issue for the back burner.

"No thanks. I'll just go straight up." If she didn't say who she was seeing, Miss Perky couldn't call ahead.

"Oh, well, all right then. Have a good day."

Selina felt the girl's eyes burning through her back as she walked toward the bank of elevators. When she looked behind her, Miss Perky looked away, hair grazing her chin as the speed of her turn whipped it around. Selina stifled a laugh and turned back toward the elevators. She considered using the stairs so it wouldn't be obvious what floor she was heading to—a digital panel ran along the top of the elevator showing where it was floor-wise—but she figured by the time it became visible where she was heading she'd already be there. No big. And, really, it didn't matter if the girl called ahead. No one would know who she was or why she was there.

She was out of her element here, and it bothered her. Typically, she was chasing creatures around deserts, in the woods, on the sides of mountains. In other words, she rarely had to worry about other people or what they thought of her, and she usually had a longer amount of time to play with, so she could dedicate herself to research for a day or two, and even dress appropriately for it. And she didn't usually have to cram so many things into one day, which made wearing the right clothes easier. But her timeframe was so constrained right now that she had to go from one place to another, prepared for whatever she might get herself into. Which meant sticking out like a sore thumb in an office setting like this one. Or the library, though no one had paid her much mind there. Librarians probably saw every type of person in existence.

The elevator binged at her, and she stepped to the side as the door slid open, vomiting a bunch of people dressed in business suits. Once again, she winced inwardly, trying to ignore the strange looks they gave her as they wondered why in the hell she was here. She pasted a big smile on her face that would make Miss Perky jealous, and stepped in when the last person exited. The scent of ten different colognes and perfumes enveloped her, and she barked a cough.

She reached for the thirteenth floor button. A man shouted, "Wait!" He rushed toward the elevator. Her finger hovered over the *close door* button, but at the last minute she moved it to *open door* and held it until he got inside with her.

"What floor?" she asked him, taking in the sweat trickling down his brow, his hair and suit in disarray. He hadn't even looked at her clothing funny yet.

"Tenth, please."

She pushed the ten and settled back against the wall, hands in a loose grip before her. She could hear Messy Guy panting, smell coffee and onions on his breath. Not a great first impression, and he sure seemed like someone about to give one. He fiddled with the briefcase in his hands, pulled out a stack index cards and looked them over, ran a shaking hand through his hair. She wished she had a mint to offer him. Or a valium.

When they reached the tenth floor and the doors slid open, she turned to him, smiled, and said, "You'll do great."

He looked at her in surprise, mouth agape, eyes wide, before stepping off the elevator.

A grin broke across her face, and she savored the humor of the moment for the next three floors.

The doors opened on a reception desk, front and center. She stifled the laugh that had been creeping up her throat. This wasn't a floor with many offices, as she'd expected, but one big room. There were a couple doors off this lobby area, but they all belonged to the same business, from what she could see.

An older woman sat behind the reception desk, her hair swept back in a bun. She'd tucked a flower into her hair, softening and livening up what would have otherwise been a harsh hairstyle. She smiled warmly at Selina and waited for her to approach.

Selina already liked her. Way better than Miss Perky.

She walked toward the desk, waiting for some reaction to her leathers, and unsure whether she was delighted or disappointed when she didn't get one.

The woman continued to smile at her, and it reached all the way to her eyes. Not a fake smile. "Can I help you, dear?" Some women couldn't pull off calling another "dear," but it warmed Selina when this one did.

"Um, yes, hi. I'm looking for Oliver Benson, III."

"Can I tell him who's visiting?"

"He won't know me. A friend referred me. My name is Selina Moonstone."

"Hold on a second and I'll call him."

This woman, with all her warmth and friendliness, had completely thrown Selina for a loop. She'd come up expecting to threaten, cheat, lie, sneak, whatever it took to get in to see this guy. Instead of telling her he was in a meeting or out of the office or unavailable due to an alien takeover, the secretary called him right away. She hadn't even asked what Selina wanted. What strange business world was this?

After a few seconds, the woman hung up the phone. "He has a phone call to make and then he'll be out to speak with you. Would you like to take a seat over here?" She indicated a burgundy upholstered love seat and a set of easy chairs to the right of the reception area. Ferns sat on either side of the love seat.

"I'd love to, thanks...," she leaned in to see her nametag, "Sonia. I appreciate your help."

Sonia nodded and answered the phone, which had let out a quiet purr of a ring. Selina walked over and sunk into one of the easy chairs. Man, this was comfortable. Benson was doing well for himself. To her understanding, he was some sort of insurance guy. His company provided life and casualty insurance, which made him a salesman. She settled back, picturing the man who would come out of the doors at any moment. She'd seen his photos, but they could be old. He might be fatter now, face aged. She knew he'd slither out like some kind of snake, all eager for a sale. Joke was on him. She already had life insurance.

Sonia walked over with a glass of ice water, which she handed to Selina. "You look hot, dear, and I can see he's still on the phone. It will probably be a few more minutes. Is there anything else I can get you?"

Once again, Selina was thrown off balance. She wasn't used to people being nice to her. "Oh, thanks. And no thank you, I'm good with this."

Sonia smiled and walked back to her desk, leaving Selina feeling guilty for thinking rude thoughts about her boss. She sipped the ice water, letting the cold rush through her body. It was hot in all this leather. Again, she ruminated on her stupidity at having worn these clothes, but she hadn't been sure where she would end up throughout the day, and she'd wanted to be prepared. At least she'd left the visible weapons in the truck. She did, however, take a second to unzip the jacket, which brought a measure of relief when paired with the ice water. Her medicine bag showed, so she tucked it under her shirt.

About three minutes later, a door opened, and an attractive forty-something male stepped out of it, straightening a well-fitted suit jacket. His hair was dark brown and neatly trimmed, though probably considered a bit long for a businessman's haircut. His light eyes met Selina's and he smiled, heading straight toward her.

She straightened in her seat then stood.

He looked like he had in the pictures, only more attractive. When he got to her, he held his hand out.

She switched her glass to the other hand, wiped her palm over her leg, which didn't do much good against the leather, then offered it to him. "Sorry for the damp hand."

"No worries. At least I know why your hand is cold and wet. You wouldn't believe some of the nasty handshakes I've gotten over the years." As with Sonia, his smile was genuine. Unlike her, his accent was lilting. Welsh, she thought. "I'm Oliver. And you're Selina? Is that correct?" He still held her hand, his grip firm, but not threatening. More an embrace than anything else.

"Yes, Selina Moonstone."

"Nice to meet you, Selina." He let go of her hand and just like that the warmth disappeared, her hand once again icy.

"Nice to meet you, as well, Oliver. I was hoping to discuss Curtis Lansing with you today. Do you have a few minutes?"

13

EVERYTHING COMES WITH A PRICE

She eyed him, waiting for a reaction. His smile never faltered, though he looked somewhat puzzled. "Sure, let's go to my office. You done with your water, or do you want to bring it with you?"

"I'd like to keep it, if that's okay. I'm rather parched."

"No problem."

He held an arm out, indicating that she should walk beside him, which she did. The door to his office was nondescript, a dark wood that matched several other doors along the wall. However, when he opened it and ushered her in, she was blown away by the room she encountered. Everything had been done up in blues and greens, and his office was set up to be welcoming. His desk stood toward the back of the room, but his chair sat on the side nearest the door, so he would face the windows while he worked. Closer to the door were four easy chairs like those in the reception area, arranged so that they all faced each other, more a diamond than a square. A thick rug lay under them, with a small table in the center. His walls were lined with open bookshelves, sporting fiction titles she recognized, not simply business books, though he did have a shelf full of official-looking tomes.

His smile widened to a grin at her reaction. "Not what you expected, is it? If I'm going to be in here for hours upon hours, it's got to be comfortable." He indicated the chairs. "Please, take a seat."

Selina sat in the one closest to her, holding the ice water on her leg.

"Feel free to put that on the table. No coaster required. It's cheaper than it looks, covered in resin so no damage can be done." He sat in the chair diagonal from her, which meant they faced each other directly due to the arrangement of the chairs. He settled back in the seat. "You said you wanted to talk about someone named Curtis?"

Ah, he was going to pretend not to know him. She'd see about that.

"Yes, Curtis Lansing."

"I know a couple men by the name of Curtis. Not sure of their last names. Is he a client of mine?"

"To tell you the truth, I'm not sure. I found your card in his home; he's missing."

His brow creased, and he leaned forward. "Missing? And he had my card?"

Selina nodded, keeping her eyes on him to gauge his reaction, but so far he wasn't doing anything that seemed suspicious. He looked troubled that a man was missing, but not stressed or panicked like he would be if he were involved somehow.

"May I ask what line of work he's in?" he asked.

"Sure. He's in oil management at the local refinery."

"Curtis Lansing? Let me look him up to see if he's a client."

He got up and walked to his desk, grabbing a laptop from its surface. He unplugged it and brought it over to sit across from her again. She waited as he opened it, typed something, moved his finger over the mouse pad, and typed some more. Finally, he looked up at her. "I don't have him in here, so he's not a client. Give me another minute and I'll see if I can do a search. I might recognize his face if he has pictures online."

Selina hadn't prepared for this level of cooperation. Most people would have fobbed her off or asked for more information already.

This odd willingness to engage and to look for him struck her as suspicious. She leaned forward to take a drink of her ice water before settling back again.

He continued fidgeting with the computer. After a minute or two, he turned the screen to face her. "Is this him?"

She nodded, recognizing the man from the photos in his hallway and his Facebook page. He looked as slimy as she figured he had been, five o'clock shadow on his chin and jaw, squinty eyes, and a wicked smile that made her feel like shriveling up to avoid it.

"Do you know him?" she asked.

He turned the screen back to face him, studied the photo, then nodded. "I believe I do. Not sure why yet, but he does look familiar."

"Did any social media accounts come up when you searched him?"

"Yes, I think so." He glanced back at the screen.

"Go to his Facebook and see if you can find more photos; he has a bunch posted. Maybe you know him through someone else?"

"Good idea. Let me see."

Another two minutes and he was nodding.

"You got something?" Selina leaned forward, eager for an answer.

"Yeah, I know the guy in this picture. He's a client of mine, and I believe he works at the same refinery." He did something on the mouse pad, typed for a moment, then nodded again. "Yep, he works at the refinery. I'm not sure I should give you a client's name, though."

"I'm trying to figure out where this guy is. Every bit helps."

"I'm sure. And I'd love to help you. Who could turn you down?" He smiled. "But it's not exactly good business to give away a client's information. It's possibly illegal. Are you with the police?"

"No, I'm a private investigator, looking into his disappearance." She pulled a business card out of her pocket and handed it to him. She had all manner of cards, but on this particular job she'd figured this one would be the best choice. "There's no evidence anything has happened, so the police can't get involved, but his family is worried."

"I see. And you came to me because you found a business card at his home?"

"Yes."

"And that's the best clue you have?"

Selina felt a flush of irritation creep into her cheeks. He was poking fun at her, being smug. "His home was clean, a couple things missing. One of his vehicles is also missing. This is one of the few clues I've found."

"How does his family know he isn't simply on a trip? His pictures show him as quite old enough to make a unilateral decision to go on a trip without telling his entire family."

"He hasn't shown up to work, either. His sister received a phone call inquiring after him. And he's been out of touch for a couple weeks."

"I just don't know how I can help you. I sell insurance. I give my card to a lot of people, or current clients pass it along. His coworker probably gave him my card."

There was more to it than that, as evidenced by the bloody circle around his name on the card, but she didn't want to tell him about that. Then again, maybe it would freak him out and he'd give her the information. She sat in silence, debating which way she wanted to go.

He studied her as she thought. He was patient. More patient than her, that was for sure.

She decided to go with the truth. Something she felt they'd both been avoiding throughout this conversation, which might give it more power. "Listen, this is going to sound strange, but bear with me. I found your card in a fetish bag of some sort. There were herbs mixed in there, along with your card. And your name had been circled in what appears to be blood. I think it's more than a referral, though I'm sure referrals are nice."

"Excuse me? Circled in blood?" He shifted in his seat and leaned toward her, closing the laptop.

"Yeah. I haven't been to a medicine man or occult expert yet to see what they say about the bag, but I figured that stood out enough to be worth checking on. If it was a curse, I'd think you guys would have crossed paths, and you pissed him off somehow."

"I'm sure I'd at least remember if I'd had an issue with this guy."

"I'm sure you would. But there is a reason he has your card. I can look into that while I'm looking for him. Maybe he's gotten involved in something bad. Maybe you should be worried about the same thing. Is there anything you're involved in that would have to do with witchcraft of some sort?"

"Certainly not. Not anything I'm aware of."

"You sure you won't tell me this other client's name? I won't tell him you sent me; I'll tell him I found his information among Curtis's things."

He slumped in his seat and exhaled, thinking. The scent of mint wafted across to her. She breathed in, getting a nose full of pleasant scents. He wore cologne, but it was mild, citrusy, a slight undertone. A touch of coffee intermingled with the cologne and the mint, and she suddenly felt hungry. Her stomach rumbled, and she placed a hand on it, embarrassed.

His eyes, which had become unfocused as he thought, focused on her face. "Hungry?"

"Yeah, it's been a couple hours since I ate. I'll grab something on my way home."

"Tell you what. Let's go grab lunch. It will give me time to think, and maybe I'll remember Curtis and won't have to give you my client's name. Besides, I'm hungry, too."

Selina frowned at him. "Are you just trying to get me out of your office so you can ditch me and not tell me the guy's name? I can look through those photos, too, and see if he's named anywhere." Of course, she'd already done that, and she knew that Curtis hadn't tagged his friends or listed their names anywhere. And most of his friends had images other than their own on their profiles. She had no idea whether this was intentional as a security precaution, or whether they didn't like their own pictures.

Oliver's lip pooched out a tiny bit, and he laughed. "You're right. You could. What will you do if his name isn't in there?"

"Keep looking." Her tone came out sulkier than she'd intended, and she hardened her voice. "I know he works at the refinery. I should probably go there anyway, just to follow up on Curtis."

"Well, that solves that problem, doesn't it? How about lunch?"

His grin was infectious, and she had to struggle not to return it. He couldn't use charisma to get out of this.

"Can I see your laptop?"

"If you go to lunch with me."

Damn, cute and persistent. Her traitor of a stomach rumbled again, and she puffed out air, crossing her arms. "Fine, but I'm not going to enjoy it."

"Fair enough. I'll enjoy it enough for the both of us. Steak sound good? Or there's a great pasta place down the street, not far. We can walk to either one. It looks lovely outside, but maybe not for someone decked out in leather. You a biker?"

She didn't have a good answer to that, so she ignored the question. "I was thinking more along the lines of a sandwich or something, but pasta sounds good."

"Pasta it is." He got up and held a hand out to her.

She eyeballed his hand, thought about ignoring it, but decided to be gracious instead. She grasped it and rose, not putting any weight on him.

He kept hold of her hand and brought it to his lips. "It's a date."

Selina yanked her hand out of his and glared at him. "You've just refused to help me on my missing person's case. Don't think you can charm me into forgetting that."

"I wouldn't dream of it."

He held the door open for her, closing the door behind them after she'd stepped out. They walked to the front desk together, where he asked Sonia if she'd like something from the restaurant.

"You know me, Mr. Benson, I've got my lunch in the refrigerator."

"Oh, Sonia, not another salad?" he asked, head tilted, a frown on his face.

She laughed and shook her head. "Nope, not a salad today. I brought 'real food' this time." She hooked her fingers into quotes to emphasize her words.

"Glad to hear it. No person can survive on salad alone. Send me a message if you change your mind. I'll be gone about..." he looked at

Selina and wrinkled his brow, "...an hour or so. Let me know if anything comes up."

Sonia winked at Selina, making her squirm. "I will. Go and have a nice lunch." She waved them off and returned to her work.

Selina followed Oliver, thinking she didn't have much of a choice if she wanted more information, though she would have to keep lunch short, and she would definitely be paying for her own food. She let him walk in front of her, enjoying the view. His broad shoulders filled out the jacket nicely, but not as well as the pants, which cupped a gorgeous backside. Lunch wouldn't be so bad after all. Especially not if she could worm some information out of him while they ate.

14

ANOTHER OPEN DOOR

The walk to the restaurant was, indeed, lovely. The sky was blue, the weather not too warm, not too cold. Oliver's sonorous voice vibrated within her, comforting her in a way that surprised her. His stories drew her in and his quick wit kept her enraptured with what he had to say. She forgot for a while that she was with him to get information, not on an actual date.

At the restaurant, she removed her jacket, allowing herself to relax. She wore a red tank top, which was comfortable, but certainly not dressy. Luckily, the restaurant he'd taken her to was nice, but not elegant, and the other diners wore a mix of business suits and jeans. She figured leather pants were dressier than jeans any day.

Oliver had taken his own jacket off, rolling up his shirt sleeves. His arms were bronzed, telling her he either spent time outdoors or enjoyed tanning beds.

Partway through dessert, shared tiramisu (he'd insisted), separated onto two plates (her insistence), he got quiet, a frown flitting across his face.

She paused, a bite on its way to her mouth. "What is it?"

"I think I remember why Curtis Lansing is familiar to me. Give me a second."

She shrugged and continued eating, watching the fleeting expressions as he tried to remember. His eyes became distant, unfocused, and he rubbed a finger over his bottom lip repeatedly, like an old, familiar habit.

"Yes, I've got it! We met at a class I taught on business ethics and climbing the corporate ladder the ethical way. He wanted to talk after the class, so I stayed behind for a few minutes. He said he'd tried being ethical, but it had gotten him nowhere, and he wanted me to tell him what he should do now. He was angry, defiant. I'm not sure why he bothered coming to the class, the way he felt. Of course, it was because he was frustrated with this job, but I've spoken to people who were frustrated and desperate, and they weren't rude about it."

"Did he leave angry? Did anything else happen?" Selina put down her fork, dessert forgotten.

The furrow between Oliver's eyes deepened as he remembered. Either he was being genuine or he was a good actor.

"He told me I was being holier than thou, and that I'd get my comeuppance. Said I couldn't have possibly been ethical through everything and reached the heights I'd reached. That I must be standing on plenty of skeletons, considering my success."

"Did he threaten you?"

"I wouldn't say he threatened me. His words were ominous, but he didn't say he would do something to me, just that something was bound to happen."

"I've heard he could be a real jerk."

Oliver laughed. "Yeah, you could say that. I remember him being disruptive during my talk, too. It happens, but it seemed intentional. He kept shifting his feet across the floor, tapping his feet, ripping paper out of the pad and crumpling it up, huffing out breaths like he disagreed with me. It was obnoxious. I can't believe it took me this long to think of where I knew him from. You wouldn't think I'd forget something like that."

"I think you wanted to trick me into eating lunch with you." *And give yourself time to think up a lie, quite possibly.* "How did he get your card?"

"I handed it to him, told him I could try to help him, that we could sit down and go over specific issues. Honestly, I figured he'd throw it away as soon as he left the room, but I guess he didn't."

"No, instead he used it to try and send something bad your way."

Oliver shook his head. "I must have merely been a good place to aim his frustrations. Good thing I don't believe in curses."

Selina figured he should consider believing, but if nothing had happened to him, whatever Curtis had tried to do hadn't worked.

"Did you ever discuss him with your client?" she asked. "Did your client bring him up?"

"Nope, he never did. And I've seen him recently, definitely since the class. I wonder if he was the one who referred Curtis to my class?"

"Good question. I guess I really do need to go to that refinery either way. I could ask your client about Curtis and you if you give me his name."

"I imagine you'll end up talking to him anyway, but I'm still not comfortable giving out his name." He scooped up another bite of dessert and slid it into his mouth, which she couldn't help but watch.

Selina thought for a moment before sitting up straighter and holding up her index finger. She reached into her bag, which rested at her feet, and pulled out the pad she'd written the names on. Smoothing the page, she set it in front of him. "Do you recognize any of these names?"

Oliver sighed, but looked at the paper. The recognition was visible on his face before he spoke. "He's on here. What are these names from?"

"These are the friends he interacted with the most online. Two of them belong to men who died on a camping trip recently. The other one, Randy Simpco, didn't come up in my searches. Other than his Facebook page, he's not in the news or other forms of social media. Considering the other two died together, I guess that's good news for him."

Oliver gazed at her across the table, eyes mildly squinted. "Okay, Simpco is the one I was thinking of. I don't know how that helps you since you're going to speak to him anyway." He used a napkin to wipe his mouth and fingers then set it down on the table. "I figure I owe you that much for the pleasant company. Do me a favor and don't mention my name. After all, I didn't give you any information you didn't already have, really."

"I won't. Thanks for inviting me to lunch, and for the information, even if it had to be dragged out of you." She winked at him. "I really should get back to work, and so should you, I imagine." She looked at her cell phone, checking the time. "Do you realize we've been here over an hour?"

"Doesn't feel like it. I don't suppose I can see you again?"

Selina warmed. "I don't know how long I'll be here, and I've got a lot to do on this investigation. I'm only here from Colorado to help a friend, so it probably isn't a good idea."

His face fell, and he reached for her hand. "I'd still like a second date. Perhaps a dinner date?"

"I don't think so. I really did have fun, though." She let him hold her hand for a second before pulling it back.

His lips turned down for the briefest of seconds, and then he grinned, the curve of his lips infectious so that she smiled back. "You'll miss me. I'll just wait for you to change your mind. In the meantime, can I have your number in case I think of anything else that might help? What if I hear from Randy? What if all my hair falls out, and I realize the curse worked? I imagine you'd want to know."

His eyes sparkled mischievously, and his grin had turned to one of cunning. But he had a valid point, so she asked him for his card and wrote her cell number on the back. He glanced at it, took his phone out, and dialed.

Her cell phone rang. She looked at him, looked at the caller ID, then clicked to accept the call, putting the phone up to her ear. "Yes?"

"Just checking. You can never be too sure." He hung up.

She laughed, feeling the best she'd felt since she'd arrived in Canada. When she stood, he did the same.

"Walk you back?" he asked.

"Sure. I'll take another card, too. One without blood on it would be nice."

BACK IN HER CAR, Selina paused to think about the date, about the liquid warmth of his eyes, the crinkle lines at their corners when he smiled. He was probably a few years her senior, but he was charming, good looking, and he really filled out a suit. She wondered what he looked like underneath it. When he'd rolled up his sleeves, his arms had been well toned, and his chest had looked solid beneath the blue button-up shirt. Images filled her mind, and she shut her eyes, enjoying them.

Too bad she wouldn't get to see him again. She let her breath out in a protracted sigh.

As attractive and charismatic as he was, it didn't feel like he'd been completely honest with her about Curtis. She couldn't put her finger on it, considering he'd appeared forthcoming on the surface. What he'd said had the ring of truth. Perhaps it had really happened, but he had left something out.

Now she needed to decide whether to go back to the library, back to Nathan's, or on to the refinery. She also needed to figure out if it was worth tracking down an expert on the occult to see what the bag and blood-circled name might mean. It seemed like something that could sidetrack her without much in the way of results. Unless the person who'd given him the information on what to do was also his sire, they were useless. Either way, Nathan would be a good source for where to go to find an expert. And she wanted to check in on him, so she headed back out of town.

She entered the woods, the truck bumping and scraping along. Her body relaxed, and she felt comforted. Nature always did that for her, grounded her. Nature could be cruel, but it would never be as vicious as humans.

As she pulled up to Nathan's, she noticed with concern that the front door stood open. She pulled the emergency brake, shut the truck off, and hopped out as quickly as she could. She crossed the yard in a full sprint and shot up the steps, calling for Nathan and Johnny.

The house was empty. She peeked into every room, but found no sign of distress, no overturned tables, nothing thrown around or broken. Where could they be? She had their only vehicle.

She stood on the porch, looking around, trying to spot anything that might give away where they'd gone. There was nothing to see other than their tracks from last night, pine needles disturbed from their passage. An inspection of the grounds showed nothing out of the ordinary. They'd walked all over the property, their footprints going in all directions. The doe's burial place was undisturbed, the shovel still tucked against the side of the house. She tried the shed door, but it was locked.

"Nathan? Johnny? Where are you guys?"

Had someone come to pick them up? Or were they on foot somewhere?

She went back into the house, seeking anything that might tell her where they'd gone. There was no note. A quick check of her phone confirmed no call had been received. Their boots were gone, plus a jacket for each. She peered into Johnny's room once more, noting that his shotgun was gone.

If they'd rushed out, as the open door would indicate, it would be odd for each to have taken the time to put on their boots and grab a jacket. Had Nathan taken off again, and Johnny'd had to chase him? It would be rare for someone to be overtaken by Wendigo during the day; they were creatures of darkness.

There were signs that they'd had lunch and cleaned everything up. Dishes were hand washed and drying on a hand towel.

On foot it was then. What choice did she have? If they'd taken off with someone, she'd never be able to locate them. She checked her weapons, grabbed her own guns, which she hadn't taken with her today, and made sure they were loaded. She took off her jacket and hastily put on a holster.

She had no idea what she might be walking into, and wanted to be prepared. Suddenly, she didn't feel half so foolish about having armed up before heading out this morning. She slid back into her coat, leaving it unzipped so she could reach her guns readily.

Selina calmed herself enough to walk around in search of a stronger scent. Once she found one for Nathan that stood out from the rest, indicating it might be the most recent, she followed it deeper into the woods.

15

ROCKY LIKES FISH

Fully armed, Selina ventured first to the small cabin Nathan had led them to the night before. There was no sign of them there. She did smell fresh gasoline and oil, as if the tenant had left only a short time ago. There was something familiar about a few of the scents, a slight nagging in the back of her mind, but she didn't have time to dwell on it. She kept going, hoping for a sign that they had passed this way, but not finding it.

The path ran alongside the cabin then wound up into the foothills, growing fainter as the greenery faded into rock, sand, and soil. Here, she caught a stronger whiff of Nathan's scent, the sickness evident. She followed it, part of her wishing she could embrace the crisp air and the dappled sunlight that shone through the trees. The woods were quiet, though small creatures scrambled and tittered here and there. She promised herself a trip back up this path when Nathan's dilemma had been solved, so that she could properly enjoy her surroundings.

She reached a point where the path began to lead uphill, becoming rockier and harder to travel. The ground was more uneven, with slight indentations carved into the ground where water had traveled in small rivulets, probably during spring runoff. Large boulders surrounded the path, sometimes encroaching on it.

Her breathing grew heavier as she climbed the hill, sometimes having to use her hands to pull herself up a particularly tricky spot. She wished she'd brought a walking stick of some sort, and even pondered how well a shotgun would have worked had she grabbed one. At least it would have been long and sturdy enough to give her a hand.

The hill leveled out less than a half-hour's hike in, and she looked down at a partial view of a canyon book-ended on the other side by another ridge. Pines climbed the ridge, as well, giving it an almost furred look. Selina rested, raking her eyes over the areas she could see below her. The path led down the other side, intersecting with a second path partway down the hill. She could either follow this one straight down or turn off onto the new one and cut across the side of the canyon.

In a curve below her, she could barely make out something flashing, reflecting the sunlight. Keeping her eyes open for any further flashes or signs of life, she moved quickly down the path, steering herself onto the new one when she reached it, following Nathan's scent, as well as Johnny's fainter scent of soap. Mixed in with these was a fishy, green smell. This trail was covered in gravel and better maintained than the treacherous one she'd just been traveling, and she was grateful she'd seen the flash, though she hoped it paid off with a Nathan sighting in the end. She wasn't picking up any voices or other indications of the men.

Just as the path began to slope down, she caught sight of the flash again. Squinting, she made out a body of water below her, most likely a reservoir in the canyon. The sunlight danced and rippled across the surface of the water until it fell out of view again, blocked by the trees and the ridge.

There was a crunch behind her, followed by the scrabbling sound of rocks falling. She turned, crouching, but only saw some small rocks trickling down the hillside toward her.

Selina moved behind a large boulder and peered toward the

disruption. She shaded her eyes and studied the boulders that rested above her. Something was up there. The wind moved in the wrong direction for her to get a scent.

Straining her eyes and ears, she waited, silent. She wouldn't be the first one to move.

Something shifted against the surface of one of the boulders.

Out of the dappling shadows of a tree came a creature, its tawny hide coming into resolution against the backdrop of the tan rocks. Once she could see it, she wondered how she had missed it in the first place. Its tail was dark at the puffy tip, which swung up in a loop from the rest of the tail. Black fur lined the white muzzle, fading to the light brown of the rest of its fur.

Its forepaws rested on the rock outcropping, face low as it hunched down, stalking her. Mountain lions rarely attacked humans, and Selina knew the best thing she could do was continue to look at the animal, watching for aggression, but acting calm. If she could find a stick, the best thing to do would be to put her jacket on it to make herself look bigger. For now, she opened her jacket, holding it out as far as it would go. Other than that, she'd do her best not to act like prey, to meet the creature's eyes and let it know she wasn't afraid of it.

Which, of course, she was. Knowing it most likely wouldn't attack her was all well and good, but it didn't stop her blood from hammering through her veins as her heart galloped in her chest. If it did choose to attack her, she'd have to kill it. Her life depended on it. She'd killed a lot of monsters in her time, but this was no monster, and the thought of having to shed its blood made her sick to her stomach. Not to mention the icy dread curled in her chest at the sight of sharp teeth and claws. Cougars were made to seek prey and take it down.

She continued looking into the cougar's eyes, entire body tensed in preparation to react to whatever it might do.

To her surprise, it lowered itself until it reclined on the rocks, front paws crossed over each other like a house cat might do. Only a house cat wouldn't look nearly so terrifying doing so. A pink tongue came out and swept over its muzzle, and it laid its massive head down on its paws. It seemed to be telling her she would be fine, though it didn't close its eyes, merely continued watching her.

Selina walked backward for several feet before taking a chance and turning her back on the predator that still watched her, its gaze lazy, squinting as if it were fighting to stay awake. She concentrated on listening for any sound of movement behind her, back stiff as she walked down the path.

The next time she turned around to check, the rock outcropping had disappeared from sight, as had the big cat. She let the tension drain from her shoulders, not having realized they were pulled up tight against her neck.

Now that she was getting closer to the canyon, she could see the dark blue of the water at all times. Sunlight flickered off water that was still as glass, and she saw a reflection of the nearby mountain peaks on its surface.

Voices sounded off to her right, accompanied by a small splash, and she broke through the trees, looking in that direction. There stood Nathan and Johnny, Nathan wrapped in a blanket as Johnny worked a fishing pole. They both looked relaxed. Nathan had his head tilted back, eyes closed, the sun caressing his skin and making him glow.

"Hey!" she called, picking up her pace as adrenaline born of relief and anger coursed through her veins. "What are you guys doing here?"

They each looked over at her. Nathan wrapped the blanket more closely around his body and rose. Johnny waved, quickly placing the hand back on the reel to continue fishing.

It didn't take her long to get to them, and Nathan said, "What's up?"

"What's up? Didn't anyone ever teach you to leave a note or something?"

Nathan looked genuinely surprised, his hand tightening on the blanket. "Why would I?"

"So I wouldn't worry, perhaps? So I wouldn't think you were tearing through the woods trying to eat hunters?"

"You know very well I like fresh fish for supper. Besides, we couldn't go to the store without a vehicle, now could we?"

He was right about that, but it didn't stop her from being annoyed. She took a moment to catch her breath and calm herself down. Had he not been sick, she would have shown up at his house and assumed he was out fishing. Instead, she'd assumed he was out eating someone. Well, okay, she hadn't really thought he was eating anyone, but she'd certainly considered the possibility that someone was going to get hurt if she didn't find him.

Her voice was softer when she spoke. "A note still would have been nice. We're in the middle of some unusual circumstances right now."

"You're right. I'll try to remember next time." He grinned and put an arm around her, drawing her into the blanket with him.

She was already warm, but she wrapped her arm around his middle and laid her head on his shoulder, sighing.

"I brought my pole, if you feel like fishing," Nathan said.

"No thanks. You know I've never much enjoyed it."

"Yep. Figured I'd offer anyway. People change, and fishing can be relaxing."

She lifted her head to look at him. "You know there's a mountain lion up the path?"

"Rocky? You have a run-in with him? He okay?"

Her eyes bulged at first, then she glared at him. "Of course he's okay. Rocky? Real original."

"Hey now, it's his name. I couldn't change it; not my place."

"Oh yeah? He tell you that was his name?"

"In a manner of speaking."

Selina shook her head and watched as Johnny pulled a glistening silver fish from the water. It flopped around, dangling from the cruel hook in its mouth. He removed the hook as gently as he could, promptly slamming its head into one of the rocks at his feet. The fish stopped flopping, and Johnny placed it in a wicker basket at his side, which already held several others.

He packed up the pole and hefted the basket. "Got one for Rocky. You guys ready?"

It was so peaceful that Selina considered asking to stay, but with so much remaining to be done, she knew better. She eased out of the blanket and rose, reaching a hand out to help Nathan up. He took it, surprising her, and she pulled him to his feet. He weighed next to nothing, and she pulled too hard, unbalancing him, though he quickly righted himself, laughing at her chagrin.

"Sorry!" she said.

"For what?" He shook his head and offered her his arm.

They followed Johnny up the path. Rocky no longer perched on the outcropping, but Johnny set the fish in the same spot the mountain lion had been reclining when she'd seen him.

"How'd you know this was where he was?" she asked.

Nathan shrugged. "It's his favorite spot when he's watching humans." He gestured at the boulder. "His namesake."

"Ah."

It took longer to get back to the cabin than it had taken her to get to the lake. Nathan couldn't move fast at all, and she and Johnny matched his pace. When they reached the bottom of the hill on the other side, Johnny waved and set out ahead of them.

"He'll get dinner started for us," Nathan said.

They passed the cabin from the other night, but now smoke rose from the chimney. A red SUV sat out front, still ticking from the heat of being driven.

They circled the cabin, leaving a wide berth so as not to be rude. Right as they got to the path on the other side of the building, a deep male voice called out, "Selina, that you?"

Her shoulders drooped, and she stopped in her tracks. Seriously? He was the new tenant. At least she now knew why something about the scents had been familiar.

Nathan looked at her, a question in his eyes, and she turned to confront the renter.

"Charles, what are you doing here?"

16

THERE CAN ONLY BE ONE

"You keep asking me the same question. One would think you'd get bored with that." Charles raised a steaming mug to his mouth and took a sip, eyes closing in pleasure. "Damn, that's good."

His smug smile made her spine crawl, and she shook her head to clear it. It was no coincidence that he was here. She had to make sure he didn't figure out what was going on with Nathan. If he hadn't already.

"Nathan, why don't you head on home and I'll be there in a few?"

Nathan looked deep into her eyes, trying to determine what was going on. Finally, he nodded, looked at Charles for a long moment, then turned his back and disappeared into the trees.

"Nice to meet you, Nathan," Charles called after him. Then he turned back to Selina. "Not very friendly, is he?"

"He's plenty friendly to friendly people. Explain yourself."

"What, exactly, do you need explained?"

"How did you end up in a cabin next door to where I'm staying?"

"I needed a place to stay, and this cabin seemed perfect. Funny coincidence, don't you think?"

"Bullshit."

"What's bullshit? Ending up here or running into you?"

"Both."

Charles laughed before taking another sip. He relished this one as much as he had the first.

Selina rolled her eyes. "Give me a break. Why are you here?"

"Hey, I've got my case, and you've got yours. It's not like we're highlanders." Affecting a bad Scottish brogue, he said, "There can be only one." He laughed at his own joke.

"Stay away from me. Stay away from my case. And stay away from my friends."

"Friends? The old sick guy and who else? Oh, you mean that young guy who came through here awhile ago? You got something twisted going on with them? You always did like the dark ones. Daddy issues, I'm sure." He smirked. "Both are a bit out of your age range, don't you think?"

"Ha ha, Charles. You heard me."

"I'd love to hook you up there, sister, but I'm certain we'll be seeing each other plenty."

Selina turned her back on him and stalked through the woods, anger seeping through her every pore. How had he known she'd be here? Had he followed them from the airport? She'd watched for a tail. There'd been no one behind them at all for much of the trek. So while it wasn't impossible, chances were slim.

What then? She cast around for any other explanation. She hadn't told anyone exactly where she was going. Brent had an idea, but he wouldn't have talked to Charles—they were bitter enemies. Cryptos, as a rule, didn't like people who slaughtered the very animals they were trying to study and protect. He was already pushing his own beliefs by being friends with Selina, but she only killed those creatures that were irredeemable.

The license plate on the truck? She supposed he could have used that information to find out about Nathan. What else? Nothing came to mind, but she was certain this was no coincidence.

Luckily, he'd seen the effects of the curse as just age and sickness. It didn't appear he suspected anything about Nathan. Right now, that was her number one concern. He wouldn't hesitate to come in and take care of Nathan, and he'd wait to do it when she wasn't there.

If she wasn't on such a pressing timeline, she'd follow Charles and see what he was up to, what progress he was making. She didn't delude herself that she was a masterful investigator. Charles had her beat in that area. No time right now, but she'd see what the evening brought. She wasn't sure taking a chance on him knowing more than she did in this instance was reasonable when it could mean Nathan's death. She'd already wasted time going out to lunch with Oliver. Her cheeks colored at the memory, the flush of shame seeping through her body.

When she stepped into the cabin, the smell of lemon, herbs, and frying fish drifted around her. Not an unpleasant smell, like fish in the microwave. She also scented baking bread, probably rolls. Her stomach rumbled in response, and she went to her room to clean up.

Nathan waited for her in the living room when she came out. "So who was that?"

"Charles. He's a Crypto-Hunter. Out for the buck and whatever publicity he can get." She paused. "It's bad that he's here, Nathan, right in our own backyard."

He nodded. "Not much we can do about it, is there? We'll just have to take extra care."

"Yeah. Johnny and I are going to have to take turns staying up with you. He absolutely can't know what's going on."

"Agreed."

Nathan pointed to a rumpled sheet of paper on the table. Selina leaned forward to pick it up. On it he'd written the word "HUNTERS," underlined and in all capitals. Under that, he'd jotted down a few names and locations. Some were home addresses; some appeared to be businesses.

"You've talked to all these?" she asked.

"Yes. You can always try again. Don't think it will do much good, so I'd save it if you've got other avenues to explore."

"Was there anything helpful you haven't passed along?"

"Unfortunately, no. No one had any ideas on how to reverse the process. They know what we know. I have to die."

"That's not going to happen." She held up the piece of paper. "I'll pursue other leads first, but thank you for the information. If I don't find anything else, this list will come in handy."

AFTER DINNER, Selina put on a pair of jeans and a t-shirt then said goodnight, making sure Johnny set up the alarms behind her. She reminded him to keep the fire stoked and stay awake, his shotgun close at hand.

"I'll take over as soon as I get home, but I need to go to the library first," she said. "You good here?"

"Yeah, we'll be fine. I've got stuff to do that will keep us occupied."

"Great. See you in a couple hours."

She kept the headlights off as she left, hoping Charles hadn't heard the truck start up. A warm amber light burned through the trees between the two properties. Whether that meant he was home or not, she couldn't say. Once she got far enough away that she figured the lights wouldn't be visible at either cabin, she popped them on and took off, hurrying to get into town before the library closed at eight.

On the way there, her cell phone rang. She pulled over to the shoulder, put her hazards on, and answered it. "Hello?"

Brent's voice came through, faint, but clear. "Selina? Hey, how are you doing?"

Their awkward last minutes together ran through her head. This was the first they'd spoken since that night, other than their quick texts. His call surprised her, considering the way they'd left things. Then again, Brent was a good guy, and not one to hold a grudge. On the other hand, his voice sounded wary, clipped, leaving her at a loss for where they stood.

"Not great. How are you?"

"Things aren't great here, either. I'm being investigated by the Crypto Council."

"The what?"

"Crypto Council. Apparently, one exists now. Not sure how they put that together, or who voted them in, but they seem to think they're in charge."

"What are you being investigated for?"

"Gog. Word got out somehow. I have no idea how. I only mentioned it to one person to see what they thought about my publishing, and she's a close friend."

"Maisy?"

Brent had introduced her to Maisy at a party a few years ago. They were close, and while she and Selina didn't get along all that well, Selina couldn't see her turning him in.

"Yep." His response was curt, but she realized now that it wasn't aimed at her.

"Is there something I can do to help?"

"Not sure yet, but I wanted to give you a heads up since you were involved." There was silence for a moment, and then Brent asked, "When are you coming home?"

"I'm not sure. It's still looking like at least a week, though."

"How is Nathan?"

"Not good. It's a long story. But this case is vital. Personal. A Wendigo case."

When he spoke this time, his voice had softened. He knew her history. "I'm sorry, Selina. Let me know if you need any help. I'm not on a current case, and it wouldn't hurt to get away from the city while the Council deliberates. Besides, they say I'm on hold. Basically, I'm grounded."

"Thanks, Brent. I don't think I'll need to take you up on that, but it's nice to know you're there if I need you." She paused. "Actually, hold on. You aren't familiar with any lore that would save someone from the Wendigo spirit instead of requiring their death, are you?"

"I'm afraid not, but I'll nose around."

They said their goodbyes, his tone lighter than it had been. She felt a measure of relief that he wasn't mad at her anymore. But she figured calling a Crypto to come out on a case that was destined to end in someone's death wouldn't be a good plan, especially not when he was already being investigated. Her stomach clenched at this thought. Cryptozoology was his life.

She shook it off and pulled back onto the road, killing the hazards. The trek to the library was short, and she took in the building's appearance in a way she hadn't before, when she'd been searching desperately for a first step. It was small, placed in what had obviously once been a private residence. A giant book had been carved out of wood and stuck above the front door, "LIBRARY" also carved in wood and placed beside it. A porch remained on the front, making the library look friendly and welcoming.

Inside, she went directly to the bank of computers she'd visited before. First, she needed the internet. She looked up Curtis Lansing, searching until she found the name Cheryl Lansing. She continued her research until she came across an old wedding announcement in the online version of the local paper. Cheryl Lansing was now Cheryl Packer. Selina found her address, jotting it down on the sheet that had the Crypto-Hunters' names on it.

Next, she asked the tiny, wizened librarian where the mythology section was, specifically local lore. The woman stood up, walking with a rapid pace that surprised Selina. She'd expected her to do the little old woman walk, but, despite her appearance, she was quite energetic.

The librarian, a Mrs. Penchant according to her nametag, settled Selina at a table in the back and held up a finger, signaling for her to wait and stay here.

Selina smiled, said, "Thanks," and pulled out her notebook and a pen, preparing to take notes if she found anything new.

Within only a couple minutes, Mrs. Penchant came back, carrying two aged books. She set these down in front of Selina, frowning. "We had a third book, quite old and interesting."

"Someone has it checked out? Would it be possible to contact them?"

"That's the thing. It's missing, not checked out. It looks like someone absconded with it." She walked away, shaking her head. Heading back to her desk, Selina figured.

The two books only held basic information and superstition, the majority of it wrong. A waste of time. She returned the books to Mrs. Penchant. "Thank you for these. I have another question. Do you know of any resources for looking at pieces of land with cabins on it, or popular camping areas?"

The woman's forehead wrinkled, and she pursed her lips. "I have some historical books about the area and local maps. Would either of those help?"

"They both might."

"I'll be right back."

Once again, she disappeared into the library. When she came back this time, she had several books of varying ages, most of them wrapped in the popular library plastic. The maps were laid out flat and laminated to keep them in one piece. She got Selina settled with these then went back to her desk again.

The maps were interesting, for sure. Selina was able to get a mental image of the main hunting areas around the city, as one of the maps showed legal hunting grounds. And though none of the maps laid out exactly where cabins were, she could see where the more rural areas were. She took photos of the maps with her cell phone, and once again took everything back to the librarian.

"Thank you for all your help," she told her.

"No problem, hon. Come back any time. Hardly anyone ever asks for specific things, and when they do, it's the title of a fiction novel. It's nice to shake things up sometimes. It's all about the internet now."

Selina couldn't disagree. But right now she could use quite a bit less shaking up in her world.

17

PIT STOP

The library hadn't taken too long. Selina, frustrated with the lack of information she'd found, decided to look up one of the Crypto-Hunters to see what he had to say. It was late, but she'd never met a Hunter who went to bed early. Not this type. These were mercenaries in a league somewhere between what Selina did and what Charles did. They took a lot of money to hunt down the same creatures as Selina, for whoever the highest bidder was, while actively avoiding the spotlight. It was useful for Nathan to be in touch with these guys, which was precisely why he'd had all their names.

She'd recognized the first name on the list: Bryan Stands Tall, a Chippewa man of long acquaintance. Nathan had mentioned earlier that he'd asked after her, and she'd hoped to visit him at some point, anyway. He'd be easy to find, even if Nathan hadn't written down the bar he usually haunted. It was Bar O'Clock, as far as Bryan was concerned. The Here You Are bar wasn't far from the library, and it only took her ten minutes to get there. Motorcycles and pickups filled the parking lot.

"Just like back home," she said aloud.

The sign buzzed, the "Y" and "O" blinking in and out, which made her laugh. It still said the same thing, whether they were on or off. And it was so apropos for the bar to have flickering lights.

Here You Are had old-fashioned saloon-style doors she pushed through to get inside. They flapped behind her before coming to rest in their original position. On one side of them stood the real door that could be closed behind them when the bar shut down for the night. The bar smelled of hops, chicken wings, cologne, body odor, and loneliness. The lighting was dim, the music loud and full of bass and guitar riffs. Men of various sizes sat at the bar, more than one showing plumber's crack. Only a couple women occupied seats, each with a corresponding male. This was not, nor had it ever been, a pick-up bar. It was a neighborhood bar, a place of familiarity for the locals to relax and shrug off the day's worries.

Loud voices shouted over the music, and she looked their way. Sure enough, there was Bryan, sitting with several other men, beer in hand. His dark hair was cut short. He wore a flannel shirt, the sleeves pushed up to show the wiry muscles and veins of his forearms. He happened to look up and catch sight of her. Raising his glass, he shouted, "Selina!"

Good thing she hadn't come to spy on him.

She nodded her head at him and walked toward the table. One of the men facing him turned. Charles. He was like a fungus. His broad grin matched Bryan's, and a mischievous twinkle lit his eyes. Her shoulders slumped as she came up to the table. She couldn't speak freely in front of Charles. Maybe he'd go to the bathroom at some point so she could get a word alone with Bryan.

Bryan slid over and patted the seat beside him. Selina sat beside him, leg pressed against his in the already crowded booth. He signaled to a passing waitress, holding up his beer and two fingers. She hurried off to the bar.

"How goes it, little sister?" Bryan nudged her with his elbow.

He always called her "little sister," though they weren't actually related, and in Native circles, it was typically cousin. He'd been around a lot during her mentorship with Nathan, had taken part in the training much of the time. His fondness for her had benefited her in the past. No one messed with Bryan and he was fiercely protective of her.

"Not great, but it feels good to be back," she said. "How about you?"

"Can't complain." His voice boomed. He wasn't a large man, was in fact rather slim, but wired with muscle. His arms were heavily scarred, and she knew from experience that his torso was, too. He'd grown up a scrapper, having to fight due to his smaller size. Though he rarely started fights, he always finished them. Even so, he was a good guy, honest and jovial. In fact, he usually took jobs that involved catching the creature alive, rather than killing something. Selina was pretty sure he liked animals better than humans, even cryptids. Had Charles not been here, she could have had a good discussion with him. The presence of the money grubber put a major crimp in her plans.

"Good haul?" she asked him. A mood this happy indicated payday.

"You bet. Closed two cases this week. Big bucks."

"Anything interesting?"

"My second Ogopogo."

Selina had experience with Ogopogo, a typically harmless snake-like creature found in deeper lakes. Most people knew of Nessie, in Scotland, but she wasn't alone. She had siblings all over the world, North America included.

"Sold it to some guy living around the Great Lakes. He wants to 'discover' it or something like that." He shook his head. "People are strange."

"That they are," Charles said, raising his glass—and his eyebrows—across the table.

Selina ignored him. She turned to Bryan, who had a sudden look of epiphany.

"I didn't introduce you around. Fellas, this is Selina. She's good people. Selina, this is Justin, Bart, Eric, Peter, and Charles." He indicated each man as he spoke.

"We're acquainted." Charles wore a smarmy smile.

Selina grunted in reply.

"Doesn't look like my sister's so fond of you, hey?" Bryan asked, gesturing between them.

"We're old friends, aren't we, Selina?" Charles asked.

"One of us is old, Charles, but neither of us is a friend."

The table laughed uproariously at this, Charles included. There's no audience like a drunk audience.

The waitress arrived right then, plunking two pints of beer down in front of Bryan.

"They're not both for me." He slid one of the foam-covered, amber beverages in front of Selina.

She held it up in salute. "Thank you." The first drink was perfect, cold and just the right amount of hoppy. She felt like she'd earned it at this point.

"What brings you up north?" Bryan asked her.

"Wendigo." She took another drink, let the warmth roll through her stomach.

The smile slid off Bryan's face. "That's never good to hear. Nathan came to me about one recently. Same one?"

"I'm not sure," she answered honestly. She didn't know what questions Nathan had asked him, or who it had been for. It had sounded like it was for his situation, though. He wouldn't have needed advice on dealing with any old Wendigo. "But he's the one who brought me up here."

His face was serious now. "I don't think I helped him much. Haven't heard anything since we talked."

"No word of anything new around here?" she asked.

He gestured at Charles with his beer. "He just asked about the same thing. None of us have heard anything other than a possible body count, but even that has tapered off. No more 'animal' attacks for the last two weeks, maybe."

"Did Nathan ask you if you'd heard of any way to remove the spirit from someone who took it willingly?"

"Those are the ones it's stuck the hardest in. Though I do remember an old story about a woman who managed to rid herself of one. It never said how it was done. I just remember it had something to do with help from a European guy. A white guy." He leaned closer to her, speaking into her ear. "He wasn't a Myth Stalker, but he was something. He had some kind of ability."

"Is this a story I could hunt down, or was it oral?"

"I'm afraid I don't even remember where I heard it, but pretty sure it was heard, not read." He grinned. "I don't read much, as you know."

She did know. Despite a college education, he was the type to charge in and deal with whatever was thrown at him, rather than to research and go in with a plan. It's why they got along so well. Compared to him, Selina was a long-term planner and master strategist. Poor Nathan had always had to be the one doing the planning, the one to wrangle them into some semblance of order. He'd called them his wildlings during her training, often throwing his hands up in exacerbation, and leaving them to their own devices to figure things out if it wouldn't cause them undue danger.

"This is an odd direction for your questions to take, "Charles said. "Why would you want to know how to dispel a Wendigo instead of wiping it out?"

"I'm just curious. Wouldn't it be nice if we didn't have to kill them every time?"

Charles shrugged, but his eyes had narrowed.

The other men at the table were carrying on their own conversation. Now they exploded with laughter at something one of them had said. To Selina, it seemed like they were safely out of this conversation, but that didn't mean they wouldn't overhear anything.

"You getting soft with age?" Charles asked.

Bryan looked sternly at him, his brows a set of thunderclouds over his eyes. Then he looked at Selina, face relaxing. "Old. She's got us beat in looks and youth." He chucked her under the chin with his scarred index finger then raised his glass to her in a toast.

She clinked her glass against his, both taking a drink. She hadn't gotten any good information out of him, and she wondered how Charles had glommed onto him, but now she had one more confirmation that there might be a way to combat Wendigo, as far-fetched as it might be. It would have to be enough for now.

18

A HUNTING WE WILL GO

After about an hour chatting with Bryan, Charles' phone buzzed. He studied it with a frown, thumb moving over the screen, before looking up. "I've got to go." Without any further explanation, he got up and went over to the bar to pay.

Selina looked after him, thinking. "What do you suppose that was about?"

Bryan shrugged, obviously happily buzzed.

"I'm going to follow him. See if he's onto anything interesting. It's too coincidental that he's here. Especially now that he's been talking to you. Want to come?"

Bryan thought for a moment, rubbing a thumb through the moisture on his beer glass. Then he brought the glass up to his mouth, chugged down the rest of his beer, and wiped a final speck of foam off his lips. "Let's do it. But you're driving."

Which was exactly what she'd intended, being only a partial beer down compared to whatever he had drunk so far. Plus, she suspected that one of the motorcycles sitting outside belonged to him, and she had no idea where they'd be heading.

"Do you need to pay?" she asked him.

"Nah, I've got a tab. I'll stop in and pay tomorrow."

"By stop in, you mean hang out and drink a few more?"

"You bet."

He had a quick word with the waitress to let her know and said goodbye to the guys at the table. Then the two of them slipped outside while Charles was still inside trying to pay, one hand waving for the bartender's attention. Bryan climbed into the passenger seat of the truck.

Selina pulled around to the side of the bar where they could watch which vehicle Charles went to. Though she'd seen it in front of his cabin, there were several SUVs here, and she hadn't paid enough attention to his to differentiate it from the others. She put it in park and turned off the headlights.

Several minutes passed before he exited the bar. He was in a rush, movements jerky, probably out of frustration for having had to wait so long to pay. At least he'd paid, or she assumed he had. He crossed the parking lot and climbed into one of the dark SUVs along the back row. His was bigger and looked more expensive than the others. She should have known he'd have the flashiest vehicle in the lot, even if it was a rental. Charles had never skimped on anything for himself, of that she was sure.

He turned on his lights and reversed, pulling onto the road.

Selina pulled onto an adjoining road, turned her lights on, and turned in behind him, hoping he would take her for another late-night traveler. She doubted he'd missed their absence, but if he was in enough of a hurry, he might not care enough to think they'd follow him.

"So tell me what's going on with you and this Charles fella'." Bryan's hand tapped on his left thigh, something he frequently did. He needed to be in action all the time, even if it was only a small part of him. She wondered if he moved in his sleep, too. A foot twitch, perhaps. She couldn't imagine him perfectly still, even while asleep.

"First, can you tell me how you know him?"

"Oh yeah. We actually met today. He was asking around about Wendigo, and Clary pointed him in my direction. I couldn't help him any more than I could help you or Nathan. I've got to say, there hasn't been this much talk of Wendigo around here for as long as I can remember.

"I don't doubt it." She kept her eyes intent on the road and the tail-lights that glowed a distance in front of her. "Hold on."

She turned off the road for a few seconds and shut off the lights on the truck, making sure it had no running lights. "Don't freak out." She turned back onto the road. Her vision was good enough that she wouldn't need the headlights as long as the moon stayed uncovered, and this way he wouldn't know they were following him. If it had been brighter, she would have been too visible, but the truck was dark, the amount of light perfect.

"If I didn't know what you were, I'd definitely be freaking out right now. I assume you can see perfectly well, right?" His voice was tense.

"Yes, I can even see the rodents running around beside the road. I bet you don't know anyone it would be safer to drive with at night, lights or no."

"All right, I'll take your word for it." His right hand gripped the door handle anyway, and the tapping quickened.

"Okay, you told me how you met him, so I'll tell you how I know him. You remember that Chupacabra case I told you about, back when I was fourteen or so?"

"Yes."

"Well, that's the guy that talked my dad into leaving me as bait. Not that my dad probably needed much convincing."

"No shit." It wasn't a question. He frowned, looking ahead toward the SUV they were trailing.

"No shit. He's an ass, and he's here investigating a Wendigo. But, Bryan, there's something I need to tell you." She looked over at him, nervous now.

He looked at her and nodded. "What is it?"

She swallowed. He was trustworthy. He'd certainly never tell Charles. Or anyone else, for that matter. Still, exposing Nathan in this way terrified her. It struck her that someone else knowing what was going on, someone who would deal with it the right way should anything happen to her, couldn't be a bad thing. Specifically, someone who cared about Nathan enough to do the correct thing.

"Nathan is the Wendigo."

His hand stilled. He sat in silence a moment. Tension built along her spine as she waited for him to respond. His hand started tapping again, but he still didn't speak.

The silence lasted so long that she jumped when he spoke again. "Now his questions and yours make a lot of sense. He did it to help someone, right?"

"Yes."

"And you think you can figure out a way to save him?"

"I'm trying to."

"Hmmmm."

Silence again. He was deep in thought, something she'd long grown accustomed to from him. He often disappeared into himself to think, working things through. She knew not to bug him when he was thinking. Instead, she focused on the road.

Finally, he said, "What do you need from me?"

"For now, what I need is you keeping your ear to the ground. Let me know if you hear about any more deaths, and definitely tell me if someone knows how to fix this. I don't suppose you remember more from that story with the woman and the European guy?"

"No, only that he was someone able to dispel the spirit. Maybe he was a priest or some other religious figure?"

That didn't jive for Selina, but she couldn't think what else it could be.

"Okay, keep trying." She shot a look his way briefly then back to the road. "I can't let him die this way, Bryan."

He reached over and squeezed her shoulder. "You'll figure it out, little sister. I'll let you know if I hear anything. And you let me know if you need anything." He looked at her until she turned her eyes back to his. "Anything."

She nodded, grateful. Somehow, she felt slightly less alone. Even if she had no intention of taking him up on it.

Up ahead, Charles' brake lights lit up. She slowed the truck, waiting to see what he'd do. He turned right, lights bouncing over what must have been uneven ground.

Accelerating, she got up to where he'd turned off, following him onto an unmarked road. Sure enough, the tires found dirt road and began to bounce, throwing the two of them around on the shoddy shocks.

Neither of them tried to talk. They wouldn't have been able to hear each other above the racket the truck produced. If Charles had his windows open, surely he'd hear them behind him. Then again, the inside of his SUV should be equally noisy.

She could still see his taillights up ahead. It was several minutes before he braked again, lights brightening. He paused, and so did she, waiting. Now he took a left turn, and the taillights began to climb. They were going up into the hills.

"Here we go," she said, following him. Luckily, the moon remained bright enough. "Luck, don't fail me now."

They climbed for what seemed like forever, Selina's hands gripping the wheel so tightly that they got sore. She let him get even farther ahead of her, sure he must have seen them by now. The road smoothed after a while, gravel crunching under her tires and pinging off the sides of the truck in a steady chorus.

"Do you have any idea where we are?" she asked.

"I don't think so. Sully's place, maybe, but it's hard to tell in the dark."

Sully had died years ago. He had been an acquaintance of Nathan, Bryan, and the other Crypto-Hunters in these parts, but he'd been a crotchety old grouch, prone to doing things his own way, and unable to work with others unless the need was dire. Even if it meant a case getting away, he didn't want to deal with other people and their methods. As far as she knew, his property hadn't been sold. It was being held in trust for someone. She had no idea how, as he'd never been married, and had no kids. No legitimate ones, anyway. For all she knew, it was in trust for a figment of his imagination so his ghost could continue living there.

The taillights disappeared around a corner, and she slowed. She set the parking brake and got out. "I'll be right back."

Setting out on foot, she went around the corner. The SUV idled up ahead, pulled over in a flat area.

Charles got out of the SUV and moved to the rear hatch. When he opened it, the overhead light did not turn on. He had to have turned off the mechanism before he got out. He shuffled through some items for a while, his back to Selina. Once done, he slung a large, dark bag over his shoulder cross-wise, shut the hatch, and continued up the dirt road.

Selina waited until he'd gone out of sight and sound distance before running back to her truck. If she couldn't hear him, he definitely shouldn't be able to hear her.

Back at her truck, she put it in drive, and went as slowly as she could, knowing there was a chance he'd hear the truck. Gravel popped beneath the tires, but the pings were fewer at this speed. She let out the breath she'd been holding once she had the truck nestled beside the SUV.

Selina and Bryan climbed out of the truck. She hadn't brought much in the way of weapons, but she did have her guns on her, as well as a few items hidden around her person.

"Do you have any weapons?" she asked him.

"Does a bear shit in the woods?"

Like her, he usually stayed partially armed. She was certain he had at least a couple knives, if not a gun, as well.

They climbed rapidly, hoping to get close enough that she could hear Charles again. Her calves burned from the uphill exodus. Next to her, Bryan's breaths huffed. When she could faintly hear Charles' footsteps ahead, she slowed their pace, intent on avoiding his notice until the last minute.

Ahead, his steps stopped.

Selina held a hand up to motion for Bryan to stop. She stepped off the gravel into the grass and dirt to the side, making her way up the hill until she could see Charles. He stood looking at a cabin, its silent hulk barely visible in the pale light from the moon. A sagging porch decorated the front, screen door hanging off one hinge.

Charles knelt, setting the bag on the ground.

Selina went back to where Bryan could see her and gestured for him to join her. He did so, quickly catching up to her. This time, she didn't attempt to mask her steps, though she didn't stomp either. Bryan followed her lead.

Charles appeared in the road ahead, a rifle aimed at them.

It cheered her to see his face go from alert to surly upon recognizing them.

"What are you doing here?" Charles asked. "And how the hell did you pull that off?"

"Pull what off?"

"You know damn well."

"I don't know what you're talking about." She batted her eyelashes at him. "So. What are we here for?"

Charles shook his head.

Selina resisted the urge to laugh. The tables were turned now. He'd dogged her steps since she'd arrived, harassed her, tried to pry information from her, looked over her shoulder, and now here she was, following him. The irony was delicious.

"Fine. Some help won't hurt, but the money's mine." He looked at them each in turn, challenge clear on his face.

Selina nodded. "That's cool with me. Bryan?"

"Sure." Bryan grinned so broadly that his teeth shone in the dark. "I'm just here to tag along. And to make sure you don't get any funny ideas."

Charles eyeballed him. He looked wary, possibly sensing the change in Bryan's attitude toward him. "I got a tip on a possible Wendigo sighting. I think it might be the one that's been killing people. Maybe we'll find some bodies that haven't been reported yet to explain the sudden gap."

Selina chose not to point out that the murders had occurred to the west, far away from this isolated cabin. As it was, relief flooded through her. At least they weren't anywhere near Nathan. A flush of excitement quickly followed. There was a chance this was the Wendigo that could save Nathan's life or that it could lead her to a solution. Could it possibly be this simple? A new Wendigo, if identified, could lead her to another, which might result in more clues as to what was happening around here, and what had occurred with Lansing.

"All right, where do we go from here?" she asked. "I don't have all my tools with me, but I have some of the basics, including a stake."

"I've got everything," Charles said. "No worries there."

He led them to the duffel bag. From its depths he pulled out knives, two stakes, and three different guns. He strapped all but the rifle to himself then flipped the rifle onto his back, where he snugged it into some sort of holster or catch. This completed, he turned and looked Bryan and Selina over. "What have you got on you?"

Bryan shrugged. "Three knives and a handgun in an ankle holster. I wasn't planning on doing anything other than drinking tonight."

Selina opened her jacket to show the knives and a gun she had strapped there. "Plus my stake, like I said, and one other gun. Spray. Oh, and these." She activated the knives at her wrists, causing them to spring out where she could clasp the handles in her hands. At his nod, she tucked them back in, always a delicate process when both were out.

Bryan looked impressed. "I need some of those." He reached out and grasped one forearm, pulling at her sleeve to study the spring mechanism, which had been disguised under wrappings of leather to simply look like a decorative wrist cover, like those often seen in fantasy films and at Renaissance Festivals.

"Steve's," she replied.

Familiar with Steve, as were all the local Crypto-Hunters, he nodded. "Didn't know she carried those."

Charles let out a puff of air. "All right, enough with the chit-chat. The guy who told me about this said he spotted him hanging out behind the cabin. Then he went off into the woods."

"Who was this guy, and what was he doing up here?" Selina asked.

"I didn't ask why, but I think he said something about coming up here to drink."

Selina looked around at the hunched building, tall grasses, and bare trees. "This seems like an odd place to come drinking."

Charles sighed. "Are you always such a pain in the ass?"

"I hope so. At least when it matters."

Bryan laughed and clapped her on the back. "I can back you up on that."

Charles ignored their back and forth. "There may be caves up here. Or he may have been staying in the cabin. The guy said whatever it was ran fast when it went into the woods, that it was light in color, tall, and covered in fur."

Selina and Bryan nodded. That could really be describing anything, though it being light in color probably indicated it wasn't a bear, a moose, or a Sasquatch, anyway. Hope swelled in her chest. If this was the Wendigo she was seeking, all she'd need would be the heart. There usually weren't a bunch running around in any one place. In fact, it was a rare phenomenon. So if there were more than one, odds are they were related in some way.

Charles handed Bryan a shotgun, and he took it happily, checking the weapon over and testing its heft.

Selina had a moment to reflect that these guys had only recently been drinking pretty heavily, and here she was, about to head out into the dark with them when they were armed and looking to score a body count. She pushed back the doubt, telling herself they were both professionals, and both familiar with the weapons they'd be using. Still, she didn't intend to stand in front of Charles if he was firing. Bryan either, for that matter, but for completely different reasons. Charles shooting her might not be an accident.

One final weapons check, and Charles shoved the bag to the side with his foot. They went to the cabin first, splitting up to move around the building and inspect it for signs of break-in, spore, and anything else that might hint at what awaited them. Bryan waited at the front to monitor the door and ensure nothing could escape while they were checking the grounds.

Selina went to the right. The wild grasses were tall, having consumed any imported grass that might have been planted. She took a second to be grateful it was too cool for snakes to be around; they were quiet, sneaky bastards. Wind soughed through the grass, causing a soft whoosh to swirl around her. Leaves shook in the surrounding trees. Small animals skittered around nearby, joined by the chirp and chitter of insects. She worked to block out these distracting noises so she could listen past them for anything larger that might come her way.

To her left, the house creaked. Movement inside or simple settling?

The building appeared to be intact on this side, the two small windows unbroken. What she could see of the roof was in good shape, and nothing indicated a basement or cellar. There were no signs of spore, but the grass had been flattened in a trail near the back of the cabin. She bent down to examine the ground. It was dry, so chances of finding fresh footprints were low. The grass stalks were pressed down thoroughly, showing her this wasn't one trek by whatever had done this, but regular transit. Several stalks were crushed or broken, so it was something or someone heavy. She turned her head to see where the path started. A small, weathered porch hunched on the back of the house, the path beginning at the steps that led down from it.

Charles came around the corner on the other side, his eyes coming up to meet hers through the bars of the porch. She motioned behind her to let him know she was going in that direction. He nodded then continued along the back of the house, bending to peer under the porch. Selina followed the path toward the woods, moving her eyes between the ground and the woods in order to track the trail and keep watch ahead of her. The trail didn't meander. It was a straight shot to the woods.

At the edge of the trees, the grasses diminished. Selina squinted into the darkness, looking for anything that might tell her where the path led. The ground was slightly worn, but not enough to indicate a trail that had been here for any period of time. A tree root stuck up above the dirt. She stepped over the root, out of the moon's light, and followed the slight trail in a short distance, but it became harder to track in the dark. Unwilling to turn a flashlight on, which would alert anything around to her presence, she paused, shut her eyes, and took a deep breath. Her nostrils flared to take in more scent.

The heavy odor of waste wafted along on the wind. Not animal spore—human waste. As if an outhouse was up here, or someone had been camping, perhaps. There was enough of it to make scenting anything else tricky, save for the stronger smells of the forest, like sap. Unwilling to advance any further without more information, she looked around one more time and turned to head back.

Ahead of her, someone let out a hoarse shout.

19

A SCOOBY SURPRISE

S elina ran out of the woods and back into the long grasses, trying to pinpoint who had shouted.

Charles stood on the porch, gun pointed at the back door. "The front!"

She steered to her left, running along the side of the cabin. Getting through the grass was like running through water, and she was high stepping by the time she got to the front.

Bryan stood on the front porch, looking in through the window to the right of the door. He waved her over, walking to the edge of the sunken wooden porch, which slanted sideways, creaking with his movements. "Something looked out the window. It's inside. Cover me."

He went back to the front door and ripped the broken screen door off the final hinge, chucking it into the grass beyond the porch before turning back to the door.

Selina moved behind him and to the side, remaining in the grass. She pulled her handgun from its holster, pressed the safety off, and arranged herself at an angle to him, aiming at the door. She took care to ensure her positioning would keep him out of any crossfire. "Go."

Bryan knocked, which struck Selina as funny, but it was always a good thing to check.

She held her breath, waiting to see if the door would open. Of course, she wouldn't open a door if there were armed people standing outside, but perhaps whoever was in there hadn't seen that they were armed. Still, they'd have to be clueless to open the door at midnight, or whatever time it was now. She hadn't checked her watch in a while.

Bryan gave it a minute, but when no one had answered in that time, he aimed a kick right below the door handle. The door bent in slightly with a splintering crack. He kicked again, and this time the door burst open, swinging against the interior wall. He ran inside before it had stopped moving, butting it aside with his shoulder when it bounced back toward him.

Selina ran up the steps behind him, registering a stench of filth and rot as she crossed the threshold. There were male yells from the back, pounding footsteps, a screech, then more yelling. A gun fired.

"Shit." Selina hurried through the front room, registering a heap in the corner that might have been a blanket or sleeping bag, as well as scattered detritus she didn't have time to identify. It wasn't empty in here, but there was no actual furniture. Squatters, perhaps.

A doorway led to the kitchen, the glass sliding door open on the far side of the room. There was no sign of Bryan, but when she raced across the porch, she spotted Charles lying in the grass below the porch. He groaned and sat up, holding his side.

"What happened?" she asked.

"Just go after them." He was winded, voice strained. "I'm fine."

"I didn't ask," she called over her shoulder, jumping off the porch without running down the stairs. She took the path back into the woods, following the sound of bodies crashing through the foliage up ahead. Someone grunted and called out.

It took her a few seconds to get caught up, but there was Bryan ahead of her, flannel billowing behind him, shotgun clutched in his right hand. He was fast, but she was faster, and she overtook him. At first, she didn't see what they were chasing, and then there it was ahead of them, white and dingy. And tall.

She passed Bryan, who huffed from the exertion. The thing ahead of them did the same, almost wheezing from the effort of running like this. She could smell filth, rot, urine, and body odor. Human body odor.

As this last scent registered, a high-pitched male voice yelled, "Leave me alone."

One last burst of speed, and Selina had caught up, right on its heels. She tucked the gun away and leapt, letting her shoulder take the brunt of her impact on the figure's back. They hit the ground in a puff of dirt and stench, and she quickly righted herself, climbing on top of the figure. She grasped what felt like fur, and turned it over, popping out the blade on her right wrist to put it at his throat.

It was a man. Filthy, scrawny, covered in some sort of white fur suit, but a man all the same. Her hope quickly deflated, the hollow space filling with anger. This was no Wendigo. "What the hell's going on?" Her heart pounded from the run and the excitement.

The man gasped for air, his breath fetid. It was apparent he hadn't bathed or brushed his teeth in quite a long time. The stench rose off him like a physical entity made of stink.

Selina pulled her head back, nose wrinkled in distaste, wishing she could turn off her sense of smell.

It took him a minute, but he finally answered. "This is my property. I've got squatter's rights."

"Is that even a thing in Canada?" she asked.

Bryan huffed up beside her, leaning his shotgun against a tree so he could bend over, hands on knees, and catch his breath. "So much for it being a Wendigo."

With an impatient shrug, she ignored the man's foul breath and bent forward, nose almost touching his. She let the tip of her blade press more firmly against his throat. "Tell me what you're doing here." She grasped the putrid fur coat, dismayed to feel a slickness to it. "And what is this?" She let it drop.

"I told you, this is my property now. I've been living up here for two years."

"Squatter's rights don't kick in around here for seven years," Bryan said, straightening. "Sully hasn't been gone that long yet."

"This isn't Sully's place." The man inclined his head behind them. "That's one road over."

"How many empty cabins are there around here?" Selina aimed the question at Bryan.

Bryan shrugged, but the man said, "Oh, lots. People lose their jobs, die. No one claims the cabins. Some of them are rentals that never get rented."

"And what category does this one fall under?" Selina asked.

"A rental, I think. The owner has a bunch of cabins, but I've never seen him at this one. I watched and waited to be sure before I moved in."

Selina had a moment to wonder whether this was another of Herb's cabins, and if he was the official cabin slumlord around here, but then something large came crashing through the woods behind them, and Selina turned to meet it. She kept her knee pressed down on the man's chest, her hand on his shoulder.

Charles tore down the path through the woods, slapping at an errant branch with the arm not holding a shotgun. He was as winded as the rest of them, if not more, but he was also older than all but the man in the fur suit.

"Finally joining us?" Selina asked.

He ignored her, eyes wide, voice excited. "You caught it?"

"Yes," Bryan said.

"And 'it' is a him," Selina said.

"How can you tell?" Charles moved up behind Selina. "Oh."

"No Wendigo, I'm afraid," said Bryan.

They all looked at the man, who asked, "What's this Windy Go you guys keep mentioning? Whatever it is, it's not me."

Selina pushed her knee in deeper, blade back at his throat. "What's your name, anyway?"

"I don't have to tell you that." He attempted to cross his arms, but it proved to be an impossible move with Selina planted on top of him. Instead, he plopped his hands on the ground, palms facing upward.

She grabbed the fur at his neckline and pulled him up to an awkward sitting position. "You just wasted my night when I'm on a serious deadline. You'll damn well tell me who you are right the hell now."

His eyes widened. He stared at her, lips pressed together. Finally, he sighed. "My name is Winston. But I'm not telling you my last name."

"Fine. Winston, explain why you're up here, and why you're wearing a fur suit."

"I put it together last time I tried to squat a property." Winston plucked at the fur on his chest. "People leave real fast if they think there's a large furry creature hanging around. Especially if I let them get drunk first." He grinned, showing rotted teeth.

Selina released his neckline and let him drop back on the ground. His head hit with a thud, and he yelped. She rose, shooting a look back at Charles. "This guy's your problem. I've got things I should be doing."

"Hey, no one invited you here, Sugar Puff."

She started back through the woods, thinking of the mess this had become. She'd known the Wendigo she sought couldn't be this far from the killings, but hope had won out anyway. The need for a quick and easy solution seduced her into a wild goose chase for a crazy man in a crappy fur suit made of lord knew what. Disappointment was a solid stone in her gut.

Bryan followed her out. They moved together past the cabin, leaving the items they'd borrowed from Charles on the hood of his SUV before driving off. The last thing she saw was Charles frog marching Winston, odd fur suit flapping on his scrawny legs, out of the woods toward the house. It was all such a Scooby Doo moment, and she briefly wondered who Scooby would be in this scenario. Winston would have to be the villainous monster wearing a mask, only in his case it was a fur suit. Then again, Charles wasn't too far from being the villain, himself. He just didn't wear a mask or disguise of any sort.

Frustration and rage coursed through her veins, but there was nothing she could do about it with Bryan tagging along. She dropped him off at the bar, figuring he was perfectly sober after a nighttime chase through the forest. He'd get home fine.

He hugged her before getting out of the truck. "My thoughts are with you and Nathan. Tell me if you need me. I'll keep my ears open. May the Myth Stalkers of the past be with you."

At this point, she could use all the help she could get.

As soon as she'd gotten back on the road, empty at this time of night, Selina let the darkness crash in upon her. All the pent-up rage and fear washed over her like a black wave.

What was her next move? She'd gotten nothing from Bryan; he would have given her any information he had. The Wendigo hunt had been a wash, and she had let herself believe that maybe, just maybe, the culprit would be up at a remote cabin far away from the killings, some minuscule chance having fallen in her lap via Charles and a stupid text.

There were too many people on the list Nathan had provided. No way could she follow up with all of them tomorrow and meet the deadline he'd imposed. Plus, he'd spoken to them already and not gotten any help. Nothing. No one knew how to save him. She was fooling herself that there was any possible ending outside of putting a bullet in his brain, ripping his heart out, and chopping him into small pieces. Her mentor. Her old friend. The man who had saved her when no one else would.

He'd called her up here to help, and she was failing him. Spinning her wheels and getting nowhere.

Now here she was, faced with an impossible task, and she'd spent the evening drinking and chasing a homeless man. Had she used her time well? Had she done everything she could? It felt like she'd accomplished nothing in the time she'd been here. Despite her big talk and empty promises.

She gulped, forcing tears away. They gathered in her chest, her stomach, and it was only by sheer force of will that she didn't break down entirely. This was no time to allow self-pity to course through her. Though she couldn't help but wonder why she had these ridiculous abilities if they didn't even allow her to save people, to save someone she loved, who trusted her to do right.

Selina felt an odd sort of affirmation at finally having this out. No more being dishonest. There was something cleansing about breaking things down this way instead of pushing on with false hope. Sometimes it's better to be honest, and to confront weakness.

But Nathan had faith in her. While he was still alive, she had to keep trying, had to push past these weaknesses, these morbid thoughts, and do what needed to be done. Wasn't that what she was good at? Action?

One more day. She had one more day to save a man who had been everything she needed him to be. There were still actions to be taken, and that she could do.

One more day.

20

NOW WE'RE GETTING SOMEWHERE

She got back to the cabin late. Both Johnny and Nathan were asleep, Nathan on the sofa, Johnny in an easy chair blocking the hall. She woke him up with a touch on the shoulder that sent him jerking up and out of his chair.

"Sorry I'm late," she whispered. "I went on a bit of a snipe hunt."

"That's all right. It's been a quiet night."

She settled in with her notebooks and sent Johnny to sleep for what remained of the night in his own bed. The hours passed with no issues. She sat watching Nathan and reading through her notes, hoping for a further clue. How was she to track down where this had all begun without more information?

Johnny relieved her at dawn. She grabbed a couple hours of sleep before taking a shower and changing into a business pantsuit she had brought in case she'd need it—she always had an array of clothes for different purposes, as one never knew where the job would lead. If she didn't have what she needed, it was generally possible to find a secondhand store. Even the smallest of towns had them.

She tucked a gun, two blades, the spray, and a stake in a bag that she stuck behind the bench seat of the truck. For once, she had no weapons on her person. There might be a metal detector she'd have to go through at the refinery, which was where she'd be heading first thing.

She felt naked without any weapons, so she pulled the bag out and grabbed the spray. It wouldn't be a big deal if they caught her with pepper spray, and they'd have no idea that wasn't all that was in the canister.

Before leaving, she ran back inside to kiss Nathan on the cheek, dismayed to feel downy fur tickling against her lips. She pulled back and studied him. The fine white hair she'd felt covered his entire body, at least what she could see. White strands ran through his raven hair, eyebrows, and eyelashes, and his eyes were lightening from brown to a murky undefined color.

He reached out and squeezed her hand. "Happy hunting, Selina."

Her stomach sank at the quiet trust implied, and she turned her back on him without another word. Mourning wouldn't help anything, but it was hard to see him wasting away like this, piece by piece of him disappearing, changing. Dwelling on this, as she'd allowed herself to do last night, would only guarantee the forcing of her hand in having to kill him.

No, mourning wasn't the answer, but it was sure an insistent urge.

THE REFINERY WAS visible from a distance, giant gray stacks rising against the backdrop of the snowcapped Rockies. White smoke or steam, she couldn't be sure which, rose high into the air from one tower, gray puffing out from another area. The metal monstrosity ruined the line of the mountains, seeming somehow harsher with that beauty behind it.

The parking lot was full of sedans and trucks, dulled by age and filth from the road. The workers here didn't make a financial killing, that was for sure. One section did boast a line of shiny newer vehicles, with upper crust makes, such as Mercedes. Management. Lansing had been management, as evidenced by his cars and home.

She passed through a gate and stepped up to a squat glass and metal booth. A guard sat inside, his feet up. His light hair was short, combed over to the side, and his face bore a smattering of dark freckles. He looked over at her with a questioning gaze that became promptly lecherous, eyes widening before he looked her up and down, a slow smile spreading over his face.

Selina sighed inwardly, but at least his obviousness told her how to approach him.

"Help you?" he asked.

"Yes, I'm looking for Randy Simpco. Is he here today?"

"Who's asking?"

She put on her best dumb bimbo expression, irritated that this was still an act she had to pull, and leaned in the window, showing a moderate amount of cleavage. "My name's Selina. I've come about an old friend of ours. Perhaps you knew him? Curtis Lansing?"

He frowned and shook his head before putting his feet down and typing something into the computer. His eyes zoomed in on her cleavage. "No idea who this Lansing guy is you're talking about, but I do show that Simpco's here. You know the drill for visits?"

She shook her head. "Can you walk me through it?"

He smiled and reached into a box below the window, pulling out a plastic badge. He held it up, the word *GUEST* visible in large red lettering. "First, I need to clip this to your shirt. You want it visible or you won't be able to go in."

He stood up and leaned toward her, staring down her top as he fiddled with the badge, taking far longer than strictly necessary. His hand grazed the top of her breast, and she almost jerked back, but forced herself to stay in place. He looked up to test her reaction, and she smiled, leaning her head down to give him a coy expression. His face heated. He licked his lips, his tongue dry and pale.

"Now I need you to sign in here. I should have had you do that first." He handed her a roster book and a pen.

She took it, purposely brushing her fingers across his, and signed her name.

He stuttered, "I-I'll just c-call ahead and let him know we're coming."

"Is that really necessary? I have bad news for him." She changed her voice to a whisper. "A death," before continuing in a normal tone. "I hate to have to express that over the phone first. Could you maybe just walk me in to be sure I get to where I need to be?" She gave him the full-watt smile, pressing her arms against the sides of her breasts to emphasize them and increase the gap so more skin showed. Having him with her wasn't optimal, but Simpco wouldn't know who she was, and she feared he'd refuse to see her if given a heads up.

"Well, it's not how we usually do it, but if it's bad news, maybe we can go in together. I can't leave you alone until I've confirmed you're with Mr. Simpco, though."

"Oh, I fully understand. Thank you."

There was a chance Oliver had contacted Simpco and mentioned her after the visit. Also, she wanted a glance at his office. Had he and Curtis shared one, perhaps? Or were they individual offices? Cubicles? Was Simpco also a manager, or had Curtis been his superior? If he chose to come out to meet her, she wouldn't have access to any of that.

The guard clipped up a sign saying, *Guard will return shortly, wait here,* then came out of his booth, locking it behind him. He glanced toward the parking lot as if for one more check, then gestured for her to follow him. She trailed him to a doorway fronted by a metal detector, and waited until he stepped through and beckoned her forward. It beeped twice as she stepped through.

She covered her mouth with her hand. "I'm so sorry! It's my pepper spray. A girl can never be too careful." She reached into her top and pulled out the canister she'd tucked into her bra, handing it to him.

He took the canister from her and had her walk through again. It didn't go off this time, and she took a moment to revel in her relief at not having strapped on her weapons.

Much to her surprise, he returned the canister to her, watching as she tucked it back into her bra. She fell in behind him as he continued down the hall, asking questions about the things they passed, burying the ones she really wanted to ask in the middle of them.

"What's that shiny globe up there? Oh, wow, there are a bunch! Why would there be mirrors in the ceiling?"

"Those are security cameras, ma'am. That way, I can track what's happening and make sure nothing dangerous is going on."

She stepped up and took his arm, pressing herself along his side as they walked. "How exciting! Can you see everywhere in here on those?"

"Well, I can't see in all the offices. You see, there are important things that go on here, and they can't risk them being seen by just anyone."

She started to pull away, lowering her gaze and putting a pout on. "Oh."

"But I can see in all the plants, all the hallways, anything other than those specific offices. You wouldn't believe some of the things that go on when people don't think you're looking."

"Like what?" She looked up at him, telegraphing eagerness in her widened gaze, watching his mouth.

He licked his lips again. "Well, for instance, one time a guy pis— urinated outside one of the offices. Guess he'd just been laid off and was mad about it."

"Wow, what did you do?"

"I called in backup. Never know with one of these guys what they might do. Getting laid off can make a man go a little crazy."

"Good thing you were here. Who knows what he would have done."

"It turned out fine." A hot red blush spread up his face.

"That would be interesting to watch on video. Did you tape it?"

"No, we don't record. All live monitoring except at night."

"I see. Hey, you said you didn't know the name Curtis Lansing. He worked here not long ago. Are you new?"

"Yeah...ah, here we are. This is the management office. Hold on."

A giant window in the wall allowed them to see into the office. Next to the window stood a thick, gray metal door. He stepped forward and tapped on the door before opening it. Inside, a secretary sat at a small desk, typing away at a computer. He had mousy hair, dishwater blond and frizzy, and wore a suit that had been in style about a decade ago. He looked up at them, eyebrows raised in question.

"Guest for Mr. Simpco," the guard said.

The secretary picked up a phone, not saying a word to the guard or asking for Selina's name. "Mr. Simpco, you have a guest." He put the phone down, and returned to his typing, speaking without looking at them. "He'll be right out."

There were four doors lining the hall behind the secretary, two on either side. One of them opened, a heavyset, balding man storming out. He wore a drab, brown suit, the blazer unbuttoned over his protruding belly. He walked down the hall, lips pressed together in impatience. "Mark, how many times do I have to tell you..." He slowed, eyes on Selina. He brushed a wispy lock of hair across the shiny dome of his forehead, pulled his jacket tight, and buttoned it up over his belly. It strained, but stayed put.

Selina stepped forward, held her hand out, and smiled.

He took it and shook with a weak grip, his hand clammy. "What is this about?"

"It's a personal matter. Concerning Curtis Lansing?"

Something flitted across his face that she didn't quite catch. Confusion? Alarm? It had been too fast before he caught himself and set his face to a neutral expression.

"Why don't you come back to my office and we can talk there?"

"That would be great, thanks." She turned to the guard, glancing down at his nametag, which had been hidden by the collar of his jacket before. "Thank you for bringing me down here, Stefan."

"My pleasure."

She followed Simpco down the hall to his office, trying to get a peek into the one across from it. It stood empty, and the others were too far to see into.

Simpco pushed the door open then stepped back, gesturing for her to precede him. The cramped office held only a small desk, two office chairs, a beat-up metal filing cabinet, and a minuscule book-shelf, which held report binders, rather than books. A small, decrepit plant sat in the room, dying from lack of sunlight and, likely, water. She wondered how long it had been here.

"Have a seat, Miss...?"

"Selina. Thank you." She settled into the chair, watching him as he sat across the desk from her.

He undid the lowest button on the way down, clasping his hands and leaning on the desk top. "What can I help you with, Selina?"

"I'm hoping you could give me some information about a mutual friend. Curtis Lansing?"

"Curtis? Why? Is he okay?"

"I'm not sure. I'm worried about him, and hoped you could help. He's mentioned you before, and I thought you'd be the person who could tell me what's going on."

"What do you mean?"

"Well, he's missing. I haven't been able to reach him. Do you know where he might be?"

Simpco diverted his eyes, thinking. When he turned back to her, his gaze had become shuttered, eyes cold. "I doubt I could be of any help. He quit weeks ago, and I haven't heard from him since."

"At all?"

"At all."

"Why'd he quit?"

"You'd have to ask him that."

Selina leaned forward. "Listen, I understand you don't know who I am, though I confess to being hurt that he hasn't talked about me as much as he talked about you, but he was acting so strange before he left that I think he might be in danger. Any help you could give me would be so appreciated, Mr. Simpco." She widened her eyes, placing her hands flat on the surface of his desk.

He sat quietly again, this time studying her. This was no man to be flirted into giving answers, which she could respect. It was a game she hated to play. Instead, she would appear to be as open, honest, and direct as possible. Only by taking him seriously would he take her seriously.

He looked down at his hands, tapped his thumbs together then looked back up at her. "I don't know where he is. All I can tell you is that he was definitely acting strange. He was losing a lot of weight, acting moody and aggressive. He trashed his office before he quit. He even...even...you know, defecated on his desk."

Selina pulled back. "That's terrible. Definitely not something I would expect from him. Did you see any physical changes in him, other than losing weight?"

He hesitated. "I don't know. I don't think so."

"Why do you say it like that?" She leaned in again. "What did you see? Please, anything might help."

"I'm sure I imagined it. Small changes, you know? I must not have noticed them before."

"Like what?"

"Like his fingers looking weird. Longer, I guess. The knuckles seemed bigger." He looked up at her then quickly away. "Like I said, I probably just imagined it. Or maybe his problem was arthritis or something along those lines. I've seen what that does to a person's hands, twisting them. Nasty and painful."

"Do you know if anything happened to him before he started acting this way? Did he say he'd had a fight with someone? Did he mention anything you found strange?"

"Now that you mention it, he came back from his hunting trip acting weird. Didn't want to tell me about it, whereas he usually brags about his prowess with a weapon. Guy's a bit full of himself." He cleared his throat and sat back. "He's not a bad guy, though. Just sometimes brags is all."

"Was he hurt on the trip? Maybe he'd had some kind of accident?"

"He had a bandage on his neck, but that was the only thing I noticed. He withdrew a lot after that, so I truly don't know if there was something else."

His gaze strayed around the room again. He twiddled with his thumbs, his foot tapping.

She hardened her voice, going an octave lower. "What are you hiding from me, Mr. Simpco?" There was always a chance this would anger him, but often the authoritative voice, when employed at the right time, did the opposite.

"What? Nothing."

"I don't believe you. If I can help Curtis, I need to know everything. Tell me. Please?"

He sighed, took his hands apart, unbuttoned the jacket the rest of the way, and looked around the room.

She sat quietly, watching him, her gaze steady and direct. She'd give him the space he needed, but make sure he knew she expected an answer. It was tricky getting information out of someone when they had probably questioned the validity of it or felt uncomfortable about it. This was something she was quite accustomed to, working as she did with creatures most people thought weren't real.

He looked up and met her eyes. "It's stupid." He paused, braced himself. "He said he was changing. He thought he was becoming a monster. I think the guy just cracked."

"What kind of monster? Did he say?"

"I don't know. It was a weird thing I'd never heard of. A Winnebago or something. Said he'd found it online."

"A Wendigo?"

"Yeah, that might have been it. He said he needed help, to be absolved of his sins."

Interesting. "What did you say to that?"

"I told him he was crazy. Told him to find a priest if he wanted to be absolved of his sins. He got pissed, said I didn't believe him. You know what? Of course I didn't. Fucking crazy talk." He looked at her, a chagrined look settling over his face. "Excuse my language."

"Anything else? Did he see a priest?"

"No, he said a priest couldn't help him, that it wasn't *that* kind of sin. Said he needed something more. So I told him about this guy. He's my insurance guy, but he...well, he specializes in helping people who have done bad things."

Selina froze, briefly taken aback. "What do you mean?"

"You won't believe me."

"You'd be shocked what I believe. I've seen a lot of strange things."

He hesitated, looking anywhere but at her. "I don't know. I can't explain it." He sighed. "I broke down one day at his office, and he, well, he somehow made it better. He gave me some kind of bag with all these herbs in it. The instructions were to take it home and circle his name on the card with my blood. When that was complete, I was supposed to bury the bag with the card in it. I had to spit in it then speak over it, some words he gave me. I know it's crazy. I think it just helped me in the way, say, a priest might if he said my sins were gone." He stared intently at the surface of his desk. "A placebo or something."

She sat there, processing what he had said. His name circled in blood. A bag of herbs. That liar.

"Miss?"

"I'm okay. This helps. Listen, what's your insurance guy's name?" She had to be sure.

"Benson. Oliver Benson. I think he's a second or a third."

"Thank you. One more question. Where was Curtis's office? Was it in here or somewhere else?"

"It was right next door, but everything's been cleared out. What he didn't take with him went into the trash. There's a new guy in there now. A new manager."

She itched to check the office anyway, but it was doubtful there'd be anything useful, and this guy would be looming over her the whole time. Breaking in probably wouldn't be a good idea, especially if there was nothing to find. At this point, she had to weigh the possible usefulness of her actions against the ticking clock of her deadline. His personnel files could help, but would they give her information she didn't already have? Doubtful. And she'd have to figure out where they were to begin with, which would take more time than she had.

"Mr. Simpco, you've helped me a great deal. Thank you for sitting down with me. I think those are all the questions I had." She stood up, tugged at her blazer, straightening it where it had crept up.

He looked puzzled, a line appearing between his eyebrows. Then his face went slack with horror. "It's because I said that weird stuff, right? I don't actually believe it was magic. Like I said, it felt more like confession. Or what I always thought confession would be like." He laughed, a short bark with no genuine feeling behind it. "Cheaper than therapy." Another laugh.

"No, no. It's nothing you said. Well, it was something you said, but only because it helped me think of something that might help me find Curtis. Truly, you've been a big help." She leaned over to shake his hand. It was damp with perspiration, and she worked to not jerk hers back.

He released her hand, leaving her to discreetly rub it on her pants, and walked around her to open the door and let her through.

"Thank you. And thanks again for talking to me about Curtis. I know telling me all of that had to have been uncomfortable, but you helped me a lot."

He nodded, standing in place, hands gripped before him.

She turned to go, a thought stopping her. She knew she must be forgetting to ask some important questions, but he'd startled her with the information about Oliver and everything else had fled her mind. "Mr. Simpco, could I possibly get your card in case I think of anything else?"

Simpco reached into his back pocket to pull out a weathered brown leather wallet. From this, he extracted a small, cream-colored card, and walked the few steps to catch up to her.

She smiled and took the card, taking in his still worried expression. It had taken a lot for him to tell her about Oliver. People not involved in the mythical world were deeply uncomfortable with anything out of the ordinary. She was usually careful about reacting in any negative way, but what he'd said about Oliver had ripped away the filter she usually employed.

Approaching the secretary's desk, she looked around, happy to find that Stefan wasn't waiting for her. The secretary didn't even look up at her as she walked by, but Selina barely noticed this. She went out the door, all thoughts of exploring the refinery gone. Besides,

Stefan would be watching via the cameras. He'd see if she went next door in an attempt to peek into Curtis's old office.

She couldn't believe it. Not only had Oliver lied to her, but he also knew some of what had happened to Curtis. She knew what he was, or suspected. And it was not human.

21

EATER OF SINS

Damn it!

She'd let Benson charm her out of pursuing her questioning of him, wasting her time and Nathan's. A Sin Eater. She'd never dealt with one in person, had thought they were extinct even, but it fit like a well-cut puzzle piece. He was a Sin Eater.

Lansing had gone to him to remove his sins, but it hadn't worked. Then again, she'd found the bag. If Simpco was right, Lansing had never completed the ritual. Why not? Had he become too far gone to do so? It was entirely possible his doubt had kept him from doing anything he'd deemed weird, but then it was odd that he'd pursued it in the first place. The question remained as to whether it would have worked if he'd completed it.

Selina called Brent once she got to her car in the parking lot. While she knew the basics of Sin Eating, she didn't know enough to comfortably go in and confront him, but Brent might know more. As far as she knew, they weren't dangerous. And Benson sure hadn't looked like he could take her out. He wouldn't be the first creature whose appearance was deceptively weak. Not that he'd looked weak. In fact, he'd looked toned and in excellent shape. Her mind was drifting in a direction she didn't need right now.

There was no answer, and she ended up leaving a message for Brent. Well, she wasn't going to wait to hear from him, especially as she was pretty sure no inherent danger existed. She thought about calling Nathan, but he was likely sleeping. No sense bothering him about this.

She arrived at the building housing Benson's office, circling until she found parking. There was a brief space of time where she regretted not having her leathers on today, but that was just silly. Still, they were a safe haven for her, letting her know she was prepared for anything that might come at her. She quickly slid a couple weapons into hiding on her person, instantly feeling better. It kept her from feeling quite so naked and vulnerable. Most things could be killed or maimed with a stake.

Slipping out of the car, she crossed the street only to be met with hordes of people shuffling out of the building in search of lunch. The press of their suited bodies made her feel like a fish swimming upstream, and she felt suddenly claustrophobic. Fight or flight kicked in, and she started shoving through them, aggression flooding her body, making her feel more in control.

Why weren't these people paying attention? They weren't fish; they were sheep. Sheeple in black and brown coats, uniforms almost, flooding out in a wave of brainless conformity. Why didn't they get out of her way?

Her rage built, becoming something white-hot, boiling within her. Here, she had no time to waste, yet everybody else kept wasting it for her. Between Oliver and Winston, how much time had she lost? Too much, that was certain.

She elbowed one guy in the ribs as he walked into her, staring down at his phone instead of watching where he was going.

"Hey, watch it!" His voice was high, indignant.

Selina turned on him, almost panting now. "You watch where you're going. Ever think about looking up at the people around you instead of staring at that piece of shit phone?"

Surprise etched his face, eyes wide, mouth gaping. He took a breath to speak, but Selina didn't give him a chance. She turned and walked away, shoving a rather burly man in a gray suit out of her way. She ignored his sputtering behind her, as well, beginning to take a wicked sort of glee in the mayhem left in her wake.

A hand gripped her arm, and she was yanked back and around. She brought a fist with her, using the force of the turn and leaning into it. Her fist met a masculine jaw before she took in that it was Oliver she'd punched. Now doubly satisfied, she pulled back her fist for another shot, ignoring the pain in her hand from the first one.

He put his hand up, the other cradling his jaw as he staggered backward, hunched over, head turned to the side. "Wait. Just wait." He straightened, but continued rubbing his jaw, moving it from side to side. "It doesn't appear to be broken."

"That's a shame. It would be if I'd gotten the second shot off."

He laughed, but there was no real humor in it. "So, I take it you know I lied to you, and you decided to come beat the crap out of a bunch of innocent suits who just want lunch in order to get your majestic revenge on me. I don't see what purpose that serves."

"There is a man dying because you lied to me. A man I have very little time to save." She paused and looked him in the eye. "You're a Sin Eater, aren't you?"

Shock flitted across his face, but she could tell she was right. He was surprised she knew, not at the accusation. They stood there, facing each other, the crowd parting around them like a stream around a rock.

"We need to go somewhere private to talk." He reached for her arm once more, but she jerked away from him.

"Don't you touch me."

He held his hands up in a placating gesture and pointed to the elevators. "Fine. Let's go up to my office. I will not discuss this with you in the lobby with all these people around. We can order in lunch."

"I don't want any damn lunch. What is it with you and food? I want answers."

"I know perfectly well what you want, but like all these people, I'm hungry. I was on my way out to grab something to eat. Perhaps if you would show up at a different time of day, you would not be subjected to my appetite." He jerked his head toward the elevator. "Let's go."

He stepped around her, straightening his suit and dabbing at a spot of blood on his lip. Without waiting to see if she would follow, he went to the elevator and punched the up button. He lifted his face, watching the floor indicator.

Selina huffed and walked up to stand beside him, careful to avoid all physical contact. She felt burned that she'd had a good time with this man, even though he'd been lying to her. She'd relaxed. Sure, she hadn't trusted him all the way, had known there was more to what he'd said, but he'd seemed so sincere that she'd allowed herself to look like a fool. She could feel his body next to hers, even without physical touch, and it fed her anger. She didn't let other people make her look stupid. Not since she was a kid.

They didn't speak a word until they arrived at his floor. His calm behavior worked to deflate her anger by a smidgeon, or perhaps it was being out of that crowd and having to stand still and focus on her breathing. She wasn't great in crowds of people, preferring instead to be out in the wild, surrounded by the peace and solitude of nature. People's energy tended to overwhelm her. Either way, she felt much calmer by the time he stepped up to Sonia's desk and asked her to order in a couple sandwiches, as they'd be having a lunch meeting.

Sonia smiled as if genuinely happy to see Selina again, and it made Selina feel bad in some strange way, as if she were letting the friendly woman down. The smile disappeared when she noticed the blood on her boss's lip, and she rose, reaching toward him. "What happened, Mr. Benson?"

"I had a run-in with a lunatic in the lobby. Can you bring me some ice when you get a chance, please?"

Selina's face warmed, a combination of anger and chagrin filling her. She shot a glare in his direction. Her hand throbbed, but she didn't want to look at it for fear of alerting him she'd hurt herself punching him.

Sonia handed him a couple tissues, pulled from a box on her

desk, and hurried off, probably to get the ice.

Oliver turned back to Selina. "You can glare at me all you want; it was a factual statement."

Selina raised her chin. "If we aren't in your office within the next sixty seconds, I will make a scene."

He nodded at her and headed toward his office, shaking his head. As soon as his office door had been closed behind them, she rounded on him. He took a step back toward the door as she got into his face, her body in his space. She slammed a hand into his chest and pushed him into the door.

"Why did you lie to me?"

He pulled her hand off his chest and stepped around her. "Take a seat. I will explain, but you need to calm down."

"I don't have to do anything. I—"

A knock sounded at the door.

Selina stomped her foot in frustration, sinking into one of the big, soft chairs.

"Willing to handle this like an adult, I see." He opened the door.

Sonia stood there, a bag of ice and a folded paper menu in hand. She handed them to Oliver, glanced over at Selina, and said, "I'm going to start thinking you're coming here just for lunch if this keeps up." Then she walked away, closing the door behind her.

Oliver handed the menu to Selina and settled into the chair across from her, placing the bag of ice on his jaw with a sigh. "Some right you've got there."

"Oh, that was nothing. Just wait until next time."

"Tell me something: How do you know about Sin Eaters, what do you know about them, and why is it you believe they're real?"

"I don't know much about them...you...but I do know they're real. Well, I knew they once were. You take in people's sins, absorb them."

"You didn't answer the other two questions." His eyebrows rose. "Has anyone ever told you anger becomes you? Your eyes are a most startling green right now. And I've failed to mention how nice you look in a suit. I almost didn't recognize you without all that leather."

Even sitting there with a bag of ice on a reddening jaw, he had a commanding and attractive presence. It pissed her off.

"Is this being charming bit part of being a Sin Eater? Some sort of hocus pocus?"

"So you think I'm charming?" He grinned, but winced and quickly stuck the ice back on his face.

"No."

This made him laugh, hard. He set the ice on the table and laughed harder when she frowned at him.

She quickly rearranged her features into something angrier, not having to pretend. Picking up the ice, she threw it at him. He apparently brought out the sullen teenager within her, but she couldn't stop herself. It seemed no matter what she tried to do, he made her lose control of her emotions.

He caught the ice with both hands in front of his chest, laughing all the harder.

Realizing she wouldn't get anywhere if she kept amusing him, she rolled her eyes and settled back in the seat, crossing her arms over her chest. She stared at him in stony silence until he grew quiet enough for her to say, "Did you miss the part where I said a man's life hangs in the balance?"

This stopped the laughter, and he sobered, wiping a tear from his face. He settled back in his chair, picked up the ice, and settled it back over his jaw. "Sorry, I couldn't help it. Where were we? Oh, before you answer that, pick a sandwich, would you? They've got great smoked turkey. Then we can be all business and discuss this like grownups."

Selina growled, but opened the menu with a jerk that tore the top of the page, which made him chuckle again, though he didn't break into full histrionics this time. The smoked turkey sounded delicious right now, but she wouldn't give him the satisfaction. "I'll take a French dip."

"Perfect. Give me a second to call Sonia, and then we'll get back to it."

He crossed to his desk and picked up the phone receiver, giving Sonia an order for Selina's French dip, two iced teas, and a smoked turkey sandwich with sprouts, cucumbers, lettuce, tomato, and pickles. As soon as he'd finished, he sat across from Selina again and leaned toward her.

"Before we return to you avoiding answering my other questions, tell me, do you think the typical person believes in Sin Eaters or even knows what they are?"

"No, of course not."

"Then why would someone give that information out when they're being questioned by a stranger?"

He was right. Of course he was right. Did she really expect that he would have come out and said he was a Sin Eater to some woman who showed up at his office one day? However, he'd lied to her about other things, drawing out her investigation, and for that she was still angry.

She skipped his question and fired back one of her own. "Are you saying you are, in fact, a Sin Eater?"

"Before I answer that question, I'd like you to tell me why you know anything about them."

"You've given me no cause to trust you, so why would I give you personal information when you refuse to answer a simple question?"

"Simple? You've just asked me if I'm a mythological creature. After stalking into the building like a murderous Amazon and throwing punches." He considered her for a moment. "I'm certain you weren't telling me the truth, either. Give me something, some speck of honesty, and I will answer in turn."

She felt fairly certain he was a Sin Eater, which meant outing herself was probably safe. It wasn't something she ever told people. They wouldn't even know what she was talking about, let alone believe her. Still, it felt wrong to tell something about herself that could be dangerous to her. And, no matter the reason, he had lied to her, led her on, wasted her time. She couldn't afford that if she was going to save Nathan.

Oliver sat there, not saying a word.

They were in a standoff, which was something else she didn't have time for. Coming to a decision, she looked up at him and steeled herself. "Have you ever heard of a Myth Stalker?"

22

MYTHOLOGICAL MATCH GAME

He sat back, cocked his head to the side, and studied her as if he hadn't seen her fully before.

"I have," he said.

"And do you believe they're real?"

"I do. I've met a few in my time."

"I'll bet. Okay, well...that's why I know about Sin Eaters." She held her breath, watched for his reaction. Her mouth had gone dry. She rarely told anyone what she was.

He pursed his lips in thought. "Interesting. You're not here for me, though, are you?" His question held no fear, despite the implications.

"No, I have a Wendigo issue, with which you seem to be embroiled."

"Why is it your issue?"

"One, it's my job to track down creatures like that. Two, my friend is the one infected. I'm trying to find a cure."

"You and I both know there is no cure once someone is infected."

"I believe there is a way. I just have to find it. One thing that might help is finding out how Curtis managed to get infected in the first place, who got infected first. I've never tested this theory, but in the old vampire tales, if you can find the lead vampire, the one who spawned the others, and kill that creature, the others can be saved. It's a long shot, but I have to try to see if finding the person who took in the Wendigo spirit initially can save my friend." Her urgency pushed her forward, leaning toward him. "Understand that I am determined to find this information. This is deeply personal to me. I will do what I have to do to find information that could help me save him. Anything I have to do." Her words came rapid fire now. "Lansing is responsible for infecting him, but I need to know what happened before that, how Lansing got sick in the first place. He doesn't seem like the type to perform a ritual, and I highly doubt he ate anyone. How was he infected then? Any information might help me save Nathan, but I don't have much time. He's already beginning his transition."

He sat back all the way in his seat and steepled his fingers against his nose, assessing her quietly. His eyes held the slightest squint, and he worried at his bottom lip with his teeth.

Waiting on his response challenged her. She wanted to leap up, grab him by the shoulders, and shake. Or slap it out of him. But she knew patience was necessary. He'd be more likely to help her if she could wait it out.

Her patience stretched like taffy until it grew too thin to not snap. "I need you to tell me if Curtis mentioned anything about how it happened. Did he even tell you what he thought was wrong with him?"

"He did. Unfortunately, that's not something I can do anything about. He was angry when I told him that, yelled at me, wanted to fight. Eventually, he returned to me and asked if I could at least help with his sins. He thought it might help somehow, even if it wouldn't cure him. How could I turn him down?"

"Did he say where or how it happened? Did he mention a location?"

"He said he went hunting in the mountains, rented a cabin with a couple friends. A freak blizzard hit, as happens in the mountains, and they were trapped up there. Something began stalking them. They heard noises outside, saw red eyes peering in the windows.

"They decided it must be a wolf or a bear, some sort of predator. One night, they decided to go out and hunt it, but their weapons had been shattered. All except for one, which they'd locked in a safe. They went out, armed with one shotgun, a shovel, and a fire poker.

"There were footprints in the snow, larger than their own. The prints were similar to a man's bare foot, but holes at the end indicated claws. Terrified, they nevertheless followed the prints, finding a cave hidden in the mountainside. Inside, there were bodies, raw meat piled in the back of the cave.

"They fled, but not before seeing enough to know the remains were human, not animal. There was not one animal carcass visible to them in that cave."

"That sounds about right for a lair," Selina said. "They don't kill animals, only people."

He nodded and continued. "Right. When they got back to the cabin, they tried to start the truck, but it wouldn't turn over. Too cold, maybe. It wouldn't have mattered, anyway, as the snow kept getting deeper and deeper, and a crust of ice had formed across everything. They were trapped.

"That night, one of his friends began having nightmares, reporting a foul smell. He thought there must be something dead in the cabin, maybe under the floorboards. Neither of the other two could smell it, and they ignored his pleas to tear up the floor.

"His nightmares continued, keeping them awake throughout the night. Every time they'd fall asleep, they'd awaken to his screams. At one point, the quality of the screams changed. He was in pain, burning, he said. They tried to help him, and ultimately to hold him down, but he kept screaming, fought them off. He got his hands on the poker, hit the third man with it.

"Lansing backed off, let him take off. The guy ran into the woods, didn't come back."

"Wendigo Fever," Selina said. "There's nothing they could have done at that point."

"Yeah. My knowledge of Wendigo is limited, but I tried to reassure him that his friend had been too far gone for him to help him, especially in the situation they were in, but he didn't want to hear it. It was one of the sins he wanted to be absolved of."

"I see, and is it one of the ones you could absolve him of?"

"It is."

"Keep going."

"They tried to barricade themselves in the cabin, blocked the windows with furniture, but when that thing came back and started scratching around outside, his other friend started acting weird, talking about the smell. Curtis couldn't smell it, but he had figured out that it was probably a bad sign. Afraid that his friend would kill him, and fearing he'd been infected, he got his friend drunk, waited until he passed out, and dumped his body outside the door. When he checked the next morning, his friend had disappeared."

A wave of disgust filled her. "What a coward."

"Perhaps. However, he was scared. I can't say I blame him, though I'd like to think I wouldn't have done the same."

"I guess."

"He paid for it. He began to hear his friends' voices outside the cabin, calling his name, pleading for help, screaming in pain. It went on the entire night, their voices rising above the sound of the storm, pellets of ice hitting the window and sounding like claws. He fell asleep around dawn, thinking the light would mean it was over, but he woke up to something standing over his bed.

"He said it was covered in white fur, emaciated to the point where its ribs were sticking out. It had talons as long as his forearm, he claimed, thick and black. He closed his eyes, waited for it to attack, to kill him. But it never happened.

"Instead, when he finally opened his eyes, the figure still stood there. It grinned, a sight that scared him so badly he wet himself. It pointed at him, leaned over, and ran one thick claw down across his neck. While he told me this, his hand went to a bandage on his neck. He said it burned like fire.

"That day, the storm abated, the wind stopped, and the snow melted. He managed to start the truck that evening, and he left, not reporting his friends missing, not telling anyone what had happened.

Neither of them was married, and apparently no one knew to come ask him where they were, though he kept expecting it to happen."

"He'd posted on Facebook that he was going hunting with friends," Selina broke in. "I'm surprised no one approached him. It's also odd he didn't delete that post. And whose name was the cabin under?"

"I believe the cabin was under his name, but the bodies were found elsewhere. He'd been following the news religiously. I imagine he didn't delete the post because social media was the last thing on his mind when he got home. He was sick. He said he finally understood that smell they'd talked about. He'd checked under his crawlspace to see if something had crawled under there, died, but he found nothing. He went online, started doing research, and that's when he found out about Wendigo and knew he was in trouble. It was then that he started seeking help, eventually finding me because of Randy."

"So you agreed to help him absolve his sins, and then what?"

"I don't know. All I can tell you is that it didn't work. I would have known if it had. Whether he was too far gone or he never completed the ritual, I can't say."

"He didn't. I have the pouch you'd given him; it's how I found you. Remember? And what happened beyond that is he infected his niece, who then infected my friend. Do you know where the cabin was?"

Oliver shook his head. "No, I never asked."

"Shit. If I can find that information, perhaps I can find the lair."

Oliver leaned forward. "Has the niece turned?"

"No, my friend took the curse from her."

"How's that possible? Does that mean someone could take it from him?"

"No, she was an innocent, which made the spirit's hold on her weak. Typically, the spirit can't get a good hold unless the person is evil, has done something horrific or cannibalized, or they've taken it willingly upon themselves. Lansing's actions at that cabin ensured he'd be infected. The Wendigo senses a kindred spirit." She paused for a moment, looked down at her hands, which were clutched in her lap. "Nathan, my friend, took the Wendigo into himself to save her."

"You'd think that would mean it would still be weak."

"You'd think so, but no. He took the curse, so it's his. However, I heard something about a man of religion or some sort of ability being able to help."

"Interesting." He looked thoughtful, lips pursed. "Not something I'd ever heard before."

"Yeah, but it also does no good unless I can find it." Selina looked back at him, studying his face.

"Would the family know where the cabin is located?"

"They might. I think they'll have to be my next stop. My friend asked me not to involve them, but I see no choice. I found an address for them, but it's in my car. I'll probably go straight there from here."

"I can help with that. I'll look it up and map it really quick so we have it for sure."

Just then, a knock sounded at the door. He went to the door and retrieved their sandwiches from Sonia, who also came bearing a fresh bag of ice and a bottle of Ibuprofen. She reached up and gently took his face in her hands, turning it to look at the left side, where some bruising was starting to appear.

"How badly did you cut your mouth?" Sonia asked.

"Not bad at all. It was a sucker punch, no real force behind it."

Selina puffed out a breath.

"You need anything else?" Sonia asked.

"No, thank you. We'll be good now that food is here."

Sonia patted his good cheek then left, shooting a look at Selina that made her shrivel up in the chair, sure that Sonia knew she had been the one who punched him.

"She mothers me," Oliver said. "Has no idea I'm about four times her age."

"You're what now?"

"A new Sin Eater hasn't been born in decades. I'm one of the youngest, and one of the few who are still alive."

"You're kidding."

"Nope." He grinned.

She looked at him in a whole new way. "You don't look half bad for an old geezer."

"Yeah, well, I'm charming. Or so someone indicated recently. It goes a long way."

23

BOUND KNOWLEDGE

Selina ran out to her car for the address, though Oliver had offered to look it up online. She wanted a minute alone before heading back in. A lot had been discussed, and she had new information to sort through mentally. Plus, some air away from Oliver wouldn't be a bad thing. She'd opened up to him quite a bit, which was a foreign thing for her, and she wasn't entirely comfortable with it. In fact, she kept running through the conversation in her head to ascertain whether she'd said anything she'd regret later. There was also the question of how much she could trust him. She understood why he had lied to her initially; she'd lied, too. But if his information wasn't solid, it could waste more of her precious time, and he had no real incentive to help her or to be honest.

On the way back in, the lobby was mostly empty, and she nodded to the perky receptionist from the other day. The woman nodded back, a big smile on her face. It didn't appear she recognized Selina without the leathers. She rode the elevator up without incident, and with no fellow passengers.

Sonia glanced up from her computer long enough to wave her toward Oliver's office then returned to whatever she had been working on. The sound of clacking keys followed Selina across the lobby and into the office, cutting off when she closed the door behind her.

Oliver leaned with his back to his desk, partially sitting on it. He stood straight upon her entrance and took a step forward and to the side. "I have something you might find useful." He gestured at a large book sitting on his desk.

She approached the desk, pausing long enough to hand him the slip of paper with the address on it. The book was so old it was crumbling at the spine, the pages thick and uneven, as if it had been hand-bound, with pieces added at different times. It was covered in gray leather. A musty scent rose from it.

Selina reached toward the book, laying a hand on the cover. It felt bumpy, but soft, and there was some give to it, indicating the leather was thick. The title had been written in gold lettering, which flaked away beneath her fingers: *A Shaman's Guide to the History of Northern Phantasms*. It was a massive tome, taller than it was wide.

Carefully, she opened the first page, the binding giving a soft creak. The pages were yellowed with age, and she made sure to turn them with caution, aware of the age and delicate state. Though the pages were made of thick paper, they were worn in places, sometimes down to the point of being almost see-through. There were handwritten notes throughout. Some pages appeared to be missing, and the ink had blurred or smudged in places, but the rest was mostly legible.

Near the center of the book, she found a page entitled "WEHTI-GO." The word was large, written in all capitals, and it had been circled multiple times. An ink sketch showed a skeletal creature with white fur over most of its body. Its eyes were orange, the pupils slit like a snake's or a cat's. Massive black talons hung from its gray fingers, and its teeth were sharp and pointed, protruding from a short snout. Its stomach was bare of fur, as was most of its face, the flesh gray.

She looked up at Oliver, who remained in the same spot, silent, watching her. "Where did you get this?"

"An old friend."

"A shaman?"

"A Myth Stalker, actually, though he styled himself a shaman, as well. He was the last of his line, and I was the only person he knew who was...like us. Supernatural, mythological, whatever term you use. I've had it a long time, waiting for the right person to come along. There may not be anything helpful in there, but I thought it might be worth a look."

"The spelling...was he Cree?"

"Yes, I believe so."

She returned to the book, scanning through the information on the Wendigo. It was quite accurate with what she knew. It even detailed how to properly dispose of a Wendigo to keep it from returning for its slayer. Interesting. She'd rarely found books such as these in her many travels. Myth Stalkers typically kept thorough notes, passing them on to a family member or apprentice. Of course, not every Myth Stalker told their family what they were, or they never had a family. Many such notebooks were lost, with no one to keep them safe and pass them on.

Selina considered what she might have done with her father's notes had she not been part of the Myth Stalker world. Her anger at him at the time of his death had grown like a living thing within her. Chances are, under different circumstances, she would have destroyed everything he'd left behind. Certainly this would have been true if he hadn't told her what he was. And he hadn't done so until it became obvious that she was more like him than he'd originally thought. She ran a finger over the book, wondering about its owner. She wanted to ask Oliver for more details, but that was for another time.

In very small print at the end, she found the following information:

A person who is infected despite being good at heart, does stand one chance to heal themselves of the poisonous spirit infection. They must first cleanse their soul of all sins before eating the heart of the originator of the line of Wehtigo that has infected them. They must do this before the thirtieth night has passed since their possession. Once the moon has completed one full cycle, the infected is stuck forever, cursed to waste away and crave the flesh of their fellow man.

Now she had even more confirmation that salvation for Nathan existed, that she could stop this spirit. Of course, there now existed yet another deadline, and she didn't have the date he'd initially been infected, but she assumed by his progression that it had been less than thirty days. This, combined with the fact that Nathan had been able to take the spirit into himself without completing any of the usual ceremonies or mechanisms necessary, meant there was a lot she didn't know about Wendigo. Which also meant she stood a chance, because the rules she'd been living by weren't unbreakable. Given, with what Nathan had done, the Wendigo would not always go for it. The spirit would have preferred a strong, healthy male to a weak teenage girl, and that was how he'd accomplished what he had. He had lived more, his soul full to the brim with life experience. A tasty treat for something that ate souls. The pure innocence of a child would have been a sweet appetizer, but not enough to fulfill the spirit's needs. The new rules had limits of their own.

How would she find the originator? Curtis's family was still her best chance. There was also the possibility that finding out who had given Charles the information that had brought him out here would answer the question. She had been working under the assumption that he had come here to track Curtis Lansing, unaware that he'd already been taken care of. She realized now that this might not have been the case. Charles might know who had infected Curtis, and might at this very moment be on their tail.

She closed the book, hope swelling in her chest. If Curtis's family or Charles had information for her on the originator, there was still time to save Nathan. Finding confirmation that there was a method to end his suffering without killing him meant he had a chance. At least she'd been on the right track, with a solid lead now on how to handle it if she tracked down the originator. She hadn't thought about feeding him the heart, only killing the creature and hoping it would magically stop his progression. The book could still be wrong, but she had to keep moving forward. She'd never know if she didn't try. But she had to speak to Charles first or find the Wendigo before him, or there would be no heart available to feed to Nathan, and then it would all be over.

She had to wonder why no new bodies had turned up since her arrival. With at least one more Wendigo operating out here, if not more, there should have been something. Wendigo didn't get full. Was someone helping this one, cleaning up behind it?

Now that was a sobering thought.

24

THIS IS WHY

After mapping out the route to the Packer home online for Selina to see, Oliver asked to go with her, saying he felt responsible for Curtis having infected people after he'd told Oliver about what was happening. Selina figured there was some truth to that, though she still found herself trying to find an ulterior motive. After a moment's internal debate she waved it off and told him he was welcome to come with her. A friendly face couldn't hurt. And if he was hiding anything else, maybe spending more time with him would out it. Plus, loathe as she was to admit it, she enjoyed spending time with him.

Cheryl and her family lived on the edge of suburbia, backing up to the foothills, which afforded them a nice sized property with a view. The houses were standard cookie cutter, nice in a uniform sort of way. The Packer home was tan with multitudinous windows, including a bay window by the front door, plants nestled in its corners.

Selina had changed into spare jeans and a t-shirt she kept in her bag, and her weaponry was minimal. Oliver stood beside her, "dressed down" in khaki slacks and a sweater. She couldn't help noticing how good he looked, all clean-cut and wholesome, and he smelled divine, a faint musky scent that made her want to jump him. None of the guys she'd spent time with in the past had been like him. Businessmen weren't her standard type of guy. In fact, they were usually a hard no for her hormones. She was sure the lust she felt in his presence had more to do with adrenaline and her emotional turmoil than anything else, but that didn't change the way she felt.

He'd driven, surprising her with his ownership of a Jeep. It was well worn, sporting scratches and dents that showed he probably legitimately used the Jeep for off-roading. She would have pegged him as the sports car kind of guy, but he looked as comfortable and at-home in the Jeep as he did in an office setting, and she couldn't help a twinge of jealousy that he fit in so well, no matter where he happened to be. She'd never fit in anywhere, even when she'd tried her damnedest. The fact that she'd come to embrace this difference most of the time didn't make her feel any less of an outsider. Then again, maybe if she'd lived as long as he had, she'd be able to fit in everywhere, too.

Nah, I'd probably be even more of an outcast. Thoughts of various vampire movies came to mind. They never fit in, and they were ancient.

As they sat in front of the house, studying its bland, but comfortable façade, Oliver broke the silence. "Do we need some manner of cover story, or are we just going to tell them that we're mythological creatures in search of another mythological creature?"

Selina barked out a laugh. "Nathan saved their adopted daughter's life. I'm telling them the truth, and they'd better be willing to help me, or there will be hell to pay."

He smiled. "All right then. We'll go in with that attitude and see how far it gets us."

"Don't worry, I'll play nice. To start."

"That'll be a new experience for me."

They approached the door together, a dog in the neighbor's fenced backyard barking at them. Its obnoxious yipping made Selina want to shoot it, but she ignored it instead and pressed the button to ring the doorbell.

Footsteps sounded inside, followed by a pause, then the metallic rasp of the deadbolt. A man opened the door a small amount and stuck his face through it. His large hazel eyes were framed by thick plastic eyeglasses, a type Selina rarely saw these days. He wore a sweater dotted with moose and pine trees, topping off pleated brown slacks.

Was he for real?

"Can I help you?" His tone indicated he was ready to slam the door the second she asked him if he believed in Jesus or if he'd like a free carpet cleaning.

"Hi, my name is Selina Moonstone. I'm looking for Cheryl." When he moved to shut the door, she quickly belted out, "I'm a friend of Nathan Thrush's."

"Just a minute." The man pulled his head in, shutting the door. Selina and Oliver looked at each other at the sound of the deadbolt turning again.

"Bit antsy, isn't he?" asked Oliver.

"Nah, you can never be too safe these days. Though this isn't a neighborhood I'd expect to see someone so drastic about it."

It didn't take long for returning footsteps, but these ones *click-clacked* like a woman's. Selina heard the sounds of a chain sliding into place before the deadbolt turned, then the woman from the photos opened the door, her face tired, lines around her mouth and eyes, and at the bridge of her nose. She'd pulled her hair back into a loose ponytail, but her makeup was impeccably done, and she wore a dress that Selina figured would be considered business casual. It was a soft red boat neck, belted at the middle with a slim black belt. Her shoes were black to match the belt, and only mildly heeled.

I guess I should have stayed in the suit. Selina ran a hand down her t-shirt, pulling the hem to straighten it.

"You're friends of Nathan?" Cheryl asked.

"We are, yes," Selina said.

"What do you want?"

"Wow, not quite the friendly reception I would have expected, considering Nathan's dying right now after having saved your daughter."

Cheryl looked down, eyes squeezed shut. She pulled back and closed the door.

Selina stepped toward the door, livid at the woman's reaction, but Oliver placed a gentle hand on her arm and said, "Wait."

He was right.

The chain slid back across the door and it opened. Cheryl stepped back, gesturing for them to come in.

Selina stepped past her, and Oliver followed. The living area was nice, comfortably furnished. The sofas were tan, glass tables arranged around them. There appeared to be one missing from the far side of the large sofa; a lamp sat on the brick of the fireplace slightly in front of the sofa instead.

Cheryl shut the door, turned and held an arm out toward the sofa. "Please, take a seat. I didn't mean to be rude. It's just...this has all been a lot. I have to ask, though, what do you mean Nathan is dying?"

Selina froze in the middle of sitting, causing her to plop down onto the sofa when she couldn't stop herself. She looked at Cheryl, studying her, but all she saw was concern. "You don't know?"

"Know what?"

"In order to remove the spirit from your daughter, he had to take it into himself."

"He...what? No, he said it was like an exorcism, that he would be removing it from Nell and sending it back where it came from."

They all sat in silence for a minute, Selina shaking her head. He hadn't told them it would cost him his life to help Nell. No, not just his life. His soul. Her anger at them dissipated, not entirely gone, but certainly deflated. They hadn't known it would kill him. And, really, knowing Nathan, of course he wouldn't have put that guilt trip on them. He would have wanted them to have a fresh start, even at his own expense.

"There's no way to do that," Selina said. "In fact, it's rare that the spirit of the Wendigo can be removed in any way, even as weakened as this one was by taking over an innocent soul. I didn't realize he hadn't told you."

"What's going to happen to him now?" Cheryl's hands twisted in a constant avalanche of fingers. Selina had begun to fear the woman would break a digit with her angst.

"Unless I can find a way to save him, he'll either turn into a Wendigo or die."

The distraught woman gasped, slapping a hand to her mouth in a move Selina had always thought clichéd in movies. She sunk down into the loveseat across from them and hugged herself, leaning toward her knees, eyes unfocused.

"I didn't know," Cheryl said. "I wouldn't have let him do that if I'd known."

"That's a nice thought, but I imagine if it came down to him or Nell, you would have made the same choice."

Oliver's head jerked up and he leveled an intense reproachful look upon her.

She glared back, but sighed. "That's not a jab or anything. Any parent would make the same choice." She shot him a look intended to say, *Happy now?*

Tears leaked from Cheryl's eyes, but she didn't seem aware of them. They sat in silence, watching her sway slightly, almost rocking. Finally, she looked up at Selina, her eyes now intense, determination showing in the press of her lips.

"How can we help him? You wouldn't be here if you didn't think there was a way we could. He was so good to us, swooped in and saved Nell when we needed him most. I'll do whatever it takes."

"If we can track down the creature that initially turned your brother, there is a slight chance of saving Nathan. From what we've gathered, he was turned on a hunting trip." At Cheryl's nod, Selina continued. "Do you know where that cabin is?"

Cheryl sat up, eyes once more unfocused as she thought. She pulled her arms from around her and rose. "Hold on, I believe I do." She ran from the room, heels *click-clacking* on the hardwood flooring, the sound changing to a *pomp-pomp* when she hit carpeting. There was the sound of paper and objects being pushed around, and something fell on the floor.

Selina started to rise, intending to join her to see if she needed help when the *pomp-pomp* once again led to *click-clacking*, and Cheryl came into the room, holding a piece of paper and wearing a triumphant look on her face.

"I've got it! The cabin is one of Herb's. Do you know of him?"

"Yes, he owns a cabin near Nathan's." Selina placed a hand on Oliver's knee and squeezed in her excitement at getting the information. "How many places does that guy own?"

"Not sure, but he has a nice business going for himself. He's actually my husband's step-brother, but they never lived together. I mean to say they're not close. In fact, they often don't get along. Herb has a full brother, Tim. They're always together. Curtis got along with both of them, probably better than my husband. That's how Curtis was able to use the cabin. Sometimes Herb lets us use them if no paying customer is. The one I think Curtis would have been at is about two hours from here, northwest. Herb's number's on there, too. Here you go." She walked toward Selina, holding the paper out.

Selina stood to meet Cheryl as she approached, reaching to take the paper. Cheryl surprised her by wrapping her arms around Selina, pulling her into a hug. Not knowing what to do, she slowly brought her arms up, patting the other woman on the back. She could see Oliver stifling a laugh, and her brow furrowed into a frown. They stood there like that for what felt like a monumental amount of time before Cheryl let her go, stepping back and wiping the tears from her cheeks.

"We used to go up to that cabin all the time. My husband wasn't a big fan of the rustic life, so it's been a while for me, but Curtis kept going year after year with his buddies. I miss that old cabin."

Selina conjured up an image of Cheryl's extremely yuppie and uptight husband. The fact that he hated going to the cabin was obvious by looking at him. He and Herb were as different as night and day, and she suspected Herb must be considerably older. No wonder the two of them didn't get along. Well, the three of them. It didn't sound like her husband was besties with Tim, either.

Cheryl broke into Selina's thoughts. "If you need anything else, please call me. I wrote my number on there, too. But first, would you come with me really quick? I'd like to show you what Nathan did."

Selina slumped, wanting to get out the door to call Herb, but Oliver came up behind her and put a hand to the small of her back. "Shall we?"

She glared at him and brushed his hand off, but followed Cheryl through the kitchen to a sliding door in the dining room. Cheryl opened the door and stepped out, Selina following, Oliver at her back, probably to prevent her from escaping. They stepped out onto a nice wooden porch that looked down onto a browning lawn framed by trees. On that lawn, a teenage girl played with a young boy of about eight. Her long black hair swirled around her as she ran from the boy, both of them laughing, his hair glowing golden in the dusky light of the lowering sun.

The girl, Nell, looked up and waved. "Hi, Mom!"

"Hi, babies. You almost ready for dinner?"

"Oh yeah." The boy rubbed his belly then lunged for Nell, trying to be sneaky. She danced out of his way, light on her feet, then stopped, letting him crash into her. They fell in a heap, her wrapping her arms around him, protecting him from the fall. Together, they lay in the grass, laughing and hugging each other.

Selina understood. This is what Nathan had saved.

25

NELL'S STORY

Despite her desire to get going, Selina needed more information. "How did Nell get infected?"

"I really don't like talking about it. I still can't believe how close we came to losing our daughter." Her eyes drifted back to her kids, and Selina could see the raw, naked emotion there. It was obvious how much she loved them both.

Having seen what happened to Nell's birth family, Selina felt a wash of gratitude that the girl had found a home like this one, uptight dad and tearful mom aside. She hated to push it, but she needed answers. She placed a hand on Cheryl's shoulder. "I understand that. But every bit of information helps."

Cheryl's eyes met hers, and with a sigh, she slumped. She directed Selina and Oliver to the kitchen table, leaving the door open so she could hear the kids through the screen door. The happy sounds of play washed over Selina as they each sat down.

"I love my brother. He's always gotten himself into trouble, been a little selfish." One hand tightened on the other as she talked about him. "I figured he'd grow out of it, eventually, that it was just taking him a while. But then he brought this into our home." A tear escaped from the corner of her eye and slid down the contour of her cheek.

She dashed it away with her hand and returned to clutching her hands together.

She'd placed herself on the side furthest from the door, her gaze straying to the window as she continued to talk. "He showed up at the house, car jerking to a stop at the base of the driveway right as I was getting out of the car with a load of groceries. I dropped them when he stumbled out of the Forerunner. It looked like he had shrunk, and he was obviously sick. It had been a couple weeks since I last saw him. When I ran to him, I could see white hairs covering his body like fine fur. My first thought was of that old movie with the guy covered in plants, only white instead of green." She looked down, ashamed. "I freaked out, pulled away from him.

"I asked him, 'What's wrong? What's going on? Are you sick?'

"He laughed at me, a humorless sound that was half laugh, half sob. Maybe more sob.

"'I'm sick, all right,' he told me. 'I need help.'"

She looked at Oliver, who gave her a sympathetic half smile and a nod. He reached out and squeezed her hand, resting his on top of her gripped ones.

"Even though I was freaked out, I put my arm around him and helped him inside. I could feel those weird hairs tickling my arm as we walked, and it creeped me out." She paused, struggling to continue speaking.

Selina waited quietly.

"He brought this evil thing into my home." She moved her hand from under Oliver's and reached for a tissue from a box in the center of the table. Tears leaked from her eyes. She squeezed the tissue in a death grip as if she could choke the past, rid herself of it.

"I got him settled in the guest room, brought him soup and water, but he couldn't eat or drink. He pushed it away, broke my dishes on the floor." She shook her head. "That's when I noticed his fingers. They were elongated, the joints enlarged. His nails were black, sharp like talons. I backed away, out of the room." She looked out at the kids again. "I left him there, went downstairs to call the hospital."

Oliver interrupted her. "Where were the kids?"

"They were at school when he got there, but they showed up while I was on the phone. I had them go to friends' houses, told them they could do their homework later." She dabbed at her eyes with the tissue. "I didn't know what was wrong with him, but I knew I didn't want them anywhere near him."

"What did the hospital say when you called them?" Selina asked to get her back on track.

"They told me I should bring him in, but he refused. He said there was nothing the hospital could do for him, nothing any doctor could do.

"I asked him what he was doing here then. 'What is it you think I can do for you?' I asked him. 'What do you want?'

"He didn't answer. Just looked away and curled onto his side, turning his back to me. I called my husband then, and he told me to kick Curtis out or he would. He said I had until he got home."

It surprised Selina that Mr. Moose Sweater could be so firm.

"I argued, but I wanted him to leave just as bad. I was scared, but it was my brother we were discussing. There was something wrong, and he obviously needed me." Here, she choked on a sob, took a deep breath then continued. "I knew I needed to get him away from my family. But how do you tell your sick brother to leave when he's come to you for help? Especially when you're the only family he has? Our parents died in a car crash when I was in college. He didn't have anywhere else to go."

"It couldn't have been easy," Oliver said. He was way better at this sympathy thing than Selina. Impatience overrode her own sympathy.

"Did you tell him to leave?" Selina asked.

Cheryl rose from the table abruptly, her chair scraping across the hardwood floor. She paced around them as she continued with her story.

"No, I didn't. The kids came home. They were hungry, so I made Kraft dinner and canned vegetables, told them to go into the living room and do their homework. I went downstairs to start some laundry, and that's when I heard a scuffle above me, screams. I dropped everything and ran upstairs, and there was Curtis holding Nell. He was staring at her shoulder. Her shirt must have slipped down while she fought him. She was still struggling, but it didn't seem to affect him at all. Her feet were kicking, and she was using her free arm to hit him, but he didn't even sway or move. He stood there like a statue, holding her, staring at her.

"I tried talking to him. 'Curtis? Let her go!'

"Nothing. I thought maybe if I spoke to him firmly, used my big sister voice, it would get through to him. 'Curtis, I'm talking to you. Let Nell go right now.'

"His eyes flicked up to mine. They were bloodshot and empty. Then he looked back at Nell. The pupils had spread, obliterating the blue of his iris, red reflecting from them, making it look as if his eyes blazed orange. I knew he was gone then, and I ran for him. I tried to stop him." She stopped, covered her face.

Selina waited, let her have a moment. Inside her head, the clock ticked toward Nathan's demise, but she obviously couldn't rush this. Cheryl appeared to be replaying every second in her head. It showed on her face, the rictus stretching her mouth, in her words. She felt responsible. And she was, to a point. Selina had never had siblings to know what that was like, but she was sure others would have done the same, would have felt inclined to help their loved one. This wasn't guilt Cheryl would ever get past, and that was something Selina knew more than enough about.

Cheryl lowered her hands and looked at them each in turn. Her eyes fastened onto Selina as she said, "He bit her. He sunk his teeth into Nell's shoulder. She was screaming and thrashing, and trying to get away from him, her own uncle. He gnawed on her like an animal." Cheryl touched her own shoulder. "She'll always have scars there.

"I grabbed a candlestick from the sideboard and slammed it into his head, over and over."

She closed her eyes then opened them and continued. "It didn't knock him out, but he let her go, and I grabbed her. I called for Timmy. The keys were beside the door, and I grabbed them and ran out to the car with the kids.

"I could hear something scrambling across the wood, like the sound my dog used to make when he tried to get enough traction to run. I could swear Curtis howled.

"I didn't look back, didn't want to see him. I slammed the car into reverse before the kids were even buckled in and took off, the tires screeching." She looked at Selina. "You can still see the tracks I made on the driveway." She turned her gaze toward the front of the house, even though there wasn't a window to the driveway within her view.

Selina prompted her again. "When did Nathan get involved?"

"We didn't go home for a week. I remembered Nathan. He was the one who helped us adopt Nell. So I did some research and tracked him down. He agreed to go with us. When we got to the house, Curtis was still here. Well, the thing that had been Curtis. The hair was thicker, more of a pelt now. His eyes were red, his nails even longer than before. I didn't recognize him anymore. Nothing of my brother existed, not even his eyes.

"He'd made some kind of nest out of sheets and towels. There was blood on them, chunks of raw meat. He'd scrounged from the freezer before he turned, his new muzzle covered with brown, caked-on blood. Only it looked like he hadn't been able to eat the meat. There was a pile of it vomited onto the floor. And so many pieces remaining. If he'd been that hungry, wouldn't he have eaten it all?"

Selina started to answer, to tell her Wendigo couldn't eat animal meat, which was one of the final signs of the change, but Cheryl broke down into full sobs, and Selina realized they'd get no more from her. Anything else she needed to know about that day, Nathan would have to tell her. Or she'd have to guess on her own. Her thoughts turned to Nathan, still able to eat the fish they'd caught. How much longer until he couldn't?

Cheryl's husband came into the room and saw her sobbing, leaning against the counter. He took her into his arms and led her into the other room, settling her on the sofa. When Oliver and Selina followed them in there, he looked up at them defiantly. "Don't you see she's had enough? What else do you need?"

Selina swallowed her guilt and went on. "Just two more questions."

Oliver reached for her, probably meaning to stop her, but she had to know. She stepped out of his reach and held a hand up toward him.

Cheryl's husband opened his mouth, but Selina forged ahead, not giving him time to refuse. "Is the Forerunner here and do you know what happened to his computer and files?"

He answered her since Cheryl was still crying, pulling in gulps of air. "The SUV's in the garage. We don't know what to do with it since no one else knows he's dead. I don't know anything about a computer or files; we certainly don't have them."

"Can I look at the Forerunner before we leave? We'll see ourselves out after that."

He nodded, turned his back to them, and returned to comforting his wife.

Selina stood there for a minute before saying, "Thank you for your help, Cheryl. I know this has been hard on you." She turned and dragged Oliver with her, not waiting to be yelled at again. She couldn't stand men yelling at her, especially ones that looked like cliched dads. They found their way to the garage, where the Forerunner sat next to a sedan.

Selina climbed into the front passenger seat while Oliver opened the rear hatch. There were the usual items in the glovebox—registration and insurance papers, receipts for work on the SUV, a pair of gloves, a tire pressure gauge, the manual for the vehicle. She closed this and moved to the center console, where she found loose change, lip balm, hand sanitizer, and a slip of paper. She grabbed the paper and unfolded it. It was the printout of the front page of a website.

The name across the top said Charles Lancaster.

Huh.

The rest of the vehicle didn't yield anything. It was clean, no hardened French fries or spilled sodas. She wondered if he had really been that tidy, or if it had been cleaned out not long before he'd been stricken, the way people did before going on trips. His car had been this clean, too. Could be he paid the maid to clean his cars out, in addition to the house. It was most likely that he really had been this tidy, possibly a touch of OCD. Losing his parents young couldn't have been easy, and OCD was an anxiety disorder.

She pushed away any thought of pitying him or feeling bad for him. It was because of him they were in this situation.

They exited through a door in the side of the garage, heading to the Jeep.

"Where are we going now?" Oliver waited, hands on the wheel, gazing at Selina as she sat, thinking.

She stared up at the house, so plain on the outside, but so full inside with a good and loving family. How had Curtis Lansing come from a crew like that and been such a terrible person? She looked at Oliver. "Nathan's place. I'll direct you when we're closer. For now, get back on the highway and head south."

As he drove, Selina pulled out her cell phone. She punched in the number for Herb that Cheryl had included with the cabin's address.

His familiar voice answered right away. "Hello? This is Herb."

"Hi. I got your number from a friend who recommended you for cabin rentals."

"Of course! What are you looking for? Family sized, couple retreat, single occupant?"

"The friend actually gave me the address of a cabin she's used in the past. Said it was perfect. 7892 Hillside. Does that sound right?"

He paused before responding. "I'm afraid that cabin's no longer available."

"Just for right now? I'm looking at renting it in the future. Maybe a couple months from now."

"I'm sorry. It won't be available again in the near future. I have others that might work for you, though. In fact, there's a similar one about ten miles from that one that fits the same number of people. It's actually nicer than the one you're inquiring about, more modern and updated. I just put in new flooring last year."

"I'll have to call you back, thanks. I was hoping for that one specifically." She hung up, not waiting for him to lob a sales pitch her way.

"What was that?" Oliver asked.

"Herb. He says the cabin's not available for rent, and that it won't be any time soon. I'm willing to bet there's a reason for it, and that's where we need to be. I want to pick Nathan up first, though."

Neither of them spoke for a while, and Selina found herself lost in her thoughts, eyes fixed on the passing landscape, but not really seeing it. This whole time she'd been so absorbed in finding a way to save Nathan that she hadn't thought about what he'd done. The reasons for it. Instead, she'd been angry at him, frustrated that he wouldn't give her more information. In fact, she'd been handling him like she would a stubborn child.

But he wasn't a child. He was the man who'd brought her up in the areas where her father and mother had failed. Not that it had been her mom's fault. She'd been kind and loving, unlike the aloofness her father had shown her. But her mom had never been able to stand up to Selina's father, except when she made him take his daughter to be trained. That had been the one time Selina had seen her mom put her foot down. Aside from that, she'd always been eager to please him. Looking back, Selina knew that she was trying to keep him close to her, to make sure he wanted to come back when he went off on his missions. Though she had been a beautiful, sweet, and intelligent woman, she'd not had the best self-esteem, always dieting and exercising to look better. Underneath it all, her issues hadn't really been her weight, but a lifetime of not fitting in outside the reservation. Her father had taken advantage of that, using her when he needed a place to come back to. As far as Selina could tell, her mother had never gotten anything back from him.

Oliver looked over, glanced down at the sheet of paper still clutched in Selina's hand, then back at the road. "Who is that? You know him?"

"Hm?" It took her a second to pull back from her reverie. "Oh, yeah, he's a pain in the ass. A mercenary, always going after the spotlight."

"Why would Lansing call a merc? He doesn't appear to be the self-sacrificing sort."

"I don't know, but Charles is here. He got here the same day I did. If I wasn't so loathe to go back in there, I would have asked Cheryl if they'd spoken to him. Surely they have. If Lansing called him out here, he'd know about him, would know to track down his sister, just like I did. He's not stupid. Just an ass."

"Do I need to turn around?"

"God, no. I know where Charles is; we'll ask him directly. I can't handle Mr. Moose Sweater biting my head off anymore, and I definitely can't deal with any more sobbing or crying. Besides, I think they've given us as much as they can."

"Do I need to change course?"

"Nope, he's right where we're headed, and now I'm more worried about that than I was before." Her grip tightened on the paper, crumpling it.

"Why?"

"It can't be a coincidence that he's in a cabin owned by this Herb guy right next door to Nathan's cabin."

"Doesn't sound like a coincidence."

"That's what I'm saying." Selina felt the change as Oliver pressed down on the gas, accelerating. At least she had someone else to worry right along with her.

26

CLOSE ENCOUNTERS OF THE MYTH KIND

They approached the cabin, Oliver wincing at the tortured sounds the Jeep made as they drove over the rutted road. It might be an off-road vehicle, but this road was narrower than most. She suspected he'd have some newer, deeper grooves in the paint by the time he got home.

When they pulled up, the front door was wide open.

"Oh, come on," she said. "I don't have time for this right now."

She hopped out of the Jeep before Oliver had it in park, running into the cabin. "Nathan? Johnny?"

A familiar—and unwelcome—voice called out from the living room. "We're all in here. Why don't you come join us?"

Charles. Her body tensed, springing into fight mode. He'd figured it out.

Oliver came up behind her, and Selina held up a hand, hoping he'd stay where he was. She started down the hall, looking longingly at her room as she walked by. She felt naked without a gun, knowing he was sure to have one, and she suspected she was going to want to kill Charles.

Nathan's quiet voice drifted down the hallway. "Do it. I'm at peace with it."

She ran the rest of the way, feeling the heat of the fireplace before she could see it. Oliver's footfalls sounded behind her.

Her heart pounded, breath pumping in and out. There was the sound of a rifle being cocked. *Click.*

"No!" The word ripped from her throat, felt like giving birth as vocal cords strained around the force of it. She burst into the room, took in the scene before her.

Charles stood, rifle butt to shoulder, pointing down. Proper stance, arms firm, eyes intense.

Below Charles, kneeling with his back to her, was Nathan. His blanket had puddled around him, over his bent legs, arms outspread. The white hair, backlit by the fire, had now become a fuzz over the entirety of his visible body, but not yet thick enough to be considered a pelt.

He turned toward her, eyes reflecting reddish-yellow. "It's too late, Selina. I will not turn."

Charles didn't even look sideways at her, just continued to stare down the barrel of the gun. He shifted a foot, planted himself more firmly. His finger tensed on the trigger, beginning the squeeze that would end Nathan's life in one final explosive act.

She sprinted forward, throwing herself in front of Nathan. "No. Charles, wait!"

"Get out of the way, Selina," Charles said, not shifting his stance. His finger remained on the trigger. "You and I both know there's nothing that can be done. Let me kill him."

"No! Listen. I think I can reverse it."

"That's impossible."

"Maybe, but maybe not. I know Curtis Lansing called you here. I know where he turned, and I think I can find his sire and reverse the process."

"Where's Curtis?" he asked.

"He's dead," Nathan said, still on the floor. "I killed him."

"When?" asked Charles. "He called me up here to take care of the problem."

"Well, he's dead," Selina said. "Your job here is done. You don't get to do mine." Her mind raced as she battled the hopelessness that tried to wash over her. How could she stop this? She was facing off against two stubborn men, neither of them willing to listen to her. She pulled the spray out of her bra and aimed it at Charles, aware that they'd all get dosed if she let loose in the small space.

Nathan placed a hand on her shoulder. "Selina, move. Let him do this. I can feel myself turning."

She turned to say something, to argue with him, to plead with him. But then she realized Charles could help them. They needed to go to the cabin, and having him along could help guarantee success. The only other person with the experience to help her was too weak to do so.

"Wait. What if we can find his sire tonight?" she asked, moving herself to more thoroughly block Nathan. Briefly, she wondered where Johnny was. She could see Oliver out of the corner of her eye, moving closer to Charles. But there was nothing he could do if Charles chose to shoot.

Charles released his finger and turned to her, lowering the gun slightly. "What if we can?"

She was pretty sure she saw dollar signs creeping into his eyes, but if that's what it took, she'd use it. There was no way he'd help out of the kindness of his own heart. If he had one. "I found a way that I might be able to reverse this for Nathan. We have to find the sire and kill him." She eyeballed the weapon. "Put the gun down and I'll explain more."

"Your friend is near the end of the change, Selina. There's no time for something that may or may not work. Shouldn't you be more concerned about his soul?"

"That is the very thing I'm trying to address. There is a way. We can go now, tonight. I have an address. Please, help us."

"And why should I do that? I've already got him exactly where I need him. I finish this now, I go back to my cabin, have some hot coffee, relax."

She swallowed her disgust at his complete lack of empathy. He was talking about her friend. "Think of the infamy. Every Crypto and

Hunter would know you'd been part of healing a Wendigo. Consider how many people we could save, cases we could close, if we were able to hunt the sires and destroy them. You could write a book, appear on TV, make a fortune. Please, Charles." It physically hurt her to beg him like this, but she had to. She set the spray down to signal her goodwill. He didn't have to know she had a knife within easy reach.

"Your 'please' won't do any good. I'd far rather see you go down than help you. Less competition." He appeared to think about it for a moment, eyes on her. "But the rest sounds appealing."

"Then put the gun down," she said.

He lowered it the rest of the way, clicking the safety back into place. He looked at her, the usual cocky smile playing over his lips. "I do enjoy you in that position. I'm going to file this image away for later."

"Save your bullshit for later, Charles. Help me get him up."

"Oh, he won't be the one getting up."

"Are you shitting me? Help me get him to his feet, you asshole."

He set the gun against the sofa, but didn't move to help her. He obviously enjoyed having their roles back where they'd started. The outcome of this situation didn't impact him one way or the other. Either way, he'd get credit for solving a Wendigo issue.

Oliver came over, bending down to put a shoulder under Nathan's arm. Together, he and Selina got Nathan to a standing position, moved him over to the sofa, and eased him down.

It was then that footsteps sounded at the front of the house. Johnny's voice called out, "Hey, guys, where are you? What's going on?"

Selina gestured with a flick of her head at Oliver, who disappeared down the hallway. There were muffled voices then running footsteps right before Johnny burst into the room. His eyes were wide, the whites showing all around.

Selina rose and turned her back on Charles. She bent down and picked up the blanket, draping it over Nathan's shivering shoulders to cover the front of him. "We have to go, but first I've got to get ready. Charles, get everything you've got and meet us back here in your vehicle. As fast as you can."

"I'm no gingerbread man, but I think I can manage it. First, I need some insurance. The address for this sire should do it."

"I'm a little busy, Charles. I've already made it clear I need your help. We won't take off without you."

"Not good enough. The address or I stay right here."

Selina rolled her eyes, ignoring him. He'd leave or he wouldn't.

"I've got it," Oliver muttered. He strode to where Charles stood, stopping in front of him.

"Are you her new pet?" Charles asked Oliver, chuckling as he picked up his rifle and headed down the hallway.

Oliver didn't answer. His shoulders were tense as he followed Charles down the hall.

Charles' lack of urgency made Selina want to scream, but she had more important things to do than prod him. Plenty of time later for screaming. First, she needed to know where Johnny had been.

"Where were you?" she asked him. "You should have been here."

"Nathan sent me on an errand. I was only gone half an hour."

"What errand?"

"I told him to feed Rocky the rest of our fish," Nathan interrupted.

Selina gaped at Nathan, but before she could ask why the hell this had seemed like the right time for something like that, Nathan shifted on the sofa, nearly toppling over.

Johnny went to Nathan and fussed with the blanket. "What happened while I was gone?"

Selina pulled back, but stayed hovering nearby. She was just as curious as he was. How had Charles ended up here? How had he found out about Nathan?"

"I called him." Nathan clamped his mouth shut, jaw firm, stubbornness evident in the way he held his body. That would explain the fool's errand he'd sent Johnny on, probably hoping he'd be gone longer.

"Why?" Selina asked. "Did you think I wouldn't do it?"

"I preferred you not having to. When I found out he was here, I figured I'd keep him as a backup plan."

"And when did you hire him?"

"Earlier today. I left a message explaining there was something odd about this house. He'd already seen me, so I'm sure it didn't take much for him to connect my behavior with this cabin."

Selina didn't want to hear any more. Nathan hadn't trusted her to do this. Her stomach sank as the shame of that hit her, and she turned away. He knew about Charles, knew their history, and he'd still preferred that greedy bastard to her because he didn't trust her.

Oliver came back into the room. He looked at each of them in turn, probably trying to figure out what had happened while he was out front.

"Oliver, can you help them get ready? I need to get some things together." When he nodded and took her place, she turned to Johnny. "Can you find everyone some warm gear? And grab your rifle with the silver shot. Once you guys are dressed, get everyone into the Jeep." She shot a look at Oliver. "I hope you don't mind. The truck's in the city at your place, and we don't have an alternate."

"Of course." He moved off to help Nathan.

She left the room, unshed tears prickling at her eyes. She didn't buy that Nathan hadn't wanted to put her through that. Sure, there was an element of truth to it, but he knew her too well to think she would have preferred Charles doing it.

No matter how sick she felt about it, she couldn't let this slow her down. She picked up speed, sprinting into her room to get her things. There was hardly any time, and she'd need an entire arsenal to make sure this went off without a hitch.

It was easy to grab the tools in her room after she'd changed into her leathers. She paused, eyeballing the box that held her father's knife. Maybe it would bring her luck. Pocketing the knife, she set out to find Nathan's things. She hadn't asked him where his materials were. Not wanting to have to ask him anything now—she doubted she could look at him without breaking down—she went through the rooms, looking frantically for his old case. Not finding it, she started back through again. Nothing. She did grab his guns and some extra ammunition from the gun case, and she put everything she already had packed into the back of the Jeep.

It was then that she saw the shed, figuring he probably kept everything in there. She ran over to it, found it locked. Frantic and impatient, she slammed her foot into the door, right by the lock. The wood splintered, but didn't bust all the way through. Two more kicks, and the lock severed from the rest of the door, the wood shattered around where it had been. Reaching inside, she felt for a light, figuring expedience called for full vision, especially when she wasn't sure what she was looking for.

No light, but her hand found a flashlight on a small shelf right inside the door. She clicked it on and a weak light spilled out before her, hardly better than her own night vision.

There was his old trunk, situated right inside the door, against the left side of the building. She directed the weak light around the rest of the shed, picking up anything that might be of use. Rope, another flashlight, batteries. She turned off the flashlight, threw it in with the other items, and hefted the trunk.

Oliver stood next to the Jeep, Nathan and Johnny already inside, when she clumped up to it. He took hold of the trunk, helped her push it into the back of the vehicle. "Anything else?"

"I have to ask Nathan. Just a sec."

She swallowed her pride enough to approach his window.

Nathan turned in the front seat to look at her through the open window. "Did you get the silver axe? It's in the shed. Grab the bag next to it, as well." He reached over and turned on the Jeep's head-lights, which illuminated her path.

It only took her a minute to sprint back to the shed and find the glint of the silver coated axe blade. She grabbed it, setting it on her shoulder, snatched up the bag with her other hand, and ran back to the vehicle where Oliver now sat in the driver's seat.

She'd intended to drive, but she might as well be in the backseat getting her weapons ready instead. He had the Jeep in first before she'd gotten the door closed all the way, and it shut of its own accord. His phone was mounted on the dashboard, a mapping service pulled up.

Selina settled back in the seat and grasped the sides to try and keep herself steady as they bounded over the ruts of the dirt and gravel road. It felt like her head would explode from all the bouncing and slamming about. Dust came in Nathan's open window, making her want to sneeze.

Nathan piped up from the passenger seat, voice weak. "We haven't been introduced. I'm Nathan, this is Johnny."

Crap. "This is Oliver. He's been helping me today."

"Nice to meet you," Oliver said.

Headlights showed off to the side where the road went to Charles' cabin, flashing as trees blocked the light. "There he is!" Selina said. "He'll fall in behind on the main road. Keep going."

Oliver sped up, gravel spitting from the rear tires. The rutted road slowed them, and she leaned against the driver's seat, squinting into the darkness off to the side, using the seat to keep her steady. There, more flashes of light. They were still in front of Charles.

They burst out onto the highway, fish-tailing the Jeep. Nathan and Johnny had desperate grips on the bitch straps, and Nathan made pained noises. She could see a muscle in Oliver's jaw twitching, knew it must be hard to keep driving this way when it obviously caused Nathan pain.

Oliver floored it, the Jeep resisting at first. He downshifted until the engine roared, and they jerked ahead, finally building enough speed for him to shift up to fifth.

A vehicle shot onto the road behind them, light from the headlights moving up then down before leveling out as he bounced over the berm. It had to be Charles. He swerved around and caught up to them.

Oliver drove over the now much smoother road, focusing ahead of him into the darkness.

In the front passenger seat, Nathan's breathing was labored, interspersed with growls and whines. He clutched the armrest, the fuzz visible against the backlighting of the dashboard as a white aura, surrounding him.

Her chest clenched. She just needed a little more time.

The map showed a good twenty-minute drive ahead of them, so

Selina started prepping, knowing her sense of urgency would lead to mistakes if she didn't rein it in. She closed her eyes and took several deep breaths. There was nothing she could do about Nathan in this moment. All she could do right now was make sure they were prepared when they arrived. Of course, she didn't know exactly what they were driving into. Whether he would be in the cabin or somewhere else. Whether Herb or his brother would even be there.

She couldn't think about what would happen if they weren't there. If she was wrong. Instead, she focused on what needed to be done, opening her eyes once her pulse had slowed. She laid out her various holsters and sheaths, matching silver knives and bone ash bullets to their holders. Strapping them on in a moving vehicle was tricky.

Johnny tried to make nervous conversation. "So...what do we do when we get there?"

"We assess the situation, figure out where Herb and the Wendigo are, and go from there," Selina said, strapping an ankle holster on.

"That's not much of a plan."

"I haven't had much time to put one together. Don't worry, this is what I do. Once there, I'll be able to formulate a full plan. Whatever we do, the plan is to kill the Wendigo and feed its heart to Nathan. Those are the two most important aspects for us to focus on. If anything happens to me, that's what needs doing. No matter what, the Wendigo dies and Nathan eats its heart."

Johnny nodded and looked back out the window. No one else made an attempt at conversation.

Selina shoved items she couldn't strap onto her body into several bags. Flashlights and batteries, water bottles she found in the back of the Jeep, a couple knives, night vision goggles, and extra ammunition. She hefted her dad's knife, which had its own clip. She slid it onto the back of her pants, a reassuring weight against her back.

Once the bags were zipped, she put them in back, facing forward.

Time to prepare for battle.

27

INTO THE WOODS WE GO

They slowed as they neared the cabin, turning the headlights off. Charles did the same behind them. The cabin was dark; it looked deserted. Icicles hung from the eaves, and snow covered the roof and surroundings in a shallow, glistening white carpet. The snow was a mild surprise, but they had gone up significantly in elevation. Being familiar with the odd weather at high elevations, Selina had packed for cold, at the very least.

While the cabin looked empty, turmoil in the snow showed someone had been here since the snowfall. In fact, there'd been quite a lot of activity on this side of the cabin. Selina got out of the Jeep to study the ground. The prints were too many and too clustered together to tell anything about any individual set of prints, but as she traced around the side of the cabin, she found that the ground was less disturbed here, and that there were at least two distinctive sets of prints heading farther into the mountains.

One set was a standard man's shoe print, the tread and width showing it was probably a pair of snow boots. The other set appeared to be bare feet, almost humanoid in shape, with claw imprints at the ends of the toes. They were larger than the boot prints and certainly weren't recognizable as any typical animal Selina had ever seen, and she was adept at identifying North American animal prints after years of tracking.

A single set of footsteps crunched through the snow behind her and came to a stop next to her. Charles bent down to peer at the tracks. "What've we got?"

"A man's tracks, maybe Herb's since this is his cabin, and then something else. Our Wendigo, fully transformed. At least I assume so. Each set of Wendigo tracks is slightly different, for whatever reason, but it couldn't be anything else that I know of."

He reached down with his index finger extended, pressing it into one of the prints. "These aren't iced over like the ones out front. They must be fresh."

"Yep. I'm thinking they headed out not too long ago. They go up the hillside, so we'll be climbing." She looked up, a frown creasing her brow. "There's something odd, though."

"What's that?"

"The way the tracks are, the human is walking next to the Wendigo. The tracks never cross. They show calm, orderly walking, not running. It doesn't make sense."

It was his turn to frown. "Good point. How's that possible?"

"Have you ever seen a Wendigo have enough control not to attack someone?"

"Never."

"Neither have I. The family is usually the first to die. They can't hold themselves back. Why is this different?"

They were both quiet for a moment, examining the footprints. Selina released a breath and turned to him. "You ready?"

"Good to go. Who are we taking with us?"

"Everyone. We'll need all the help we can get, and I'd like Nathan close, so I can keep an eye on him." A ball formed in the pit of her stomach. "I won't know if it's helped if he isn't right there. If I need to show him the necessary mercy, it might as well be right away. There's no time to find the sire if this isn't the one. Plus, he'll have to be there to eat the heart."

"They're going to slow us down."

"I know, but not significantly. Well, except for Nathan, but he's the one that really needs to be there, and I need them to handle him. That leaves our hands free."

"All right."

Charles turned to head back to the vehicles, feet crunching through the hard-packed snow once again.

Selina lingered, squinting into the trees, wondering if the man and his cryptid friend already knew they were here. No answers came from between the ice-crusted trees, even with the light of the moon reflecting off the snow and illuminating the area around the cabin. She followed the path Charles had taken, his bigger footprints making the trek easier than it had been to get to the back. He'd skirted the other sets of prints to forge his own, not wanting to disturb the evidentiary tracks. Maybe Selina didn't give him enough credit, and he wasn't just a blowhard out for glory. Her father certainly hadn't minded working with him all those years ago. Of course, her father hadn't been a joy to work with either, so maybe they'd simply neutralized each other.

She'd see soon enough.

HER PREPARATIONS on the drive over made it easier to get everyone out of the car and armed. Each person except Nathan had a small pack with the necessaries she'd split out, such as water, batteries, flashlights, and night vision goggles, two from Nathan's trunk, one from hers. Everyone would also be armed. Johnny had a spear he'd made himself. Typically, Nathan would have wielded the axe, but he was too weak, and Selina preferred her knives and guns, so Oliver offered to carry it. Nathan strapped a buck knife to his thigh just in case, though nobody thought he'd be using it. Each also got a stake.

Charles had his own weaponry, which he gathered efficiently from the back of his rental. His silver axe rested in a specially made sheath on his pack, criss-crossing with a rifle, so he could draw one or the other by reaching behind him. He had as many guns and knives as Selina, as far as she could tell.

They bundled up and set off around the side of the cabin. Selina took the lead, with Charles in the rear to cover them in case anyone tried to sneak up behind them. There was no way to know if their presence was known or not, so they had to move forward with the assumption that someone knew they were here. Quite possibly, that someone was watching them, prepared to attack at any time. The big concern being whether a Wendigo was standing next to a regular guy, or one had followed the other up into the hills. Would they come upon a body or an ally to the creature? The irony of her own situation with Nathan didn't escape her.

The path they were following narrowed, and they had no choice but to disturb the previous tracks, as there wasn't enough room to skirt them or try to step around them. The trail sloped upward, and they were forced to climb, scrambling over icy rocks at times. The higher they climbed, the colder it became, the chill biting Selina's nose and ears.

Behind her, Selina could hear Nathan, his breathing growing increasingly growly. She figured a less stubborn man would have turned by now, but he still fought as much as he could. He had to be in considerable pain at this point, yet he pushed forward. Of course, it was his life that hung in the balance, but not everyone would have fought like he had. It would have been easier to give up.

She peeked behind her to check on him, saw a strained, pale-furred face, his eyes intent on the ground. Johnny walked right behind him, one arm on his back, his eyes cast warily at his mentor. They were keeping up, though, and the fact that Nathan had features to read at this point was good enough for her. For now.

Quiet masculine rumbles sounded from the back of their party. Oliver and Charles talked, keeping their voices low. It was always amazing to her that two men who didn't appear to like each other much could get along, setting aside those differences. Selina tried to make out what they were saying, but the sound of footfalls and

Nathan's strained breathing were too much, drowning out their voices just enough that she couldn't make out the words.

The slope lessened gradually, then more. Selina looked up. Sure enough, it looked like they were about to reach level ground. More level than what they were on, anyway. She picked her way over one last set of rocks and ended up on a shelf of sorts. The snow was thicker on the ground, but footprints marred the surface, leading off to the right.

Selina turned to lend a hand, gripping Nathan's forearm and pulling. She could feel the press of his nails through her coat and it scared her, pushed her to move faster.

Following the footprints, she soon sighted an opening in the face of the cliff before her. Snow had partially fallen over it, covering the rest of the prints. She had no doubt this was where they led. Had the two they were tracking caused this miniature avalanche or had it happened naturally? It could really go either way, considering the depth of the snow and the looseness with which the rest of it hung to the sides of the cave opening. She had to figure an intentional avalanche would be hard to do just right.

"All right, guys, we still have to assume they know we're here," she said. "That avalanche could have been done purposely to block the tunnel. Nathan, I'm going to need you right behind me. Johnny, I'd prefer you stay at the rear with Oliver. Stay out of this unless we need you. I'll call you in when we've cleared the area first."

"I want to help," he said, quickly shushed for being too loud.

"I know you do, but the biggest help you can give me is backup. This may be a trick. They may have set it off and hidden somewhere, waiting for us to go into the cave."

Oliver opened his mouth to protest, but caught himself. Instead, he nodded. She saw the muscle in his jaw jump as he tensed it, but he didn't argue. Good. She wasn't sure what he could do. Yes, he had been around far longer than she had, but he wasn't a hunter or tracker. He definitely wasn't a Myth Stalker. He was a businessman with a lot of experience, and that wouldn't help them here. Another set of hands couldn't hurt, though, which is why she'd opted to bring him along. She doubted he would have stayed behind had she tried, anyway.

"Charles, I need you with me from the start. We're limited by not knowing what the setup is in there, so we'll have to go in hot and heavy. There's a human in there, but he appears to be part of this in some way, so I'm not worried about keeping him safe right now. We move fast and we take out anything and anyone in sight. Any human standing with the Wendigo is collateral damage." Once again, she thought about the fact that she happened to be lugging around her very own Wendigo-to-be.

"Now that's my kinda' party," Charles said.

"I figured you'd like that. Oliver and Johnny, I need you to keep Nathan safe and moving. If Charles or I are taken down, do what you can to finish the Wendigo. If that's impossible..." Here, she paused, swallowing the balloon forming in her throat. "If that's impossible, your job is to ensure Nathan does not turn."

Charles scoffed, coughing out a short sound. "Speak for yourself, sister. I won't be going down. Maybe later." He winked, teeth showing in the dim light as he grinned.

Oliver shook his head, looking grim.

Selina ignored Charles. She'd thought that now, in the thick of things, he'd be done making idiotic comments, but there were apparently a few left. She figured his last words on his deathbed would be something both smartassed and perverted.

She continued. "You'll have Nathan to advise you. The basics are that silver will slow it down, but will not kill it. You have to shatter its heart and chop its head off. Stakes are the easiest way to shatter the heart thoroughly. Johnny, have you been trained on Wendigo and how to take care of the body afterward?"

Johnny nodded.

"Okay, good. Then I don't have to go over the details. You're in charge of dispensing the creature if something happens to Charles and me." She paused to study the embankment. It rose high enough that they'd have to work to get over it, but it was doable. "All right, Charles, when we get inside I go left, you go right. Stay five paces behind me so we're staggered. Nathan, five paces behind him, but left with me. Johnny and Oliver, once I call you in, stick to the rear center, and keep an eye out behind us."

She and Charles both did a weapons check, making adjustments where necessary. Bundled up as they had to be, it was quite the trick to have everything where she needed it. She made the decision to take off the bulky overcoat she had on, but kept on her bike jacket, figuring the spine guard was a good idea. She'd still have more flexibility than with the overcoat, though less than without, and the adrenaline and movement would ultimately keep her warm enough. At times like this, she wished one of her powers was body heat.

Charles removed his coat, leaving him in a long-sleeved Henley. He had weapons strapped across his chest and waist that she hadn't been able to see under his coat earlier. Yep, they were both obviously fond of being well armed. This served to reassure her. Between the two of them, this Wendigo was going down.

She tested the placement of the silver swords crossed at her back, adjusting them a smidge. She nodded, satisfied. Several stakes were located on her person, one of these strapped to her thigh. She also had a gun on her ankle, one at her other thigh, and two in a cross holster so they hung on either side of her rib cage, high up. Even so, she knew they might be in an area too enclosed or unstable to use them. Better to have them and not need them, though they would only slow the Wendigo, not kill it. In addition to the stakes and guns, she had knives planted on her person. She pulled a walkie talkie out of its own clasp at her waist and tested it. Her voice came out of its partner at Johnny's waist, staticky and muffled, but clear enough to make out.

Weapons in place, she double checked that the men all had the night vision goggles she'd given out at the vehicles. She wouldn't need them inside, as they needed a mild source of light to work, just as with her own eyes. Her enhanced vision was like that of a cat's, not perfect, but it gave her a slight edge over prey. Charles had his own goggles.

This was as prepared as any of them were going to get. With more time, she would have been able to research the layout of the cave system, but they'd have to go in blind.

She nodded once to Charles as he and Nathan put on their night vision goggles, then turned to the cave. Studying the pile of snow and detritus close up, she found it lower on the left side, and fairly solid. Perhaps there were rocks underneath. She tested it, putting some weight on it, then more when that held. She grabbed the coat she'd shed and laid it over the surface.

Charles looked at her, an eyebrow cocked with impatience. He settled his hands across his chest and sighed.

"If you're so intent to go, feel free," she said. "I'd like to make sure I don't get stuck in a pile of snow while something's trying to eat my face off."

This elicited a snicker from Charles, and he waved a hand, signaling she should continue.

Selina stepped up onto the snowbank, stilling as it settled beneath her. When she didn't sink through, she continued, grasping the stone to her right for balance. Once over the top, she hopped down into the darkness of the cave, pulling one of her swords as she went. Sword raised, she looked around, wary of movement. This part of the cavern was shallow. The snow had gone to the back wall on the right-hand side. Something caught her eye, and she peered more closely at the snowbank. A small object jutted out from the bottom. She walked over and squatted, peering closely at it.

It was a leg. A human leg. The snow must have covered the pile of bodies Oliver had told her about. Luckily, the bodies were frozen, keeping the stench at bay. Exhilaration coursed through her veins. She had the urge to run forward like a charging knight. They had reached the right place.

Charles grunted his way over the snow while Selina swept the darkness with her eyes, straining for either a sight or sound should anyone be approaching. With a grunt, Charles sunk into the snow near the top.

Selina stifled a laugh, holding steady. Now was not the time to be distracted, even by Charles making a fool of himself.

He struggled behind her, trying to work his way up and out. Snow shooshed down the side, tinkling on the cave floor at the base.

As amusing as it all was, Selina grew impatient. "It's snow; go forward instead of trying to lift yourself up."

He grumbled, but the sounds behind her changed as he tried the new tack. Snow rained down on her and she shifted to her left to avoid it. Finally, he jumped down, feet smacking the rocky surface and echoing down the cavern.

"Now that you've blown any element of surprise we may have had, let's get Nathan in here," she said.

Charles groused, but she heard him scuffling around behind her.

Nathan took about the same amount of time as Charles to scale the wall of snow. He was weaker, but also lighter than either she or Charles at this point. Plus, he had to get over the Charles-shaped hole that had been left behind.

Oliver's voice, muffled, sounded from the other side of the wall of snow. "I gotcha'." He must have been giving Nathan a boost.

As soon as she heard Nathan's feet hit the ground, she asked, "Good?"

"Yep." Nathan panted, and she turned briefly to look at him. He had his hands on his knees and was bent over trying to catch his breath. He'd already put his goggles on, which was good.

She started forward, scouring the darkness for a flash of light, a scuff, anything. Behind and to her right, Charles moved, making the barest of sound. He was certainly good at this when it didn't involve climbing piles of snow. Too bad he had to be such a money-hungry, perverted creep or she might actually respect him.

Normally, Nathan would have been quiet, too, but in his current condition she was surprised he had made it into the cave, let alone up the hillside. He stumbled here and there, his breathing labored. She attempted to block out the sounds he made behind her, to keep from being distracted.

They'd gone several yards without being attacked, so Selina pulled the walkie out. "You guys can head in. So far, nothing." It would take them time to get over the snow, and there'd be enough distance to keep them safe if someone were waiting in the shadows ahead.

"Got it." Johnny's voice came out more muffled than hers had.

Up ahead, Selina heard a dripping noise. A warm draft rushed by her, completely unexpected in the frigid cave. "Something's up ahead," she whispered.

Nothing was visible. They were too deep for any outside light to penetrate. Selina bent over and nudged a switch at each knee, turning on LED lights to help illuminate in front of them and give the goggles and her eyes some light to use without having to hold a flashlight on the ground.

"Nice," Charles said. "I need to get me some of those."

The walls were unnaturally smooth here. This was no weather-worn cave, but something that appeared to be manmade. She had no idea what might have done this, but figured perhaps mining had occurred in these mountains. Certainly, there'd been a ton of mining in the lower Rockies in Colorado. Typically, those tunnels were more rough-hewn, with wooden support structures bracing the walls and ceiling.

"You'd think we'd be approaching something, anything. How is this tunnel so straight?" asked Charles.

"And why aren't there other tunnels leading from it?" Selina started forward again. Behind them, Nathan made pained sounds that made the hairs on Selina's neck rise. "You okay, Nathan?" Turning, she found him crouched over, one arm against the wall. He was bent at the waist, his head down. "Nathan?"

"I'm okay, but we need to keep going. Hurry."

He didn't need to tell her twice. She increased her speed. The ground began to slope downward ever so slightly, making forward progress that much easier.

"Down slope," she said, just loud enough so they should be able to hear her, but hopefully not so loud as to bring attention to them.

The temperature warmed as they moved deeper into the mountain, which seemed wrong. Shouldn't it have been cooling as they moved downward? Then again, she recalled touring Cave of the

Winds in Colorado, and they said the temperature stayed consistent all year. It was in the 50s, she thought. This must be the same sort of thing.

Probably due to whatever they'd heard dripping before, tiny rivulets of water ran down along the stone pathway. The actual dripping had been lost behind them somewhere. She turned to Charles, intending to say something about the water, but before she could say anything, a massive cacophony began. At first, she thought the sound was Nathan having fallen, but he was right there in front of her. The rumbling grew, and now came the sound of rock hitting rock.

"What the hell is that?" she called, no longer determined to keep her voice low.

"I think our mini avalanche just met a jumbo avalanche." Charles whipped out his flashlight, shining it back the way they'd come.

A shooshing noise sounded in that direction, building to a roar. A massive wall of snow and debris moved toward them, creeping steadily along the floor, crashing against the wall like a herd of wildebeests in a narrow canyon.

Without another word, the three of them broke into a sprint, Nathan channeling some last vestige of adrenaline. Air rushed over them, nudged forward by the snow. If the tunnel ended ahead, they were all dead.

The rumble increased, shaking its way through her body, making her teeth chatter. The ground vibrated, bits of rock falling from the ceiling. Her jaw clenched, and she increased her speed, hoping both men were doing the same.

Up ahead, she saw a slight difference in the tunnel wall, a deeper shadow on the left side. Selina shouted, "Follow me left!" and hoped they could hear her over the sound of the rumbling snow. "Left, left!"

She dove for the shadow, bracing herself for impact. There was no time to investigate. Either they'd slam into a wall and be smothered by the snow or they'd be safely tucked out of the way from the wall of snow crashing their way. This was their best chance.

28

A RIVER RUNS THROUGH IT

Selina went through a narrow archway, rolling as she hit the ground to try and take some of the brunt of the impact. Charles landed next to her, dragging Nathan with him, who landed partially on top of him. Both men grunted.

The snow didn't fully cover the doorway, having slowed to a stop, but it did cover about half of it. Peeking out over the snow that blocked the opening, she saw that it had filled at least three-quarters of the height of the tunnel in the direction they'd come from. It petered out as it progressed downhill. She lifted the walkie to her mouth. "Are you guys okay?" Only static responded. "Johnny? Oliver?"

Nothing.

Her chest squeezed in panic and horror, and she fought against the pressure. "I hope they made it." Thoughts of what might have happened to the two men when that snow came down pulsated in her brain. There was no way for her to go back and check on them. Her friends could even now be smothering under a horrible pile of snow, or somewhere farther down the mountain where the wall of snow might have forced them. Her pulse throbbed in her throat, her breath quickened, and she placed a hand on her chest in order to try and bring herself under control.

Sticking her head out above the snow, she yelled, "Oliver? Johnny? Can you hear me?"

When she received no response, she took out her cell phone, knowing it was a long shot. Sure enough, no signal.

"Does anyone have a signal so we can call emergency services?" she asked.

Charles, who had been standing over Nathan impatiently, pulled out his phone to check. "Nothing."

Selina started to ask Nathan, but remembered he didn't own a cell phone.

No, there was really nothing she could do to help. The tunnel outside was full of snow. If she tried to climb it, she'd be wasting valuable time and sealing Nathan's death warrant. She had to make a choice between looking for Johnny and Oliver or moving forward with Charles and Nathan.

As if tuned into her brain, Charles said, "There's no way we can get back there to check. We have to hope they're okay." He helped Nathan to a sitting position.

But when Charles went to let go of him, Nathan slumped over. Selina knelt next to him and touched his face. He was out cold.

"Crap," she said. "I imagine this is the most peace he's going to get tonight."

"I'm sure you're right. I can carry him for a bit, but I'll need your help getting him over that snow. If that's where we need to go."

"Hold on. Let me look around."

They were in a wide tunnel, this one with posts bracing along the sides, and beams overhead. The ceiling rose to a height of about six feet, and that and the walls were rugged, rather than smooth like the tunnel they'd started in. In fact, looking at the doorway they'd come through, the wood there looked newer, less weathered. For whatever reason, someone had built a new tunnel that joined with this one. Rubble covered the ground, scratching and popping across the rock as she walked over it.

Behind her, Charles' feet scuffed across the ground. She glanced back to see what he was doing and watched as he arranged Nathan against a wide pillar of stone, his head lolling onto his shoulder. Charles looked up, caught her watching, and said, "I'll come with in case it branches into multiple tunnels. We need to get going."

With a nod, she proceeded through the tunnel, careful of her footing. Some of the rubble was quite large, and the ceiling dropped below six feet at various places, making them both have to bend forward to progress. The LEDs lit the tunnel just right for her, but Charles snapped on his flashlight behind her, rather than use his night vision goggles. At this point, they weren't so worried about trying to keep quiet and be discreet. They needed to find a way out.

Another tunnel did branch out up ahead. She approached with caution, wary of ambush. She stopped about a foot shy of the entrance and pressed her back to the wall, waiting for Charles to catch up. As she waited, she pulled one of her swords out, holding it before her.

Charles joined her against the wall in order to pull his axe out. She wasn't positive he could get a good enough swing on it in the tight space, but then again, there'd been men in here however long ago swinging picks at the walls to knock valuable minerals loose.

He nodded, axe firmly gripped in his hands.

Selina nodded back then stepped out, sword held low and at about a forty-five degree angle. Her pulse pounded.

Nothing there. Just more tunnel.

"Clear."

Charles crossed the entryway, heading down the main tunnel. The light went with him, fading the farther he got.

Selina followed this secondary tunnel, which was slightly smaller than the one she'd just come from. This one held far more rubble, and she found herself sweeping her eyes across the ceiling for weak braces. There were several posts broken or missing, and a shiver crawled up her spine. What would it have been like to work down here, knowing the tunnel could collapse at any minute? What about the men who'd forged the tunnel to begin with?

Her foot hit a larger piece of rock, sending it forward with a clack. A couple more steps brought her to a flow of rocks, tumbled together and spilling down the passageway. There'd been a cave in. At least she wouldn't have to choose which tunnel to go down. Unless there were others ahead.

She followed the tunnel back to the bigger one, thinking about what might have happened to Oliver and Johnny. Her concern wormed through her brain. She tried the walkie one more time, but still heard only static. Even so, she turned the volume up so she could hear if they tried to reach her. Guilt gnawed at her.

Charles' voice startled her from up ahead. "Selina, I hear running water." His voice was quiet, his light a tiny pinhole in the dark, but the walls of the tunnel must have bounced his voice around just enough to get back to her.

She sprinted in the direction of his light. There'd been water in the tunnel, so perhaps Charles had found an alternate way to whatever body of water existed in here.

AFTER CHARLES SHOWED her where the sound appeared to be coming from, they'd gone to retrieve Nathan. Now they walked down a steeply downgraded tunnel, Nathan across Charles' shoulders. She had to admit that Charles was a nicer guy than she'd previously thought. Well, maybe nice wasn't the right word, but...decent?

There was only one more tunnel branching off this one, and it had also been blocked by a tumble of rock, this one much closer to the main tunnel. She was surprised there weren't any cave-ins along the main tunnel, but maybe it had been better fortified to begin with. Perhaps the little ones branching off it had been the newest ones before they bailed on the mining operation.

Charles breathed heavily, thanks to the extra weight across his shoulders. Even as emaciated as Nathan had become, he was still a dead weight. He'd started mumbling, though his eyes hadn't opened yet. She couldn't make out what he was saying, but she heard enough to know it wasn't English he was speaking.

She'd tried the radio several more times with no response, and had finally turned it back down to the lowest volume so as not to alert anyone ahead, though the mumbling and heavy breathing weren't exactly discreet, and their footfalls weren't too quiet as they worked down the slick, rubble-strewn rock. She tried to shove the guilt and horror down, compartmentalize it to keep it from distracting her. But she was all too human in her emotions, and she felt ill at leaving the two men to fend for themselves.

Charles grunted, almost tripping over a rock the size and shape of a football. They wouldn't be making a surprise appearance with all the noise. The sound of water grew louder, signifying rushing water somewhere below. It could be a river, perhaps a waterfall, though she figured that would be a slightly different sound. They'd find out soon enough, considering how loud it had gotten in the last few minutes.

Sure enough, they reached a raging river, the water flowing under a low ceiling. Their path ended there, no other outlets showing themselves. Their route appeared to be down to either jumping in the river or climbing over the snowbank made by the avalanche. Neither one was a great choice. Or a safe one.

"Do you need to rest, Charles?"

"Yeah."

Carefully, she helped ease Nathan from his shoulders and settled him on the ground. She looked at the water, pondering how much bacteria likely flowed right along with it. Was it worth risking it for something to drink? They'd long exhausted the water they'd brought, which hadn't been much since they'd sort of expected to find the Wendigo in a shallow cave, rather than having to journey to the center of the Earth. Or so it now seemed.

"So, boss, what do we do from here?" Charles asked, settling himself next to Nathan and leaning his back against a large boulder. His feet were just shy of the river in the narrow space.

She slumped. "I don't know. There's no way out from here. Every route is blocked."

"Unless we jump in the river."

She laughed, a quick outward puff of breath. "Yeah, sure. Who knows where that would take us. For all we know, the ceiling gets lower and stays that way. We'd drown." She thought for a moment, considering the alternative. "Maybe we should go back up."

"I'm not sure I can carry him back up, not and get anywhere fast." He hung his head, still trying to catch his breath.

"You're right. And I suspect things aren't going to be good when he wakes up. Look at him." Her fear and grief threatened to overwhelm her. All this, only to ultimately fail. Not only would she not save Nathan, she might have brought all of them to their deaths here. At least everyone would still have their souls. All except Nathan.

Charles looked over at Nathan, whose closed eyes were deeply sunken into the bones of his skull, his cheekbones almost razor sharp. His lips were thin and gray, almost black. Tufts of white fur covered his fingers and face. The nails were full-on talons, long, thick, and black. His ears were elongated. In short, he looked very little like Nathan and very much like a Wendigo.

"Yeah, pretty sure he's going to try to eat us when he wakes up," Charles said.

"I'd say that's not funny, but you could be right. We may have to try the river." She shivered as she looked at that frothy white water. Wave upon wave cavorted over the others, smashing into the rock precipice that hung over the river. She could see that the rock's surface had been worn smooth over time, even as the flow of water had eaten away at it.

She stood and looked back up the tunnel where they'd come from. The path disappeared around a bend a ways up, and even that visible stretch seemed like one hell of a long walk at this point. And then what? She hadn't found an alternate way out of that cavern back there unless they wanted to dig their way through one of the smaller tunnels. The snow blocked the tunnel mouth. They could climb up over the snow and make their way down to wherever it ended, but that would take forever, and there was no guarantee that tunnel even continued on. After all, it was different than the older tunnels, and she wasn't confident it had been a part of the old system.

Helplessness washed over her in waves, threatening to pull her down.

Ignoring it, she sighed and wiped her hands on her pants. This wouldn't end here. She looked at Charles. "I guess if we're going to do it, we might as well get it out of the way. We live or we drown."

"Or bash our heads open on the rock."

"Yeah, or that. But we'd still end up drowning." She studied the water before speaking again. "I'll go first with Nathan, try to keep his head under so he doesn't hit the overhang as we go through."

"I'm heavier. I might have more luck keeping him down."

"I suppose, but you've also just lugged him for what seemed like a couple miles. You come in close behind us and do what you can. That way, if I lose him, you can still nab him."

Charles nodded, eyes serious, mouth grim. "Do you really think he'd want so many people to give their lives to save his?"

This caught her by surprise. She jerked her head around to look at him. "What do you mean?"

"I mean we've probably lost those other two, and now you're talking about how I save him if something happens to you. I don't really know this guy, but he was ready to die a few hours ago. You think he would have chosen this method if he'd known how it would turn out?"

"Of course not, but it's not up to him at this point. We've come too far not to try."

Charles shrugged. "Okay. Let's do this thing."

Selina shot him a wry smile and walked over to Nathan, grabbing him under the arms. "I figure I'm gone as soon as I'm in that water. Grab his feet." She hooked her hands up against his chest and gripped his jacket tightly in her hands, tensing her arms to hold strong.

Charles looked into her eyes, holding Nathan's ankles. "Good luck."

"See you on the other side."

She took a deep breath and jumped, Charles swinging Nathan's feet as she went, so his body would hit the water at the same time.

The shock of the ice-cold water hit her, and she gasped, taking in a mouthful. She had just enough time to push through it, wrap her arm around Nathan's throat and push them both down before her back grazed rock, slicing her skin, and her world became a roiling gray abyss.

She was thrown all over the place, striking different surfaces with just about every part of her body. She wondered if it would be worse were she not somewhat anchored by the limp form of her old friend. Her chest burned with lack of oxygen, and it took concentration to not breathe in, against her baser instincts.

Despite her efforts to keep Nathan safe, she felt each impact as he slammed into the stone around them. Their heads emerged enough for her to knock her head into rock, her chin bouncing off Nathan's forehead. Then they were back under, once again rolling with the current of the rushing beast around them.

Her lungs were on fire. She wondered if Nathan had already drowned. She couldn't control it any longer, heaving in a breath. Ice filled her burning lungs, the two sensations merging in an odd fashion. Impossible, she thought, that one could feel both fire and ice at once.

Just as she thought it would never end, that this would go on until she finally passed out, the darkness around her lightened. Her head bobbed up out of the water, closely followed by Nathan's. She winced, waiting for the impact, but nothing happened. The ceiling had risen, though they were still in close quarters. It felt like it, anyway. Lack of light made it impossible to see what lay around her. Her gasping breath brought in mostly air, and she coughed, hacking water out of her lungs then gurgling as more water shot into her mouth.

And then there was sudden brightness, and it was as if the ground had dropped out from under them. She felt the void at her back for a second before falling headfirst. Nathan's body, still wrapped in her arms, trailed along above her as she fell vertically.

She took a deep, burning breath as a new roar filled her ears, figuring she'd hit bottom any time, and hoping desperately that she wouldn't, that it would at least be deep enough not to shove her spine through her skull.

Her grip on Nathan tightened, and she closed her eyes.

She'd managed to hold Nathan this whole time, but when her body slammed into the water's surface it felt like she'd jumped off the Empire State Building, and he slipped from her arms. There was a surprising lack of give to the water, or so it felt, and she came close to losing consciousness, white bursts of light dancing in the darkness. Her head became cloudy, a rush of a different kind filling her ears. It felt peaceful to drift in the water now, no longer a frightening scramble. Her thoughts were messed up, body aching everywhere.

Hands grabbed her, pulling her up, and she resented the intrusion. The cool air of the cave hit her wet clothing, making her colder than before, and she wrapped her arms around herself, unwilling to open her eyes and look around. Besides, it was probably just more darkness, and she'd likely lost the LEDs. It didn't feel like there was a point.

She heard the sound of Charles retching, and then, "Open your eyes. You're not going to believe this."

She shook her head, squeezing more tightly into herself. Shivers wracked her body, and she coughed, unable to stop. It felt like she'd inhaled a gallon of water into her lungs, but it wouldn't come out.

Charles jerked her up into a sitting position. It was then that she noticed the warm glow coming through her eyelids. When she opened her eyes, she found they were in another large cavern, this one with a hole at the top that let in moonlight. Not only that, but lit torches cast a warm amber flicker around the cavern. Her body yearned for the heat promised by those flames.

This time, she sat forward of her own volition, looking around. The waterfall they'd just come down was monstrous, or so it looked from here. Nathan lay on the flat rock surface beside her, still unconscious. He had even more fur, or perhaps it was the effect from being drenched. No, it looked like there was a lot more there. He barely appeared human anymore.

Charles knelt beside her, braced on one arm, one knee underneath him. His blond hair, darkened by the water, lay in sheets down the sides of his face. He looked as tired as she felt.

She stood up and looked around. Though the cavern had been lit with torches, there was no one in sight. Roughly squared entryways scattered around the cavern indicated this was where the different tunnels emptied. The walls and ceiling were ragged, and near the waterfall was a grouping of stalagmites and stalactites, a couple meeting to form angular columns.

It was then that two unexpected things happened at once.

29

JUST DROPPING IN

From their right, out of a small entrance in the rock face, a roar sounded. In stepped a giant, filthy white beast. The torchlight turned its eyes red, and its pronounced snout sported jagged teeth. Its broad shoulders filled the mouth of the tunnel in which it stood.

There was no time to process this. A shout came from behind them, and Selina turned, confident Charles had her back. Out of one of the entryways, Johnny appeared, followed close behind by Oliver. They were bedraggled and wet, though not dripping as she and Charles were.

"You're alive!" she said.

"Looks like we got here right on time," Oliver said, nodding behind her before leaning over to take a breath.

Johnny looked around, a frown on his face. It eased when he saw Nathan, but only for a moment. "We found a different way in," he said.

Selina faced the Wendigo again, striding up beside Charles. She pulled her swords from her back, relieved to find them still there. Luckily, she had the best fittings. She'd have to hug Steve for it later. She had to assume her rifle would be useless to her after the dunk in the water. There was a chance her guns would be okay, but this was no time to test it. Better to use weapons she knew she could rely on than to risk something going wrong with a gun in the thick of the fight.

Behind them, Nathan whimpered then growled.

Around the creature stepped Herb, wearing overalls and a baseball cap that read *Herb's Car Repair: Faster Cheaper Better.*

"Gee, Herb, fancy meeting you here." Selina was unable to keep her lip from curling in disgust. "What are you doing in this place?"

"I'm only trying to protect my brother. We can stay here where he can't hurt anyone."

"Really?" she said. "You've done a real knock-up job so far."

Charles snorted at this, but kept his eyes on the Wendigo, body rigid, his axe held out before him. Selina held the silver-coated swords to either side of her.

"That was before. When I was trying to stay in the house." Herb held his hands out, palms toward them. "But I'll stay with him now, keep him here. I can control him."

"You can't control a Wendigo," Selina said. "You're lucky he hasn't ripped you apart yet."

"He's my brother! Besides, I made him what he is. It's my fault. I have to make it right."

Selina was taken aback. "What do you mean you made him?"

"*I* did the ceremony...the ritual. Whatever you call it. He brought that stupid book from the library and I was making fun of him, so I did it to show him he was an idiot. But it worked." He choked, rubbed at his eyes. Then he lifted his chin and stared defiantly back at her. "What matters is that I can control him."

"I'm sure you only think you can control him. Give it more time, he'll turn on you and destroy you like he will everyone else who crosses his path. Best to take care of the problem now."

"He won't! Leave here and leave us alone. I've got this. You just want to kill him."

Charles turned his head partially toward Selina and said, "I'm tired of listening to this clown. Are we going to take care of this or chatter like monkeys for another hour?"

Heat rushed through Selina. What was she trying to accomplish, anyway? Herb and the creature that had been his brother weren't going to listen to reason. And nothing they could say would change what had to happen next. They needed to do something before Nathan turned.

"All right," she said "We need to get this done."

"So tell me, boss, what needs to happen?" Charles asked.

"Give me a minute."

For the first time since they'd landed in this cavern, Charles lost his composure. It would have been comical had these been different circumstances. The hand holding the axe dropped slightly, and he turned to look more fully at Selina. "You don't know?"

"I just know this guy sired Nathan's Wendigo, so we have to take him out. I'm still working on what happens after that. Proceed as you would with any Wendigo."

Charles sighed, and as he turned his face back toward Herb and the creature, a flash of grimy white struck out at him, knocking the axe from his hands and sending him flying. Both body and weapon landed on the rocky floor at the same time, one falling with the *clank* of silver, the other with a meaty *thunk*.

Selina sprang between Charles and the Wendigo, swords out, tight in her grip. She tried to keep an eye on both threats, but they'd spread out as the Wendigo had hit Charles. She could hear him moving behind her, likely collecting his lost blade.

The creature before her feinted as if he would attack, pulled back then lunged toward her.

She jumped to her side and rolled, bringing one sword up. The blade caught the creature along the calf, blood spurting out and slicking the fur down.

It screeched then growled. Its paw swiped over her head, catching her along the back and sending her sprawling.

She regained her feet, not happy to have her back to Herb, who appeared to just be standing there. However, the greater threat was the Wendigo, and there were three men in this cavern who could back her up. She had to trust that they would.

"We need to do this fast." Charles' voice sounded strained, and she darted her eyes to the side to look at him, face still aimed at the Wendigo. Charles stood over Nathan, who lay on the floor, clawing at the rock, thick claws extending from his hand and scraping runnels in the stone. "You get that creature down; I'll watch Nathan and the thing's brother."

"Quit calling him a *thing*!" Herb shouted, hands balled into fists. "His name is Tim."

"Yeah, yeah, he ain't heavy, he's your brother," Charles said. "You're an idiot."

Selina turned her attention from them, unsure where Oliver and Johnny were. The creature blocked her view behind him, and that seemed to be the only place they could be. With no time to waste, she couldn't continue on in defense posture. She would instead need to focus on getting the creature down.

She adjusted her grip on the swords as she thought.

The creature watched the blades, so she moved them in alternating circles to keep its attention on the silvery gleam, rather than on her.

She lunged, one blade before her, the other swinging sideways.

It easily sidestepped her, covering more ground with that one movement than she could cover in two steps, but she sliced it across the middle with the first sword, blood now coursing down its stomach and leg.

She twisted around, this time crossing the two blades and aiming higher up. Metal scraped metal as she pulled them apart. Twin gashes appeared in its throat, and it held its hands up to the injury, gargling.

It didn't go down.

This time she aimed for its eyes, jumping as high as she could to slash at it then landing with a tuck and a roll. She'd only managed to slash one eye, but the creature wailed, hands at its face. It stumbled about, partially blinded.

Johnny stepped around her, a short spear in his hand. He jabbed with it, hitting the creature in the chest. It went in nowhere near its heart, and the Wendigo grabbed the spear, pulling it out of Johnny's hands. It turned the spear on him, and before Selina could stop it, sent the spear through his stomach.

A look of shock crossed Johnny's face, jaw slack, eyes so wide there was more white than brown visible. His hands moved to grasp the length of wood sticking out of his middle. He stumbled back a step.

Selina reached for him, but Oliver was already there, supporting him to the ground. He tossed her Nathan's axe, which she caught after dropping one of her swords. He waved his hand at Selina, signifying she worry about the creature, and bent over Johnny.

"This ends now," she said.

She dropped the other sword and switched her axe to her non-dominant hand in order to pull the handgun from the left holster. Sliding the safety off, she fired, willing it to work. The shot caught the Wendigo in the chest. Before the vast echo had died down, she shot again, this time catching it in the stomach.

The next attempt at a shot dry clicked. She dropped the gun, grabbed the axe with both hands, and ran at the Wendigo, swinging it wide. It buried itself in the creature's side, eliciting an inhuman scream.

She pulled it back out and swung again, this time embedding it in its thigh. The creature grabbed the axe handle near the blade and swiped at her with its other hand. She let go, unwilling to wrestle for it.

Instead, Selina gathered herself then threw her body on the creature and rode it to the ground, hands gripping the thick, rough fur.

She grabbed her father's knife and took out its other eye. Blood gushed from the new wound.

Springing the knife from her left wrist, she punched the creature repeatedly, burying the blades in its flesh in quick punctures. The fur was so thick it acted as a shield against the knives. Its hide was also resistant, and it felt like the blades weren't getting in deep enough to make a difference.

It reached up and grabbed her, its hands so large they covered her entire ribcage. It squeezed, howling with pain and rage, and her screams joined. It felt like a vice, pressure on every inch of her torso. Her ribs would crack at any second.

Her lungs couldn't inflate all the way.

The pause allowed exhaustion to start creeping in, muscle fatigue descending.

She'd dropped her father's knife, but slashed at the creature's hands, fingers, and wrists with the knife at her wrist, trying desperately to make it free her. She freed the second wrist blade.

"Hold on!" It was Oliver's voice. Selina couldn't see him.

She landed blows wherever she could now, slashing with the knives, punching it in the face, lashing out with no real control or aim. Nothing seemed to faze it enough to make it stop squeezing.

Her vision faded, black forming a tunnel. She felt light-headed.

Her arms were still moving, but they were useless. It felt like everything had switched to slow motion.

She heard one of her ribs crack, then another, the sound like that of a dry stick breaking. Fire rushed through her ribcage, and she struggled to breathe against the pain. She grunted, jerking backward to try and loosen its grip.

It worked for a moment, and that was all she needed to get into better position. Its hands slipped back, claws raking her sides, but the leather protected her, and the pain was nothing compared to that inside her from the broken ribs. Hopefully, there wasn't organ damage.

She kicked out, her foot slamming into its face, and when it put its hands up once more, she quickly cut across the inside of one of its wrists, finding her mark this time. It grasped the wrist with the other hand, and she cut that one, too.

It swiped at her, but its efforts were useless, the hands unable to grip. She kicked at its face again and grasped a handful of greasy hair to stay on top of the bucking creature.

Charles appeared at her side, dragging Nathan with him, who looked more Wendigo than human at this point. Nathan didn't appear to be conscious. Oliver was there, too, and he reached for her.

It was then that she knew what to do, Bryan's words tumbling through her mind. A European could help. A white man with special powers. A man who could dispel the spirit, remove the sin. The book had said the sins had to be removed.

And she had a Sin Eater with her.

30

BAM, BITCH GOES DOWN

I t hurt to talk, but she managed, keeping her breaths as shallow as she could with her heart pounding the way it was. "Oliver, I need you to touch both the Wendigo and Nathan. Charles, where's...?" She looked around for Herb and found him sprawled on the ground, also apparently unconscious. "Never mind. Just keep Nathan up for Oliver to be able to touch him. Oliver, can you move Nathan's sins into the Wendigo?"

"I've never tried, but it might work."

"Good enough. Do what you can. Funnel as much of the bad as you can into the creature, away from Nathan. Tell me when you think you're at your limit."

He nodded, and she grasped the thing's fur more tightly with her left hand, squeezing her thighs as if she were riding a bucking bronco. The fur felt rough against her skin, the smell of rancid meat strong. She grabbed the silver coated stake with her right hand, and grasped fur with that one, as well, as much as she could. "Go!"

The creature went rigid beneath her, and then it began to scream.

Nathan's voice joined his, and she could hear Charles grunting. It sounded like Nathan must be fighting back. She buried herself in the fur, holding on for all she was worth, pulling forth the last of her reserves.

She couldn't see what was happening, but someone yelled, "No!" followed by a crash and Charles calling out. The creature jerked to the side, and she raised her head, trying to see around its body.

Nathan and Charles had dropped out of sight, and Oliver listed to the side, his face red with exertion, almost closer to purple. His eyes were squeezed tightly shut, lips pulled tight in a grimace.

As she looked on, his eyes popped open, red from burst blood vessels. "I can't hold the channel any longer. Whatever you're going to do, do it now!"

Selina didn't need to be told twice. She held up the hand with the stake and drove it into the Wendigo's heart with all her might. Her ribs protested. The Wendigo bucked even more, and she knew she hadn't driven the stake deep enough. She released its fur with the other hand, put it on the stake so she now held it with both, and pulled herself up enough to yank it out.

She now knelt on the creature, stake held high above her head. This time, when she drove it down it found its destination in the heart of the beast. The Wendigo let out a sound that was part gurgle, part roar, hands finding the stake, but unable to grasp it and pull it out.

Before it stilled, its eyes met Selina's, and she saw the human eyes of Herb's brother staring back at her. Instead of anger or fear, she saw only relief. A smile ghosted across the thing's muzzle. The hands fell at its side, head landing with a thud on the hard surface.

She climbed off the Wendigo, hands nearly numb from the force of the stake when she'd driven it in the second time. Oliver lay on the floor next to Nathan, both unconscious. Nathan still looked like Wendigo, and she wasn't sure it had worked. She had to hold out hope that it had. Still, she prepared to do battle with her mentor should he awaken and attack them.

Johnny was conscious, blood seeping around the spear. He grimaced as she looked at him, but gave her a wary thumbs up.

To her right, Charles stood behind Herb, arms wrapped around him as if they'd frozen mid-fight, which is exactly what appeared to have happened. Herb dropped to his knees, and Charles let him.

"What did you do?" Herb whispered. "Is Tim dead?"

"Your brother died a long time ago," Selina said. She gasped at the pain. It hurt too much to draw breath, let alone push it back out again.

Herb whimpered, body limp on the ground. He crawled over to the creature, laid his head against its chest. She couldn't help but take pity on him. After all, she might be going through the same thing in the next few minutes, and it wouldn't be her first time.

"If it helps, Herb, it was him in the end, and he looked peaceful before he died. He didn't want to be that monster any more than Nathan did."

Of course, they had quite possibly double cursed him in death by moving Nathan's sins into him, but she'd needed to get as much out of Nathan as possible in the hopes that the creature inside of him would go with the sin. All she could do was hope that those sins had let go in the end.

There was one more thing she needed to do before she could rest. She limped over to the body of the Wendigo and slumped down next to it. Rolling it the rest of the way onto its back, she drew her dad's knife again, raised it above her head, and stabbed the Wendigo in the chest. She sawed with the knife, a loud, raspy *skritch* and resistance telling her when she hit a rib. The blood that spilled over her hands felt warm and wet, thick. Her arms and ribs screamed with the effort of cutting it open. Finally, a rough hole cut, she dug the flesh and fur away from the excision and plunged a hand into its chest.

The heart was still man-sized, despite the beast's size, and she wrapped her hand around the firm, damaged muscle. It was black instead of the red or pink one might expect. She shoved the knife in with the other hand, and severed the heart from its cradle, pulling it from the chest with a sucking noise. It looked so sad in her hand, this small organ.

She dropped the knife next to the Wendigo and got up once again, body protesting every move. Only now did she go to Nathan and kneel beside him, pulling his white-furred head up onto her lap. "I need you to wake up."

He didn't awaken, but he stirred. She slapped him across the cheek. "Wake up!"

His eyes fluttered. He opened them, but they didn't focus. She held the heart to his mouth. "Eat."

His mouth opened, but when she stuffed the heart past his lips, he didn't bite down. He recoiled at first, eyes still unfocused, then brought his mouth back to the organ and began to suck at it, grimacing.

"This isn't going to be good enough." Frustrated, she looked back at her knife, too far away now. Looking with disgust at the heart she held in her hands, she swallowed, took a deep breath, and leaned forward, biting into the organ. It was thick and resistant to her teeth, but she gnawed at it until a chunk came free and into her mouth. Coppery blood squirted across her tongue, followed by the wretched taste of raw meat. She'd never liked giblets.

She chewed rapidly, choking back the vomit that tried to rise up the back of her throat. Her eyes were closed, and she focused on breathing deeply through her nose. *Not for anyone else*, she thought.

Once she had sufficiently chewed it up, she spat the mush into her hand and shoved it into Nathan's mouth. Nothing happened for a minute, and the frustration grew inside her like a physical being, swelling up through her back and chest. Tears stung her eyes. She couldn't make an unconscious man eat, even to save his life.

"Please," she begged.

Then his jaw moved. His lips closed. And he began to chew.

"Oh, thank you," she said.

A few more bites, and he stopped responding, but at least he had eaten some of the heart. She wrapped the rest in a strip of cloth and set it down next to him so it wouldn't be forgotten. He'd have to finish when he came to fully.

Exhausted, she moved to Oliver's side. "Are you okay?"

He stirred.

"Oh, sure, ask *him* if he's okay."

"I can see—and hear—that you're fine, Charles."

Oliver put his hands up to his head, grasping at the temples. "I'm fine. Sin eating always leaves me with a whopper of a headache, but this one might beat all."

"I wouldn't be surprised," she said.

"Are you okay?" Oliver asked her.

She winced and put a hand to her side. "I think I've got a few broken ribs. Other than that, I'm fine."

Selina stumbled over to Johnny. He looked pale, but there wasn't an awful lot of blood around him. Of course, if they removed the spear that would likely change. Yet they couldn't get him out of here with a spear protruding from his stomach. It might snag and do further damage. Her thoughts flip-flopped until she came to a decision.

She placed a hand on his shoulder. "I think I have to remove this, Johnny, but let me look at it first."

He sat still while she checked behind him. The spear hadn't gone all the way through. Maybe it hadn't punctured anything important, either. She had no idea how to tell.

Grasping the spear with her right hand, she placed the left against his cheek briefly, giving him a reassuring smile then moved it to his side to brace herself. "Three, two..." and she pulled. It offered some resistance, but came out, not as deep as it had been.

He gasped, his hands going to the hole in his abdomen.

She dropped the spear and placed her hands over his. Pushing hard against him, she put pressure on the wound. "Charles, I need a piece of fabric. Quickly."

She heard something ripping behind her, and then a rectangle of ragged cloth was shoved over her shoulder.

"So now I'm your bitch?" he asked.

"I wouldn't go that far. Though I like the sound of that." She took the cloth, folded it, and nudged Johnny's hands out of the way, placing the cloth over the wound. "Put pressure on it for me, Johnny." She removed her belt, pulling it through the loops, and put it around his stomach, cinching it as tightly as she could when he removed his hands.

It hadn't spurted blood. She decided she'd take that as a good sign.

She crawled over to Oliver, the adrenaline having departed her body, and laid her head across his chest. She should check on Nathan, but couldn't bring herself to do so. They'd know when he woke up if anything had changed.

Oliver moved his arm under and around her, bringing her in close to him. He kissed her on the top of her head, and left his mouth there, breathing against her damp hair. Herb's sobs still sounded from the direction of the giant white heap at their feet.

Charles sat next to Johnny, heaving a sigh, and Selina bent her head back to look at him. He looked as tired as she felt, dark circles under his eyes, deep lines around his mouth. His big chest moved rapidly with his breaths.

"How the hell do we get out of this place?" Charles asked.

"That's a damn good question," Selina said. "Certainly not the same way we came in."

She didn't intend to go near a river for a long, long time.

31

BACK TO REALITY

harles was the first to be up and about, the others lying in general disarray around the cave floor. He questioned Herb about the way out, but the little man was unresponsive, sobbing intermittently. Neither Oliver nor Johnny could remember how they'd found the cavern, having been shunted through the tunnels in a tumbling mass of snow after they'd climbed in. They'd found a tunnel in which water dripped from the ceiling, huge puddles covering the ground. The best anyone could figure, they'd been under the river, and there was likely no way out the way they'd come, the avalanche having sealed them inside. Frustrated, Charles took off in the opposite direction of where they'd come in via the underground river. A set of tracks came in through a wide tunnel, and he followed these, disappearing for about an hour.

When he returned, he wore a look of triumph. "I think I've found a way out. If you can get him to pull his head out of his ass," he inclined his head in the direction of Herb and the dead Wendigo, "maybe he can tell us how to use the tram that goes on those tracks. It's our best bet to get the injured out."

Selina tried to sit up, but her aching ribs made it slow going. Oliver sat up beside her and helped her the rest of the way, supporting her with an arm across her back. From a sitting position, she could see everyone else. Nathan had yet to come to. Johnny appeared to have passed out, which was a blessing. The rise and fall of his chest reassured her that he was at least still with them. Herb lay silently against his brother's side, tears still sliding down his cheeks.

Charles offered her a hand, and she took it, grunting as a sharp pain shot through her ribs, making her instantly nauseous. Once on her feet, she figured she'd never sit again. Anything to avoid the searing pain.

"Even if we get the tram working, how do we get them on it?" she asked.

"I'm sure I have enough left in me to carry Nathan and Johnny to the tram if we can get it in here, assuming he doesn't go psycho on me and gnaw on my head partway there. It would be easier if we could put together a stretcher for the kid, though. Moving him too much doesn't seem like a good idea."

Selina nodded. "It won't do to jostle him around any more than we have to. It's bad enough I pulled the spear out, but I didn't see another way."

She moved over to Herb, an arm wrapped around her ribs. "Herb, you need to go with Charles and help him get the tram going."

He looked up at her, eyes bleary, cheeks wet. His brows drew down, face scrunched up. "Tram?"

Selina snapped her fingers in front of his nose. "Come on, Herb. Wake up. We can't stay in here all night. The kid needs to get to a hospital. Now."

Herb blinked and looked around, rubbing a hand on the back of his neck. When his eyes returned to hers, they seemed to have cleared. "Okay, but I don't want to leave my brother here."

"I promise we'll come back and help you with him, but we need to think about the living first." Of course, she knew there was work still to do on the Wendigo's body in order to ensure he couldn't regenerate. This wasn't the best time to enlighten Herb.

"I'm not coming back to help with that thing," Charles said.

"Whether he comes back or not, Herb, I'll help you. Okay?" she asked. "Now show Charles how to work the tram."

Herb rose, obviously hesitant to leave his brother's side. He gazed down at the body for a full minute before turning his back on it and heading in the same direction Charles had come from.

Selina looked at Charles and jerked her head in Herb's direction. He nodded and closed the space between them, keeping close in case Herb bolted. She suspected Charles wouldn't continue to be so easy to work with, but she was going to take advantage of it while she could.

She turned and scrounged around the ground, squinting into the unlit portions of the cavern. There were plenty of branches that must have washed in along the river, but how to connect them into anything useful? If Oliver and Charles were wearing belts, she could use those. Rope? Did they still have any? She'd had a length of it coiled on her hip, but it was no longer there.

Oliver came up alongside her, eyes squinted, likely from the headache he'd mentioned earlier. "What are we looking for?"

"Something to make a stretcher with."

"Hmm." He moved off to look along the water's edge. Bending down, he picked up a substantial branch and brought it over. He froze, looked over toward the waterfall, dropped the branch, and took off in the direction of the falls.

Selina watched him go, curious. He bent down to pick something up, something heavy, as it caused him to stumble. It was large and dark, but that was all she could tell from this distance.

As he got nearer, she realized he held his coat. It was sodden, water pouring from it. The falls must have been splashing on it where it lay through the fight. But it was also big enough to help with the litter.

They found another large branch and a series of smaller sticks, still sturdy, but they had give to them. Oliver pulled a small knife from a sheath at his waistline and cut a series of holes down each side of the coat.

She grabbed one of the large branches and threaded it through the holes he'd created, doing the same on the other side once he completed cutting that side. The smaller sticks went side-to-side through the same holes.

Standing back to survey their work, Selina smiled and looked up, meeting his eyes. "It's not perfect, but it will do. Let's see if we can get him on there."

Moving over to Johnny's side, Selina waited while Oliver brought the makeshift litter over and laid it beside the boy. She gently grasped his ankles while Oliver slid his hands under his back, taking hold of him by the armpits.

Selina's eyes met Oliver's, and she counted backward, "Three, two, one."

Johnny groaned as they lifted him, shifting him onto the litter.

Selina brought the sleeves under his arms and tied them securely across his chest, careful to avoid the belted area. He opened his eyes and looked up at her. His face was pale, the sclera of his eyes blood-shot. She figured she didn't look any better.

"Hang in there, Johnny," she said. "We're heading out soon, and we'll get you to a doctor."

She buttoned the coat up over him to keep him warm, noticing the chill for herself now that no adrenaline coursed through her body. They'd freeze when they left this cavern, which appeared to be naturally heated somehow. She eyeballed the fur on the Wendigo, but shuddered at the thought of skinning it. It didn't matter. It would take too long, and there wasn't enough fur to go around.

With Johnny as settled as he was going to be, Selina went to Nathan. Were her eyes deceiving her, or was there less fur than there had been when she'd last checked? She couldn't be sure, but his breathing sounded even and he didn't appear to be in distress. The growls had disappeared. She figured that was the most they could really hope for right now.

Oliver had sat down next to Johnny, talking to him in a quiet voice. Selina sat next to him, leaning close for warmth. "What are you guys talking about?"

"I was just telling Johnny about a situation I got myself into when

I walked into a Vegas casino for the first time. I hadn't realized how hard all the sin in that place would hit me. I could feel it like waves of tar against my head, pressing on my entire body, sticking to me. The client was waiting for me in the bar, and by the time I stumbled over there, I had become overwhelmed, full-blown migraine, and I wasn't purposely eating any of the sin; it just kept washing into me. My speech slurred and I missed the chair the first time I tried to sit in it. He thought I was some drunk and walked away, disgusted." He laughed here, shaking his head then stopping with a wince. "It took me a week to recover from that one casino. I've never been back.

"Surely you've been other places that were full of sin?" she asked.

"Of course, but nothing as bad as the casino. You'd be surprised at the sin waiting for me in churches, though. I avoid them like the plague. I don't know how the priests do it."

"Well, they're not physically relieving the sins like you, so it wouldn't bother them the same."

"Most priests who take confession are descended from Sin Eaters, even if they don't realize it."

Selina pulled her head back and looked at him. "Seriously?"

"Seriously. They really are getting absolution, but not the way they think."

Johnny's laugh ended in a grunt of pain, and Oliver placed a gentle hand on his shoulder.

A metallic clang sounded. Then clicking that grew louder, getting closer. The sound echoed around the cavern, bouncing from the rocky surfaces. After another minute of this, a yellow vehicle appeared from the wide tunnel Charles had disappeared down. It was boxy and narrow. Charles looked like a giant behind the wheel. He pulled it to a stop, releasing a lever that let out a puff of air.

"If you guys are done sitting on your asses, let's get out of here," he called.

That's when Selina remembered her previous vow not to sit down ever again.

32

TRUE COLORS

As quick as Charles had made his way out and back again on his own, getting out the injured members of the party was a laborious process. Everyone was drained. Charles and Oliver worked together to transport first Nathan then Johnny to the tram, getting each settled the best they could. It had been designed to move people sitting up. Nathan had to sit, leaning against the edge of the tram car, which came up only about two feet.

Getting the stretcher arranged was trickier, and involved sticking Johnny in at a weird angle, his feet tucked against the side of the tram car, upper body propped at a standing angle over the end. Oliver climbed in and put his back to the stretcher, an arm up to support it and make sure it didn't topple.

Herb had not returned with Charles. When Selina asked where he'd gone, fearing the worst, Charles reported that he had said he'd be in the cabin, and he expected them up there the next day to take care of his brother's body. Selina wondered how Charles had responded to that one.

Now, three days later, Johnny was in the hospital and Nathan was recovering at home. Selina, ribs wrapped, was caring for him. She and Oliver had been talking on the phone, but she hadn't heard from Charles since they'd left Herb and the cabin behind.

Selina settled next to Nathan on the sofa, picking his feet up to lay them across her lap. "You were right, you know." Her voice was quiet.

He opened one eye to look at her. "About what?"

She cleared her throat. "That I was thinking about my dad through all this. Constantly. I still feel guilty about how things went."

"It wasn't your fault. You have to face that."

"I was afraid I'd have to do it for you, and that I'd choke the same way." A sob escaped her throat.

He sat up as much as he could, reaching out a shaking hand to touch her face. "I never feared you would choke."

"Then why did you call Charles?"

He pressed his lips together, eyes boring into hers. "Because I knew you were thinking about your dad, and I didn't want to be responsible for you feeling that way about a second human being. I doubted my own decisions, my choice to call you here and put you through this. I never doubted you."

All the hurt she'd been holding onto was driven out of her. She'd been sick over him wanting Charles to help instead of her, had felt like he'd turned on her. "I don't think I could have lived with Charles being the one who took care of you."

"No, I don't suppose you could have." He sighed. "But I had to do something."

They sat together a few minutes until he fell asleep, face relaxing. She studied him, allowing herself to relax. He was healing. It had worked. The fur had receded most of the way. He was still weak, his face heavily lined, which Selina figured might be here to stay. He had been aged by everything that had occurred, but he seemed to be safe from the worst of it. Unfortunately, his fingers had stayed somewhat elongated, the nails black, and she had no idea if that would improve or if they would stay that way. It was the same with his feet, which meant a shoe shopping trip loomed in his future. He'd finished eating the rest of the heart today, so there was the possibility this would improve, too. There was no telling.

And now she knew there existed a different way to handle Wendigo. Given, she wouldn't always have a way to find the sire, nor would she have a Sin Eater handy. Probably. She wished there were a way to have Oliver around. She was enjoying their talks. Now that she didn't have to worry about saving Nathan, she felt free to explore her feelings for Oliver, to consider what dating him might be like, and exploring the possibilities. It had been quite some time since she'd felt this way about someone.

She brushed a lock of hair out of Nathan's face, tucking it behind his ear. Then she set her head against his and closed her eyes, drifting into a light nap.

A KNOCK at the door woke Selina. She let Oliver in, a smile on her face. "He woke up today!" He'd slept the last few days, worrying Selina, but she'd figured as long as he continued to breathe, she'd leave him be. Never having had a survivor before, she didn't know what to expect. And Nathan had been in no condition to tell her what had occurred with Nell after he helped her.

She led Oliver into the living room, where Nathan still slept on the sofa. A blanket had been draped over him, the lumps where his feet rested looking bigger than they should in the dim light.

Oliver slid into the seat directly to the left of the couch. "How are you feeling, Mr. Thrush?"

Nathan moved his head a tad to look at Oliver. "Alive. Other than that, okay. And the person who was instrumental in saving my life can sure as hell call me Nathan."

Oliver chuckled. "Nathan. You've got it."

"Where are you two heading today?"

"We're going to help Herb bring his brother out for burial then we'll check on Johnny. They moved him out of intensive care today."

Selina said, "And we've got to head out soon or waste daylight. It will take the body a while to burn. You sure you're going to be all right for a bit until Steve can get here to stay with you?"

"I'll just sleep," Nathan rasped. "Not much can go wrong with that. Steve knows to let herself in."

Selina set her father's knife on the table in front of him. "Can you tell her this came in handy?"

"Of course."

"I'll refill your water before I go. We'll update you on Johnny when we get back."

"Tell him hello from me. I wish I could go visit him. Oh, and don't forget to take him his notebook. He loves to write in it." Nathan pointed at a spiral bound notebook sitting on the end table.

"Look at you. Like a mother hen over that boy." She laughed, and he waved her off. Still smiling, she fussed over his blanket before grabbing his cup and going to the kitchen to refill it. He had already fallen asleep when she returned with the sweating glass. She set it down on the table as gently as she could and beckoned for Oliver to follow her.

She left the front door unlocked so Steve could come in when she arrived. Selina hoped she'd get to see her when they returned.

They climbed into Oliver's Jeep and headed out over the rutted dirt road. There was a comfortable silence for a few minutes before Oliver broke it. "Have you seen or heard from Charles?"

"Nope," she said. "Not that I'm surprised. He's not a teamwork kind of person. I'm shocked he helped as much as he did."

"He's not as bad a guy as he first comes across. A lot of his personality seems to be for show."

"Yeah, I'll withhold judgment on that." She turned to look out the window. "You don't know what he did when I was a kid. A teen, I guess. The guy will do anything for a buck, even sacrifice another person to ensure he gets what he's after."

"Sounds like a story I'll need to hear."

"Someday. Anyway, the cabin's empty. I'm not sure when he took off, but he's gone."

The trek to Herb's felt different this time. Calmer, the roads in better shape. They weren't heading for possible danger. Selina settled back into her seat, enjoying the scenery. This was familiar ground to her, had been since her childhood. If Nathan hadn't made it, she probably wouldn't have come back to this small Canadian town in the boonies ever again. Now she could keep it close to her heart for a while longer.

She studied Oliver out of the corner of her eye. His handsome face was golden in the sunlight streaming in through the driver's side, hair a surprisingly auburn halo. She could see fine lines extending out from his eye, something she'd not noticed before. Being a Sin Eater couldn't be a life of ease. She wondered what a Sin Eater's life span might be, if it impacted his health at all. He certainly seemed healthy.

And what would it be like to be in a relationship with one? Was that even a possibility for them? After all, she'd be going home soon. Johnny and Nathan would be able to take care of each other as soon as Johnny returned from the hospital. Where did that leave her and Oliver?

Would he be able to sense her sins? She knew she had many. How many times had she had to take a life, such as with the Wendigo? More times than she cared to admit. Was lust really a sin? Was it one he could eat? What if the person lusted for him? She definitely needed to have a talk with Brent when she got home. And to do some research on her own. Eventually, maybe she'd be comfortable enough to ask Oliver himself.

Fine hairs were visible on his hands as they held the steering wheel. They were strong hands, despite the manicured fingernails. This wasn't her usual kind of man. She tended toward the blue-collar guys with grease or dirt under their fingernails. Yet here he was, a clean, handsome, white-collar guy, the scent of his cologne just enough to entice her, which was a good trick, considering her keen sense of smell. She wondered if he'd lightened it for her or if he always wore it so faint.

She felt warmth deep down in her belly. When it moved up into her face, she turned away, looking out her window instead. There was a light dusting of snow on the ground from a small storm the day before, but most of it had melted away. For now. A new storm was moving in within the next few days, and there'd be fresh white snow covering everything again. Winter came early in the mountains. The barren trees stood like sentries along the road, branches reaching out in helpless submission, so naked without their leaves.

Oliver's voice brought her out of her reverie. "You're quiet today."

She looked back over at him. "I'm thinking about having to leave soon. I need to get back to work."

"Me, too."

"I appreciate everything you've done for me, for Nathan. You didn't have to, but without you he would have turned, and I would have had to kill him."

He took his eyes off the road to look at her, face creased, eyes sad. "Would he have been the first person close to you that turned?"

Selina looked down at her hands. "No. My father was the first."

This time quiet invaded the car like a wet blanket, suffocating and heavy. They drove for several minutes, Oliver looking straight ahead, Selina watching out her window. Then Oliver said, "I'm sorry."

"I wasn't. He earned his sins. Nathan never wronged anyone."

"We all have our sins." Oliver's voice was low, sad.

If anyone would know, it would be him. She changed the subject. "When are you heading back to work?"

He glanced over at her again. "I need to be back by Monday morning. Sonia will have probably pulled her hair out by now."

"Nah, she's probably running everything better than it would be with you there to screw it up. That woman is the definition of capable."

They laughed together, but it died away.

"Selina, would you go out to dinner with me tomorrow night?"

"I'd like that."

"Good. I'll figure out somewhere you'll like. Did you bring any dressy clothes with you?"

"No, but I'm sure I can find something."

They lapsed into conversations about local sites and all the places she should visit next time she came this way, carefully skirting the topic of her leaving. It felt nice being able to talk to someone like this.

Oliver was charismatic and easy to get along with, and the drive passed quickly.

Too soon, they arrived at Herb's house. He waited outside for them, pacing in the filthy, crusted snow covering his lawn. When he saw them he froze, waiting, whole body tense.

Oliver parked the car. They climbed out as Herb ran up to Selina's side of the vehicle.

"I wondered if you guys were going to show," Herb said.

"We're exactly on time, Herb." Oliver shook his head.

"Yeah, well, I wanted you guys to come two days ago. I—"

Selina broke in. "We had other things to take care of."

Herb gestured toward an ATV with a trailer. "This should work to bring Tim out. It's all gassed up and ready to go."

"It would have been nice to know you had that the other day," Selina said.

"The battery was dead. Got a new one yesterday. I thought about going in on my own, but I don't think I could have lifted him. You guys can ride in the trailer if you want. Selina, it might be easier for you to ride in the seat with me."

She eyed the four-wheeler and the trailer, sizing up the amount of pain it would probably cause her ribs to bounce along in it. They were healing quickly, and would likely be back to new by the end of the week, but they still hurt. "I don't think that'll work for me right now, but thanks for the offer. How about we meet you at the mouth of the tunnel?"

"Fair enough." He started the four-wheeler, the engine puttering like the tired cartoon version of a tractor. The smell of gasoline filled her nose, and she stepped back out of the cold spray of snow that sprang up behind the machine as he took off. She looked down to find her pant legs were damp, but not sopping. Brushing at the snow, she joined Oliver, heading in the direction Herb had gone, following the stench of gasoline and the high-pitched cough of the engine.

The outside of the mine, which she hadn't paid any attention to on the way out, was a rectangular opening in the rock, braced by large round logs. On the outside of the entryway, planks created walls that ended at large boulders. Grass grew over the top of the structure, but the logs and planks looked whole and sturdy.

The tram sat about ten feet inside the entrance. They climbed on, Herb driving this time. A distance that had felt unending a few nights ago now felt much shorter, and it wasn't long before they entered the massive cavern again. Herb climbed out and used a flashlight to get to a couple of the torches so he could light them and illuminate a portion of the cavern. The warm light suffused the darkness, lighting their way to the body still lying on the cold, hard ground.

But when they arrived at the body, something was missing. His head. A bony stump remained, dark blood pooled around it. Herb screamed and went down on his knees. "Who did this?"

Selina and Oliver looked at each other.

Charles.

33

A HAIRY PAIN IN THE ASS

*Y*ou've reached Charles Lancaster, monster hunter extraordinaire. *If you have a monster that needs disposing of, leave me a message with a brief summary, your name, and your number,* and I'll call you back with a price. If this is Selina, sorry, gorgeous. You had to know it was coming. These trips don't finance themselves.

Beep.

"Charles, you bastard! How could you leave me to deal with that without any warning? Herb practically lost his mind. He—" The beep of the voicemail cut her off. "How in the hell is that enough time for a client to leave a detailed message, jackass?"

She stood behind Herb's cabin, looking down into a hole where a pile of gray fur lay. Oliver and Herb stood on the other side of the hole, looking down at the Wendigo's body. Herb hadn't stopped sobbing the entire time they'd been moving his brother's corpse, but now he merely let out jittery breaths, hiccupping occasionally. He sniffled, wiping a sleeve across his nose.

"You still think he's a good guy?" Selina asked Oliver as she jammed the phone into her coat pocket, tearing the lining.

"I never said he was a good guy, just a better person than he at first appeared. Despite this, I think he could have done a lot less to help, but chose to stick around. He could have killed Nathan at any time. Or left us in the cave. But he didn't."

Selina made a raspy sound in the back of her throat, scoffing at his words. She crossed her arms and tapped her foot on the ground.

Oliver moved around the hole, coming to stand beside her. "Besides, you're more upset he made you deal with the fallout, not so much that he stole the head."

Her foot froze and she turned slowly to look at him, eyes wide, mouth set in a grim line. "How dare you?"

"How dare I what? State the obvious? Dare to speak truth to you, even if you don't want to hear it?"

She spluttered, hands flying through the air as if she could lasso the words she wanted to throw his way.

He merely chuckled.

Herb was in his own world, slumped at the side of the hole, feet dangling over his brother's body. He didn't appear to hear any of what they said.

"What do we do now?" Oliver asked.

"I have to chop it up with the silver axe, salt it, and burn it."

Oliver looked down at her torso. "How are your ribs? Need me to do the chopping?"

"I've got it, but I might need you to spell me for a while." She rubbed at the ache still in her ribcage, and figured it was healed enough to allow this without delaying the rest of the healing by much.

She climbed down into the hole, careful not to step on the Wendigo. While she couldn't say it looked frail now, it certainly looked smaller and less frightening this way. It was just a dirty, bloody set of lumps, covered in grimy fur. Dead.

Oliver lowered the axe to her, and she grabbed the handle as high as she could to keep it from falling when he released the weight. It still dipped at first, but she righted it and stepped over a limp leg to stand at the creature's side. Raising the axe high and to the right, she brought it down on the hip joint. It bit through with a soggy crunch, cracking the bone and severing all but a small piece of flesh.

A gasp sounded above her. She looked up. "You might not want to watch this, Herb."

"Why are you doing that?"

"I told you the body had to be destroyed. Now that your brother's gone, the spirit can possibly resurrect the body without even that small piece of him inside to mitigate his behavior. The spirit would destroy you first. This has to be done."

Oliver walked around the hole and took the small man by the shoulders. "Let's go inside where you can't hear it, okay?"

"She has no right!"

"Come on inside."

Selina waited until she heard the door shut, figuring she'd at least give Herb that tiny benefit. Then she went to work again, hacking at the body, severing each major joint. Her arms, back, thighs, and ribs all ached by the time she'd finished, but it was worth it to wash her hands of this creature and his idiot brother.

It took her two tries to crawl out of the hole, as deep as it had been dug. Herb must have hired someone to dig the hole. She wondered what excuse he'd given them? A tiny in-ground pool? A deep garden? Sump pump? Perhaps he'd given no explanation at all. It was doubtful, with Herb's familiarity with everyone around here, and his unassuming friendliness, that no one would question his reasoning for digging a hole in his backyard after the ground had begun to freeze.

She grabbed her bag and dug out the big, dark blue canister of salt. Standing over the hole, she sprinkled it over the body, listening for the telltale hiss that it was working. The sound was a sick magic to her ears, and she emptied the canister before chucking it aside. Next, she sprayed lighter fluid over the corpse and threw a match in.

The body went up with a whoosh, followed by a roar from the flames catching. She settled in, resting on the cold ground beside the hole next to a pile of wood she'd requested be waiting for her. She'd have to wait until it burned itself out before it could be buried, and she'd need the wood as fuel since Wendigo didn't have the fat a normal human body would have to keep the flames burning. Luckily, burning a Wendigo only took about half the time of a normal human body due to the desiccation that occurred in the process of turning, so she only had about three-and-a-half hours of waiting in front of her.

From inside the cabin came a muffled wail. She turned and found Herb at the window, a hand against the glass. Oliver's face appeared behind Herb, and they both disappeared from the window once more.

Better Oliver than her. If she'd been here alone, she would have had to knock the guy out to keep him away while she did her work.

Selina's phone rang. A glance at the screen showed it was Brent, and she swiped her thumb across the screen to accept the call, grateful for a distraction since the one she'd planned on was currently inside the cabin corralling a sobbing man.

"Brent? Hey, what's up?"

"Our not-so-little friend appears to have gotten out of the cavern. Looks like there must have been an alternate way out."

"What do you mean he got back out? Have you seen him?"

"No, but the same issues have started back up. Pets disappearing, property destroyed. I've been scouting around, but haven't found him yet. When do you think you'll be coming back?"

"It looks like I've got another week here, maybe less."

"How's your friend? Were you able to help him?"

A smile spread over Selina's face. "Yes, he appears to be recovering. I doubt it will be a full recovery, but he's not turning into a murderous monster anymore, so I'd call that a win."

"I'm glad he's okay." There was a pause, then, "Does that mean you found a way to handle a Wendigo without killing it?"

Selina studied the blackening crisp in the hole below her. "It does, but it's not a method that can be used on a regular basis, unfortunately. I'm not sure it can even be duplicated again."

"That's too bad. I hoped...well, you know what I was hoping for."

"Yep."

He sighed. "I'll keep looking for Gog, see if I can't find the other exit he used. If I could find him and follow him, it wouldn't be so hard, but he's moving around more than before. Guess he got smart."

"It could be he had a friend. Maybe without another Sasquatch to keep it in one area it's been meandering."

"Shit, I didn't think of that."

She laughed. "Sorry. Hey, how's the Crypto Council thing going?"

"I haven't heard any more about it. It's making me nervous, actually. I'm sure it's not over. There have been rumblings in the forums and local Crypto community about a big political-style shakeup."

"Maybe they'll leave you alone since it appears Gog is fine and back where he started. They don't have to know the other theory. I'll let you know when I'm on my way back. Let me know if anything more urgent comes up, or if you hear anything from the Council. Otherwise, I'd like to stay until there's someone with Nathan."

"I'll keep you updated. And Selina?"

"Yes?"

"I'm glad you're okay."

"Thanks, Brent."

She hung up the phone and watched the flames, throwing several pieces of wood on top of the remnants of the body. The wood crackled pleasantly, popping here and there when a bit of sap heated up. She sighed. Killing Gog wasn't something she wanted to have to do, but if it came down to him or the continuation of the problems, she wasn't sure what choice she'd be left with. Maybe she could lure him up into the mountains. Then again, was that similar to what Herb had done? Would she be endangering people if she hid him away in the mountains, much as Herb had tried to do with his brother? Sasquatch and Wendigo were two very different creatures, but she found herself questioning her decisions.

"A hairy pain in the ass is what it is."

34

IT'S SO HARD TO SAY GOODBYE

Evening had fallen by the time the body burned out. Herb told them he would bury the body, so they left him standing beside the open grave, staring down at black ash. It was the only way they were going to get a visit in to Johnny before visiting hours ended.

They spent only about twenty minutes at the hospital with him before he fell asleep. Tired, but in good spirits, he'd spent most of the day arguing with his parents, who insisted he stop working with Nathan. He insisted, in turn, they wouldn't be able to sway him, but Selina wasn't so sure they wouldn't find a way to put a stop to it. Fear for a child went a long way.

After Johnny assured them his guts were intact, and he'd be out within the week, they headed back to Nathan's place. A rusty old trap of a truck and a nicely polished motorcycle sat out front. Selina jumped out of the Jeep, eager to see Steve and Bryan. At least, she assumed that's who the vehicles belonged to.

Sure enough, their boisterous voices greeted her upon entering the house. Steve and Bryan were both loud and unrestrained, exuding energy that Selina usually lapped up. She could feel it surrounding her as she entered the room, Oliver in tow. "Hey, guys!"

"Hey yourself, little sister. Who's this?" Bryan asked, indicating Oliver with a nod of his head.

"This is Oliver. He helped with Nathan. Oliver, this is Steve and Bryan." Selina bent over to give both Steve and Bryan hugs. "When did you guys get here?"

"Not long after you left, for me," Steve said. "Bryan arrived about an hour ago."

"I'm glad you could come visit Nathan," Selina said to Bryan. "Steve, thanks for staying with him so I could go take care of business."

"I can tell from the smell of smoke what that business must have been," Steve said.

"Good news is, you guys shouldn't see any Wendigo activity around here for a while. Hopefully."

They all chatted for a while before Oliver said he had to leave. "I'll pick you up in two days for our dinner?"

"Sounds good. What time?" Selina asked.

"Does six work?"

"See you at six in two days."

After he'd gone, Bryan turned to her. "You're dating him?"

"We're going out to dinner, yes. Why?"

"I don't know." He looked in the direction Oliver had gone. "He doesn't seem quite your type."

Selina laughed. "Maybe that's a sign it'll work out." She sobered quickly, though. "Not that it matters. I'll be going back to Colorado soon, and we'll probably fall out of contact. Look how much I talk to you guys, and I've known you forever." The happy mood she'd built up was gone, eradicated in a moment of doubt.

Steve shot Bryan a look. "If you want to make it work, you'll figure out a way. In the meantime, go out, enjoy a nice dinner. He looks like he's got some money. Either way, I bet you can have fun with him." She winked.

Bryan nodded. "I didn't mean to spoil your fun. Just be careful, and call me if you run into a problem with him. Not that you can't take care of it on your own."

Physically, she could take care of it, but what about emotionally? She hadn't let anyone get close in the past. Not even a friend like Brent, who wanted more than she could give. Oliver didn't seem to have expectations greater than she was willing to give, but she'd see in two days.

Pushing it aside, she decided two days was plenty of time to worry. Until then, she wanted to enjoy what would likely be the last visit with her friends for a while. She'd already packaged up the weapons she needed Steve to ship, leaving it open to add her dad's knife. Steve would be taking it all with her tonight. Everything was settling, as it did at the end of any good case. Now it was goodbye time with her old friends.

NATHAN SQUINTED at her from his place on the sofa.

Selina paced through the living room to the kitchen then back out. When she stopped short and stared back at him, he laughed, slow and quiet, and shut his eyes against the dim light filtering into the room.

"Why are you laughing at me?" she asked, indignant.

The same eye eased back open. "You're acting like a teenager waiting for prom."

"I haven't dated anyone in a while, okay? Too busy."

"So most people avoiding intimacy often say."

Selina glared at him. "I'm not avoiding intimacy. I'm going on the date, aren't I?"

His response was a grunt, and his eye slid shut again, lips turned up in a smile.

She huffed and turned away to march into the kitchen after the sandwich she'd made him and forgotten on the counter. She plopped it on the table in front of him, still eliciting absolutely zero reaction, stared at him for a moment more with her hands braced on her hips, then turned to stalk away toward the front door.

Pulling the aged, dusty curtain back, she peered through the small window to the side of the door just in time to see the Jeep pulling out from the trees, dust cloud billowing up behind it. She placed a hand on the doorknob, but a quiet, yet firm, voice from the other room called out, "Don't you open that door until he knocks. A gentleman comes to the door to pick his lady up."

Selina turned, hand still on the knob, expecting him to be standing in the hallway, but he wasn't there, nor did he have line of sight from the sofa to where she stood. "Who says I'm a lady?"

A knock sounded at the door, and she jerked her hand back as if burned. Letting out a bark of laughter, she straightened her skirt, touched her hair, and took a deep breath.

"Well, let him in," Nathan said.

"That's enough out of you, old man."

A chuckle sounded from the living room, and she reached for the knob again, slapping a smile onto her face as she pulled it open.

Oliver stood there, handsome in a dark suit. He had combed his hair to the side, leaving it soft and bright in the sunlight that backlit him. Her smile faltered, and she let out a small "oh" of pleased surprise. He looked good enough to eat.

His smile widened as he looked her up and down, eyes moving slowly.

Warmth spread from her middle to her face, and she knew she was blushing, hoping he couldn't see it in the shade of the alcove.

"You look gorgeous," he said.

"So do you."

With a flourish, he stepped to the side and offered his elbow.

Flustered, she took the proffered arm and moved through the doorway, pulling the door shut behind her.

Just before the door closed, Nathan's voice slipped through the crack. "Have fun, kids."

Oliver laughed, the sound rich and full. Together, they walked down the porch steps and over the rutted ground to the Jeep, where he moved ahead of her to open the door, giving her an arm up.

She wasn't accustomed to this treatment. In fact, she would normally have been indignant about it, but it felt good to let him treat her this way, so she went with it. She didn't even know why it usually bothered her, other than a man's assumption that she needed his help. In this case, nothing about Oliver's actions expressed doubt at her abilities.

When she'd pulled her feet in, he closed the door and walked around to his own door, climbing in and starting the engine. He looked over at her one more time. "I almost couldn't imagine you wearing a dress."

"Almost?"

"I've got a great imagination." He put the Jeep into drive and made a tight turn to take them back onto the dirt road through the trees. The sun was heading south for the night, and the golden light that spilled through the trees left giant shadows across the road. It also hit Oliver on the right side of the face, making him glow. It must have done much the same to her because he glanced up at her and did a double take, eyes lingering on her as she looked back at him.

"I'm finding it hard to drive with you sitting there looking so beautiful."

"Eyes on the road, mister!"

They made friendly conversation for the twenty minutes it took to get to town. It surprised her how comfortable she'd become with him in such a short time. Normally, she couldn't talk to anyone she hadn't known for years, but it was different with him, and she soon forgot her nerves.

The restaurant was in a lovely stone-faced building, a green awning stretching over the front walk. He stopped directly in front of the awning, where a young man in a red vest jogged around the nose of the Jeep to his window. Handing the keys over, Oliver climbed out and came around to open the door for Selina, once again offering his elbow.

Inside, the delectable smells of cooking meat, garlic, and vanilla teased her nose. She took a deep breath then squeezed his arm where she still held it, leaning her head on his shoulder as they waited for the hostess to make her way back from seating someone.

He pulled his arm out of her hands and slid it behind her waist, his hand warm right above her hip. Her stomach did a flip.

The hostess led them to a booth that required a step up, handed them their menus, and said, "Your server will be with you momentarily." She smiled at them then pulled a set of thick green curtains closed. The sounds of the restaurant faded to a quiet hum, utensils clinking on plates here and there, voices murmuring.

The light was dim and pleasant, and Selina relaxed back into the cushions. It felt nice to have her senses muffled for a while. "This is lovely. How do you rate this booth?"

"I bring clients here a lot. It's a bit of a drive from work, but worth it."

Selina raised an eyebrow. "Just clients?"

His eyes met hers. "Just clients. Until now."

A shock thrilled through her, and she took a deep breath.

He reached across the table.

Without hesitation, she stretched her arm out and met his hand with hers. His hand was warm and strong, and she enjoyed the feel of his skin on hers. If she'd ever been tempted to have a one-night stand, it was now.

Because it would have to be a one-night stand, wouldn't it? The thought pulled her back from the pleasure she'd been feeling. What was she messing with, anyway? She wasn't a one-night stand kind of girl, yet they had no future. They lived too far apart, each with their own life, and she still didn't know if dating a Sin Eater in her line of business was a good idea.

Some of what she was thinking must have shown on her face, because his expression changed, a frown furrowing his brow. His grasp tightened. "What are you thinking about?"

Laughing at the clichéd question, she tried to pull herself out of her thoughts. In the movies, it was always the woman who asked that question. "I was thinking about having to go home. What are we doing here? What are you hoping for from this?"

"I'm hoping for a nice evening with a woman I'm attracted to, not just because of her glorious good looks, but because she's intelligent, strong, and capable. Because she makes my stomach twist when she's around. No more than that."

She squeezed his hand then pulled hers back, settling both her hands in her lap where she rubbed them together nervously. "I wish we'd had more time together, Oliver. To really get to know each other. But then part of me knows that's silly, because it would be all the harder for me to leave."

Slowly, he pulled his hand back across the table, resting it on the surface by his plate. He tapped his index finger on the wood and looked down at it for a moment before raising his eyes back to hers. "I wasn't thinking of your leaving as a permanent goodbye. I can't say what we'll be able to do, but we don't live all that far. I'd like to keep in touch, to continue getting to know you. To take it one step at a time, one date or phone call at a time. If we decide it isn't worth it, we can end it."

"But you have a life here, and I have one in Colorado. We can't go out on dates. We can't—"

"We can talk on the phone. We can send emails and texts. In this day and age, nothing's stopping us from being together. I'm asking you to not close this door unless a better reason comes along. And you know what? I enjoyed helping you with this. I could do that again in the future. You'd only need to call."

"What about your business?" she asked. "You have to be here to run it."

"Weren't you the one that pointed out how efficient Sonia is?"

"Yes, but I..." She tapered off, not sure what to say next. She wanted to go with what he was saying, to release the responsibility of looking ahead and embrace the moment. She'd held herself back with him due to the circumstances already, too busy focusing on Nathan and the mission before her. It had seemed tacky just to be attracted to him, to consider wanting more, to envision what lay under that suit as she drifted off to sleep.

"Let's just enjoy this evening and see where it takes us," he said. "We don't have to plan our lives tonight. I want to enjoy your company, talk to you, get to know you. And it doesn't hurt that I get to look across this table at such an amazing woman."

Warmth flooded her body. It was astounding how easily that happened in his presence. She made the conscious choice to relax, releasing a breath she hadn't realized she'd been holding. She nodded once and started to speak, but someone stepped through the curtain, all bustling efficiency, and they both turned to look at the newcomer.

Wearing a white shirt, a black tie, black pants, and one of those pocketed waist aprons servers so often wore, a middle-aged man with perfectly coiffed hair and a smattering of freckles gave them a faint smile. "Good evening, Sir, Madam. Can I tell you about our specials?"

Selina looked at Oliver, took in eyes that said so much, lips she wanted her own to touch, body she wanted to caress and feel against her. "One question first. Can we get our order to go?"

THE DRIVE back to Nathan's took forever, the food cooling in plastic containers tucked into a bag. The scent of beef filled the car, making Selina salivate. But it was the man sitting beside her who really got her juices flowing. She'd decided that her obsession with doing things the right way, planning for the future of the relationship, holding herself back, all this must end. She was typically a spontaneous person, yet never with men. Trust was hard earned, but hadn't Oliver earned it?

He pulled up in front of the cabin, turned off the engine, and turned to look at her, his eyes intense. "Where do we go from here?"

She placed a hand on his arm. "Do you trust me?"

"Of course."

"I want to go for a walk."

"A walk?"

"Yep, but first I have to change my shoes and grab a few things." She looked at him, pulled out the lapel of his jacket. "Are you worried about scuffing this suit up?"

"It's the least of my worries."

"Good. Wait here."

Selina raced inside, making a point to go into the living room first. "Just grabbing something, and then I'm going back out."

Nathan looked at her in surprise, but merely nodded.

"Oh, do you have a blanket I could use for a picnic?"

"A picnic? It's 7:30 at night."

"There's still some light left."

"In the hallway closet."

She ran to the closet, shoved fabric around until she found a thick blanket, shot into her room to remove her high heels and put on socks and boots, then went back outside, where Oliver leaned against the hood of the Jeep. He'd removed his jacket and rolled up the sleeves of his button-front shirt. The tie was also gone, the first two buttons of his shirt undone. A burn started in her abdomen and worked its way up.

"You got the food?" she asked.

"Right here." He lifted the bag from behind him.

"Let's go." She tucked the blanket securely under her right arm and wrapped her left arm around his.

He crooked his elbow, bag in the other hand, and let her pull him along.

She'd promised herself a visit to the lake before she left. This wasn't what she'd originally planned, but this would be more fun. Following the path, she led Oliver around holes and rocks that might trip him. The fact that he trusted her to lead him through the dark this way increased the pleasant sensations running through her body. Her nerves were on high alert, sensitive to every brush of his skin against hers, every bump of their bodies.

She might not make it all the way to the lake.

When they neared Rocky's ledge, she stopped, pulling her arm from his. "Can you take out the fish?"

"Sure." He untied the bag, which took some time in the dark. She'd had them put the fish in last so it would be easy to grab, not explaining herself to Oliver. Now he handed her the container.

"I've got to leave an offering, so Rocky will leave us alone."

"Who's Rocky?"

"A mountain lion."

He tensed next to her. "There's a mountain lion around here?"

She snickered. "Probably more than one, but Rocky's a friend."

"All right." He didn't sound too sure, but still he went with her when she once more took his arm.

Moonlight glinted off the lake below, and the sight of it melted the last of her tension away. Water lapped softly at the shore. Somewhere, an owl hooted.

When they got to the lakeshore, Selina set the blanket out, straightening it as much as she could. She took the bag from Oliver and set the burgers out. "Hope you don't mind giving up a steak dinner for our picnic. I figured the burgers would be easier to eat with our hands."

"I would have eaten jerky to spend more time with you."

Selina whispered, "Me, too," leaning into Oliver, eyes looking into his in the low light.

He reached for her, placing one hand behind her head and pulling her into him for a kiss. It was soft at first, almost tentative, but when she responded to him the kiss intensified, deepened. His lips were soft and warm, and he tasted of mint.

She slid a hand up his chest, feeling the firmness of the muscles beneath the soft fabric of his shirt. He smelled of soap and leather underneath the faint cologne, an intense combination.

He pulled back and looked into her eyes. "Are you sure you want to do this?"

"Positive." She captured his mouth with hers again, groaning into it when his hand found her breast.

His touch felt feather light as he teased the backs of his fingers around the curve, up the side. He stroked downward again and cupped her breast in his hand, stroking his thumb over her taut nipple before gently circling its shape through the thin material of her dress.

It had been so long since she'd been with a man, which heightened her response. The raw nerves telegraphed every touch, and she yearned for flesh to press against flesh, to feel every part of him. Her core was on fire, an ache in her groin that made her feel out of control, desperate for more.

Still, she felt herself resisting, holding back. They barely knew each other. Doubt settled in, and she pulled back, looking into his eyes. He gazed back, eyelids heavy.

But they'd been through something together. Something intense and deeply meaningful that transcended getting-to-know-you conversations. She always did this, pulled away, shut herself down. It was time to be brave and to open herself up to someone.

Pushing the doubt away, she came up to a kneeling position and moved her legs over his, straddling him. It was his turn to groan as she found the warm, hard press of him against his pants with one hand as they kissed. She pushed him back to the ground and leaned down to kiss him, rubbing her body along the length of his.

He slid his hands around to her back, finding the zipper there. He pulled down, slowly, a finger tracing the skin of her back just above the zipper, leaving behind a trail of fire. When he'd unzipped it enough, he pulled her dress down, baring her naked breasts. He broke their kiss, lifting his head to lick her nipple lightly. Then he pulled it into his mouth, moving his tongue over and around it, nipping gently.

She gasped, heat racing through her body, and pressed her cheek to the top of his head, reveling in the sensations coursing through her.

His hand slid up her thigh, caressed her through her panties, and she moved against him, wanting this to go on and on, but also needing something more.

She undid his shirt buttons, pulling it down his arms so she could rub her hand down his chest, his flat stomach. Her fingers caressed the hard ripples there, moved down. It took two hands to undo his belt, unbutton his pants, and pull them open before sliding her hand against his erection.

He let out a deep moan and slid a finger under her panties, hot against her skin, working her with a skilled touch.

Their mouths met once more, and she circled a finger around his nipple, enjoying the feel of it growing hard against her skin. She used the other hand to shove his pants and underwear down.

Then she let herself go completely and utterly, and delighted in his body as he delighted in hers.

35

HOME AGAIN, HOME AGAIN, LICKETY SPLIT

Too quickly, the trip came to an end. Selina hugged Nathan, who had started moving around the house more. While he remained emaciated, she could feel his wiry strength in the hug he returned. She was confident his health would continue to improve, though she didn't know if he'd ever be back to full health.

Johnny had returned, and the two men were eager to get back to normal, though both still moved with caution, somewhere just south of the speed of sloth. She gave him a hug, too, giving him a quick peck on the cheek.

"We'll miss you, Selina," he said.

"I can't thank you enough for what you did for me, sweetheart," Nathan said, leaning in to hug her one more time. "I didn't expect to be alive."

"If it hadn't been for everyone's help, you wouldn't be. I'm glad I was able to help this time." A pulse of sadness went through her as she thought of her father and the last time she'd seen him. At least this time it had gone differently.

Oliver stepped in through the open door and leaned over to pick up her trunk. Straightening, he nodded at each man in turn. "Hi there, Nathan, Johnny."

"It's nice of you to drive Selina to the airport," Nathan said, nodding at him in return.

"I'm glad to be able to."

They said their goodbyes, and Selina grabbed her suitcase, following him out to the Jeep. He slid the trunk into the back and stepped aside for her to add her suitcase between the trunk and the wall.

As he pulled onto the road, Oliver said, "You're going to miss him a lot, aren't you?"

"Yes, but I haven't lived near him in a long time. And I'm glad he's still here for me to miss him."

"I'll drop in on them occasionally, make sure things are going all right. Maybe I can even persuade them to come into town for dinner sometime."

"That would be great." She placed a hand on his arm, memories of the other night still nestled inside her. "Keep me updated. I know I won't be able to get anything out of either of them on how the other's doing."

Feeling slightly better about leaving Nathan behind—something that was never easy, but somehow seemed much harder this time—Selina settled in for the drive. There was a lot to do when she got home. There were messages for her to return, cases to work. And she had her furry friend to deal with. Glancing over at Oliver, she placed her hand on his thigh, warm and firm. She gave it a quick squeeze then left her hand there.

He turned and smiled, and she marveled at this thing blossoming between them. Instead of feeling sad about leaving him, she was excited to see what happened from here, something she hadn't felt in a long time.

POST NOTE

I have obviously taken liberties with many things in this book, it being a fantasy story, but as someone who is part-Cherokee, but has never lived on a reservation and is not a registered Cherokee citizen, I have been careful to ensure my main character is like me. I have friends and relatives from many indigenous Nations, so throughout these books, Selina will also have friends and relatives from those Nations. However, she will have never lived on a reservation, because I cannot appropriately represent that life, nor would I have a right to try. My story and background are my own, and while no one has a right to my personal history, elements will likely make their way into these stories, as will my experiences with bigotry and insecurities about not fitting 100% into any single world. All I can do is represent my experiences. I cannot speak for others.

My goal is to represent our mythologies as accurately as possible in a fiction setting. The mythologies have been twisted in media to barely resemble the real lore passed down. But I did also take liberties here. For example, "Wendigo" is not the standard spelling/pronunciation used by many Cree and related Nations. I've instead used the version that is most known to U.S. Nations, except for a quick reference in a document within the story. I've done this for the familiarity, so more people would recognize the lore I was addressing. For this same reason, I have chosen to have even the Cree characters stick with "Wendigo" to avoid confusion throughout the book, rather than switching references back and forth. I apologize if this has caused anyone harm.

I hope for and appreciate your understanding.

~Shannon

ADDITIONAL THANKS

I can't forget to thank my beta readers, who gave me helpful feedback! Thank you to Donnell Bell, MB Partlow, Jade Farrar, Katie Redinger, and Charise Simpson. And to my critique group when I first started writing this, who put eyes on those first couple chapters and encouraged me to keep going: Michelle, Jen, Becki, and Ray-Ray.

As always, a big thank you to my kids, who have to split their mother's time with jobs and passions on the side. I know I live in my head a lot. I love you both. I'm proud of the wonderful humans you've become.

To my godmother, who was instrumental in my learning to read.

To my parents, who read to me and shared their love of books and movies so I could revel in so many different types of stories.

And to anyone who has ever supported my writing or storytelling in any way.

Finally, to my readers. If you've ever picked up a story or book by me, I appreciate you. To those who've read my work and told other people or shared it in any way, you are helping to change my life. Thank you so much for taking a chance on me.

OTHER BOOKS BY SHANNON LAWRENCE

Short Story Collections:

Blue Sludge Blues & Other Abominations

Bruised Souls & Other Torments

Happy Ghoulidays

Happy Ghoulidays II

Nonfiction

The Business of Short Stories: Writing, Submitting, Publishing, and Marketing

ABOUT THE AUTHOR

A fan of all things fantastical and frightening, Shannon Lawrence writes primarily horror and fantasy. Her stories can be found in over fifty anthologies and magazines, as well as her own collections. You can also find her as a co-host of the podcast Mysteries, Monsters, & Mayhem. When she's not writing, she's hiking through the wilds of Colorado and photographing her magnificent surroundings, where, coincidentally, there's always a place to hide a body or birth a monster. Find her at www.thewarriormuse.com or sign up for her newsletter at http://eepurl.com/dl2YTH to get advance news about upcoming publications and appearances.